SHELTERBELT

SHELTERBELT

MARY ANN SEITZ

WESTERN PRODUCER PRAIRIE BOOKS
SASKATOON, SASKATCHEWAN

Softcover edition 1981

Jacket and book design by Ray Statham

Printed and bound in Canada by
Modern Press
Saskatoon, Saskatchewan

The poem, by George Eliot, "O May I Join the Choir Invisible" on
page 168 is from *Palgrave's Golden Treasury*, Oxford University Press,
London, 1928.
This text was used by Grade XII students in 1947-48 in Saskatchewan
for literature.

Western Producer Prairie Books publications are produced and
manufactured in the middle of western Canada by a unique publishing
venture owned by a group of prairie farmers who are members of
Saskatchewan Wheat Pool. Our first book in 1954 was a reprint of a
serial originally carried in *The Western Producer*, a weekly newspaper
serving western Canadian farmers since 1923. We continue the
tradition of providing enjoyable and informative reading for all
Canadians.

CANADIAN CATALOGUING IN PUBLICATION DATA

Seitz, Mary Ann, 1930-
    Shelterbelt

    ISBN 0-88833-083-9

    I. Title.
    PS8587.E49S5 C813'.5'4 C79-091035-7
    PR9199.3.S44S5

To Our Magnificent Parents

ACKNOWLEDGMENTS

The author wishes to express sincere gratitude to the Saskatoon Media Society, the Saskatchewan Arts Board, and the Canada Council for their assistance in writing this novel.

CONTENTS

CHAPTER ONE

"Francie's playing again."

She started, her hands frozen over the bird nest she had been making from the feathers.

"*Ya tobee skazow!*" their father shouted at her from the dim corner of the kitchen where he worked at the harness machine.

Across the table Joe smirked as she began stripping feathers quickly, pulling the downy sides from the quills. She darted a look at her father. He glared at her, although his shoulders slumped with fatigue.

It was the doll that always got her into trouble. Not the old one whose yarn braids Joe had torn off in a fight, its blind, shapeless body sagging with the misery of too much loving and hating. A new doll with a painted face and real shoes.

It would be her last chance to get a new doll, because on Sunday she would be eight and after that she would be too old for such toys. She would have to help around the house more then because she was the only girl and a family of eight boys made a lot of work for a mother.

Working around the house was awful. Like tonight. All of them, from Harry down to Danny, had been stripping feathers since suppertime.

"Look, Francie. See how big my pile is." Danny squashed his feathers into a mound.

"Ya. Dat's good," Mrs. Polanski said. "You will sleep under a nice big *perina*. It be smooth, not all needles like da ones Prosvigs making. Dey jus' putting da feathers in da bag and sewing dat shut. I don' like dat way. Iss lazy way."

Prosvigs' *perinas* wouldn't be as warm, Francie thought. Prickly like straw. Prosvigs didn't care about making feather ticks the right way. They had their horses and guns to look after. But then, Rosy Prosvig, her very best friend, didn't need a big *perina*. She was jolly and round, and she never got as cold as Francie did.

She thought again of the big brown parcel that had come from Eaton's the day before.

"Frynca," her mother had said. "Take da basin down cellar and bring me potatoes."

While Francie was downstairs, her mother could have taken the doll out of the parcel first and could have hidden it until Sunday. Under the tick, maybe, or a pillow. The doll could be nestling secretly with its little button nose warm in the darkness, waiting for her. She had seen the other things in the parcel. Underwear and warm socks for the boys, sheepskin coats for Harry and Joe.

And on nights like this, when the whole family sat around the kitchen table stripping the down off feathers, she could set the doll beside her and show her how to pull the fluff off each side of the quill. The doll would know that the Polanskis made their ticks the right way, out of soft duck down that didn't scratch. The doll would learn things fast, not like Johnny Szoda at school. Already he was twelve years old and still in grade two.

She would have to watch Joe. He would tell on her again if he saw her playing, sure as anything. He liked to see someone get heck.

It was hard being the only girl in the family of eight boys. A girl couldn't lift the heavy pails of chop or stook as fast as the boys could. She got tired more easily and wasn't much help to her dad. Even when he sent her to the shop for a wrench or a hammer, she wasn't much good because she couldn't tell the different pliers and wrenches apart. And when her dad got angry with her for not knowing, she became still more mixed up because she was scared of his big voice and the strap he kept hanging in his bedroom.

"Tell us about the olden days," Eddie begged his mother. "What was it like when you went to school?"

Mrs. Polanski shifted her weight in the straight-backed chair. "You want to hear about dat again?" she sighed. "I tell you already so many times."

"We like to listen." Eddie could coax her better than anyone else.

She tilted her head to one side. "Grandpa, he not like our daddy, he don' want us to go to da school all da time," she began. "But he haf to listen to da law. So we go to da school da mos' in da summertime because we don' haf shoes and warm clothes for da winter."

"It wass wery cold in da winter in dose days. In summer we goes barefoots like you's do, but in da winter only one person can go to school at one time. Because Grandpa can afford only one pair of shoes in da fall. He goes to da Army and Navy Store an' buys da man's boots.

"Grandpa wass scared we would wear out da shoes too fast. He not let us war dem until da snow cover da groun'. Sometimes it get real cold in da fall before it snows. In da morning we see da frost showing in all da low places. Den, our bare feets get so cold!

"Den we see some cows laying down beside da road, on da way to school. Dey laying dere maybe all night an' dey warm up da ground. We chasing dem up and den standing dere warming up our feets. Den we run a little bit more."

Francie could see her mother as a girl of seven. An old snapshot in the Other Room showed her mother wearing a long-sleeved white blouse and a black skirt with bands of black ribbon around it. Had she too stood on the bleached autumn grass, one foot up under her skirt, trying to coax the numbness from her toes, worrying about being late for school?

"Didn't such big shoes hurt?" Bennie asked.

"Ya, dey wass hurting. But what you could do? I come home at night, my feets sure hurting from dose shoes. But den I stay home for t'ree days. Uncle Pete and Aunt Caroline and Uncle John take dere turns. Den my feets ready to go again."

"How far did you go in school in them days?" Bennie hated teachers and school.

"Oh, I finish grade t'ree like Daddy do, but he goes to school in da Old Country an' dey learn lots more dere. He can do more arit'metics dan I do."

"How come you can read all the farm papers then?"

"We learn. I always like to read da farm papers, see what other farmers iss doing. Daddy like to read too. He always haf to read da weterinary book when da cattles is sick. He like to read about da warss in da Old Country too. He interesting in dat. You read more, you learn more."

"What were the teachers like in those days?" Bennie asked.

"Dey wass always da mans. An' dey wass wery hard on da kids, not good to dem like dey iss now.

"I remember one boy came late for school. It not his fault. Da horse t'row him off an' hurt his leg. But he late, so da teacher make dat boy kneel on a poker on da floor."

"A hot poker?"

"No, no. It wass a cold poker, but poker hard to kneel on, hot or cold. You try dat once. He fall down after a little bit."

"Then what did the teacher do?"

"He didn' do nothing at first. But when dat boy wakes up again is the teacher ever giving him a hard licking. *Boza, Boza.*" She sighed with pity.

Francie wondered what it would be like to faint. She wished that she could faint too, so that the next time her dad strapped her she could do it. Maybe he would get scared and pick her up and call her name. Maybe he would even hold her a little, like a doll.

3

Something hard slammed into her back, and she straightened with an involuntary cry. Her father had thrown a shoe at her.

"I tell you before, get busy! What you good for seeting dere and playing?"

She stripped feathers blindly, tears brimming her eyes, then splashing down in great wet blobs. By the silence she knew that they were all looking at her. She kept her chin high. Danny looked up at her, then moved a little closer on the bench.

The big clock whirred and struck tock-plock. Francie sneaked a look at it. They should have been in bed long ago, but stripping feathers made a big mess so they had to keep at it.

In the corner the harness machine measured the stitches. Dad was lucky. No one kept after him to hurry. And leather smelled a lot nicer than feathers did.

Hands scooped holes out of the shrinking piles of feathers in the center of the table. In front of him each worker stripped a pile of down. When the pile was large enough, he stuffed handfuls of the down into one of the pillowcases standing at intervals around the table. Quills were dropped on the floor to be swept up later.

Francie looked at the pillowcases. Fat on the bottom but limp and beseeching at the top, they looked like dumpy little grandmothers. Would they ever be full enough, or would they have to strip feathers until spring came? They never had enough *perinas*. Winter was too long.

"Were Dad's parents as poor as yours, Mum?" Harry asked.

"T'ings wass not da same in da Old Country. Daddy's parents wass better off dan mine. An' da winter was not so cold dere."

She thought for a moment. She was the only one who called their father "Daddy".

"Daddy leave his home when he wass very young. He comes to Canada when he jus' eighteen yearss old. It wass wery hard for him den. He don' know nobody. When he get off the ship he have only ten cents in his pocket."

Francie imagined her father, a tall, thin man emerging from the dim blue distances of the Old Country.

"He start looking for da work. But dere iss no work on da farms den. And he a farmer. So he go to work for da railroad. He get board and room and twenty-five cents a day."

Francie froze. She had heard her father get up. She did not dare turn her head to look at him. She began to strip the feathers quickly.

He laid down a leather strap that he had been sewing. He loomed behind her.

She ducked her head as she saw his hand come up. Then he unhooked the gas lamp and set it on the table.

4

"Bring de pump," he said, a cigarette stuck between his lips.

She flew to the windowsill and back again. He pumped swift, strong strokes into the lamp, the mantles whitening and hissing with a new supply of energy. He returned to the harness machine.

"Den, Daddy save his money and buy da homestead in Poplar Walley. So he can start to farm."

She always stopped there.

"How did you meet Dad?" They shot sideways glances at him bending over the leather.

"He come to Varsovia, where my daddy live. He is Ukrainian, but he want a Polish wife. He need somebody to cook for him.

"An' Daddy ask Grandpa to marry me, but Grandpa think I too young. I only fourteen. But in dose days it not so young to be married when the girl is fourteen. Den we get married."

"Didn't you even go together for a while?" Joe asked.

"Oh, no. In dose days man see girl what he likes, he ask her daddy right away if he can marry her. Nobody waste time chasing around like dat.

"Den we homestead in Poplar Walley. In da sod shack. Dat no good farming country. It never rains there. So after a few years Daddy sell out and we move here, to Field. It don't rain here all da time either, but we haf better land here. Some places is worse. Dis place is not so bad."

This place was all that Francie could remember. The two-storey house with a big kitchen and the Other Room. The bedroom in the curtained partition off the Other Room. The two small bedrooms upstairs.

This place had a big gray barn with lean-tos and a loft. The busiest place in the summer was Dad's blacksmith shop. A small coal shed huddled near the house. Beside the hen house two old granaries leaned toward each other. Around the yard on four sides waved the young shelterbelt, holding the human and animal life in its arms, protecting them from winter gales and summer storms. It parted on the east, toward Field.

"Dis summer we going to build a pantry on da north side da kitchen." Mrs. Polanski yawned. "We will haf lots more room den."

Harry lifted the stove lid and placed lumps of hard coal over the hot ashes. Soft coal was cheaper, but it was saved for the daytime because it burned so fast.

"How did yous keep the houses warm when yous were little?" he asked as he straddled a chair backwards.

"Oi, it wass so hard, da winter. Grandpa, he don' believe in buying da coal. He jus' buy wery little. He believe in using da t'ings dat grow, like straw and wood, for da fuel.

"We haf to take turns sitting by the stove all day an' twisting flax straw in small bunches. Flax straw burn good. It give so much heat. Grandpa keeping da straw on da floor in da corner, an' we twisting dat an' twisting

5

dat. Den we push da flax in da door on da side of da stove. We keep da fire going all day. Grandma she didn't haf to bother with da stove. She just washing and cooking all day."

"A pile of straw would look funny in our kitchen," Bennie laughed.

"Ya, but what you could do? In dose days we not even have da paper box. It big t'ing to have a box. An' when da calf wass born on da cold night, Grandpa he bring him to da kitchen an' put him in da straw. It haf to dry out in da house or it will freeze out in da barn. Da barns wass poor den. Dey not warm like dey iss now."

Francie's back was beginning to ache from sitting on the bench so long. She thought of the little grandma who walked so straight and so fast and who got mad easily too. She lived eighteen miles to the west in the house where her mother had twisted the flax for the stove.

The big clock bonged twelve times.

"Lookit my pile, you guys," Bennie boasted.

Joe swept Nick's pile into his. "That's nothing," he grinned. "Look at mine."

Francie scooped up her small pile of down and thrust a fist into a pillowcase. Now all they had to do was to sweep the floor two or three times over and then they could go to bed.

"Francie, you can do the sweeping. You don't have to get up early and do chores like we do." Joe handed her the broom.

In front of Dad she didn't dare argue. She had caught heck enough times tonight. Boys never cleaned up messes in the house.

She swept the last feathers into the black dustpan her father had made and tapped them into the stove. Her father turned out the gas lamp as she scuttled into the Other Room. She was more than ready for bed tonight.

Francie undressed behind the heater. In the summer she shared a bed upstairs with Danny and Stanley, her two younger brothers. But in the winter the unheated upper floor turned bitter cold, and then the boys needed two *perinas* on each bed to keep warm. Then she was allowed to sleep downstairs on the fold-out bed with the younger boys.

"Aren't you in the bed yet?" Her mother's voice came sharply from behind the curtain.

"I'm saying my prayers." Francie dived to her knees. The worn linoleum felt hard and cold. She closed her eyes and whispered her way through the Our Father, the Hail Mary, the Glory Be, shivering and longing to be under the covers. But there was still the Act of Contrition. If she said it and died during the night, she would go straight to heaven. And it was a big sin to say prayers in bed. God would be mad at her if she did that, just as mad as her father often became with her. He could make her die during the night.

Creeping in beside the warm, drowsy boys, she turned her face toward

6

the far wall. Her father lay in the big bed, reading by the kerosene lamp. Shafts of soft light poked long fingers through the curtain closing off the partition. The kerosene lamp did not talk to itself like the gas lamp did. Its flame bobbed in silence.

Only Dad could read at night after they all went to bed. Kerosene cost too much for everyone to use.

Firelight from the slotted door of the round heater danced soundlessly on the far wall. Francie could hear the ticking of the clock and the wall fighting the wind that blew through the thin branches of the shelterbelt.

CHAPTER TWO

Early the next morning she was awakened by the clank of the heater door, then a shaking of the grates. In the dim light she could see her father standing tall in his white underwear and bare feet, stoking the heater in preparation for the morning rising. Her father never wore anything on his feet when he walked around the house at night. He even slept with his toes sticking out from under the tick. He couldn't stand to have his feet covered. He was very strong, her dad.

Upstairs, the boys could risk staying in bed and getting a furious second summons, but downstairs that would be an open invitation to disaster. Francie pulled on one heavy cotton stocking under the tick, dressing herself under the covers because the room was so cold. She adjusted the elastic bands that held up her stockings around her thighs; they settled into the grooves that still smarted from yesterday.

There was little talk on cold mornings. The boys pulled on the heavy felt socks that had been drying overnight beside the heater. Strapping their felt helmets under their chins, they slipped on their sheepskins and went out to do the morning chores.

Francie was glad that she didn't have to leave the house so soon. As the heavy inner door swung open, she could see that the hard snow had blown between it and the storm door. Snow curved all the corners. When the boys closed the door, cold air rushed into the kitchen like a fog.

The water in the pail on the washstand had frozen solid. Usually a thin crust of ice formed over its surface and her mother could easily break it with the dipper. This morning she chipped ice from the drinking water barrel that crowded the stove.

"Good t'ing we make da lunch last night," she muttered. "Da butter is frozen too. To make da lunch in da morning take too much time."

The kitchen ran along the east side of the house, and at night the fire in the stove was allowed to go out. Only the heater in the Other Room was replenished once or twice a night. On cold days the kitchen did not warm up until noon.

Francie shivered. The wall at her back was cold.

"Eat a bite of porridge," their mother urged. "It will help you stay warm."

Francie and Bennie pushed their spoons around in the pale cream of wheat. The cereal stuck in their throats. It tasted a lot better in the summer when the cows gave milk; in the winter with a tablespoon of lard it tasted gluey.

"I t'ink it be maybe forty below again today," Mrs. Polanski said, trying to scratch the frost off a kitchen window. "Yous can go in da cutter. Be careful and not chase da horses."

Francie's spirits lifted. She tucked her faded red flannelette dress into a pair of Bennie's overalls and closed the bib fasteners. Riding in the cutter was a lot better than walking and facing the wind.

They dashed out of the house and clambered over the sill of the cutter. Joe hooked the door as Francie and Bennie scrambled to the bench that ran across the back wall and burrowed their toes in the straw. The other boys knelt on the floor and looked out of the window at the rumps of the horses. As the runners squeaked over the snow, Prince and Rob began to trot reluctantly. They resisted motion in the mornings, pulling unevenly through the shelterbelt.

Joe poked at the horses with a long stick. It was rough riding in the back of the cutter. They were jolted from side to side. The cutter's short runners did not take the frozen snowbanks well. Sometimes the front end went up, hung poised for a second and then came down with a sickening lurch. To the smaller children, who could not see out of the narrow front window, the ride seemed endless.

Frost thickened their lashes above their scarves.

"Let me out," Francie said, gagging as the porridge rose within her. "I want to run. I'm cold."

"Me too," Bennie insisted.

"You get too far behind, we ain't gonna stop for you," Joe warned. But he unhooked the door and the two children tumbled out.

The snow lay in cold blue banks, and the air burned into their lungs. They followed the narrow tracks, trying to keep their balance by walking with one foot in front of the other.

"Hoi!!" Joe menaced with the stick, slapping the lines hard on the horses' backs. They broke into an awkward trot.

The children knew what Joe was doing. He had waited until they got a little tired, and then he had sent the horses running. Francie stepped on the end of the runner, lost her balance and sprawled into the snow, Bennie running frantically after the retreating sled.

Francie struggled to her feet, tears gathering. Joe wasn't supposed to chase the horses like that; he had waited until they were too far from home for Dad to see. He was laughing at them now, running like clumsy snowmen, their heavy boots slipping off the track. But that was Joe. He didn't even care if they all got a licking afterward. Joe didn't hurt like the rest of them did. When they gave up trying to catch the cutter, Joe slowed the horses. But as soon as the children neared the sled, he shouted at the team and left them behind again.

Maybe Eddie said something, or maybe Joe started thinking that they would tell on him, because the next time Francie and Bennie plodded close to the cutter, Joe hung out the side door, grinning like anything.

"Well, wanna ride now?"

She hated him. She'd hate him forever. He was thirteen and mean. Every time she started to trust him a little, he always spoiled it. Eddie was a lot nicer.

Gratefully they climbed in. The running had warmed them, but their frustration had wearied them. The crazy streak was in him now.

"Giddy-up, you two crow-baits!" He leaned out the window and smacked Robbie with the lines. The horses lunged, broke into a gallop. The cutter lurched and tipped over the hard snowbanks. Bennie fell against Francie and she fell against the side. They couldn't get up again.

"Hoof it, you scrawny two-bit nags!" Joe hooted as the cutter flew through the schoolyard gate. With a final jolt they stopped beside the faded red barn.

Francie filled her arms with the round jam pails that served as lunch pails. She and Bennie had to carry them in and place them beside the furnace to thaw. Bennie took a little time to climb out. He made it over the sill, then vomited his porridge over the snow.

Happiness swelled like a bubble through Francie as she dashed into the school. For a few hours there would be books to read and pictures to color. She plunked the lunch pails down beside the black metal jacket that surrounded the furnace. No one took his coat off until the bell rang; sometimes they wore their parkas all day. Then the desks were pushed up to the furnace, so close that they had to shuffle them around to let the teacher in to open the heavy iron door and feed more coals to the red grates that always demanded more fuel.

Her favorite spot was at the rear of the furnace where a rectangle had been cut out in the jacket to allow heat to escape. Back there she could sit on the bench and prop her feet up and toast her toes. When the leather began to smell, she would pull her feet away until the hot feeling passed. On the very worst days the furnace had not yet warmed the building. Then she would pull off her boots and hold her stinging toes in her hands to get them warm.

On the coldest days everyone played tag around the desks before the teacher came. Joe always broke the rule that they couldn't jump across the desks. But most of them tried to catch one another by sheer speed alone. The teacher didn't mind the running, unless one of them held on to the last desk in the row, giving it a pull as he sped around, spilling the contents. Today all the ink would be frozen solid, and pencils would have to be used until noon.

"Prosvigs are here!" Francie flew to the door, and in stamped Rosy, her green eyes gleaming above her round, colored cheeks. She wore one of her brothers' discarded sheepskins, and a pocket hung, half-mast, at the front. What shocked and delighted Francie was the way they just laughed when they tore any clothes.

They crowded into the school now, and the last one in did not bother to shut the door. Francie ran to close it and save the precious heat, then back to Rosy, who was shrugging off the old coat.

"Why are you taking off your pants?" Francie asked. "It's going to be cold all day."

Rosy kicked the boys' overalls up to her hand. "It gets too warm wearing these all day. Mother makes me wear these damn bloomers; that's why I get so hot."

Francie caught her breath at the sound of the Bad Word. God would get Rosy for talking like that. Maybe not today, but someday. He never forgot. But then maybe He felt a little kind toward Rosy, because her father was dead. He had died just last year, on the couch at home, with all the Prosvigs standing around him. That's how it was when a person died; no one could do anything for him, not even a best friend.

Rosy tugged at the top of her stocking.

"Where are your 'lastics?"

"Boys got 'em last night and shot at each other until they stretched 'em too big."

How are you going to keep your stockings up?"

"Easy. I'll show you." They turned their backs so that the boys couldn't see. Rosy pulled the top of her stocking sideways. She twisted the slack tightly into a little rope, then deftly tucked the knotted part under. It made a bump, but the stocking stayed up.

Francie was entranced. "What if it lets go?"

"So what. I'll just wind it up again. Stockings stay up good on fat legs."

That day the grade two boys did not care much for the poem.

I once had a sweet little doll, dears,
    The prettiest doll in the world . . . .

It could be about a new doll. The one she might get for her birthday. But in the poem the doll got lost somehow. It couldn't be found

11

anywhere. Perhaps it was lying in among the clumps of sagegrass, out in the pasture.

And then the doll was found. In a mess.

> Folks say she is terribly changed, dears,
> For her paint is all washed away.
> And her arm trodden off by the cows, dears,
> And her hair not the least bit curled.

Hurry, hurry. Pick her up before the coyotes get at her.

That afternoon the weather changed. The air mellowed, and at recess a host of large, blobby snowflakes began to fall crazily over the prairie. Francie lifted her thin face to the snow. She and Rosy slid down the smoothest banks, catching the flakes with their mouths.

"Maybe we'll get let out early, in case of a storm," Rosy said, puffing. "What would you do tonight, then?"

"Look at the dolls in Eaton's catalogue. I hope I get one for my birthday."

"I got a doll last year. Mother says I'm getting too old for toys. My uncle gave it to me. I don't play with it much."

After recess the science lesson continued as usual. Mrs. Kyraniak showed them colored pictures of butterflies. Francie knew several right away. She had chased after those very bits of color many happy times.

A butterfly was a signal to run free. By the time one was captured there was little of it left, but then it was the glorious chase that mattered, over school fences, grain fields and gardens. They paid afterwards for trampling the garden by staying in to do the dishes an extra time. Dad got really mad if they ran over the wheat.

Rosy didn't like chasing butterflies. She didn't mind the coloring, though. Teddie, the teacher's son, sucked noisily on his soother as he colored. He always carried it in his mouth. It was one of those brown rubber nipples that mothers pulled over baby bottles. Francie tried to not let it bother her, that silly sucking sound, because Teddie was funny and Mrs. Kyraniak's boy. But sometimes when he ran around with the rest of the kids with that thing in his mouth, she thought she'd like to bop him one. If she were to hit Teddie in the belly by surprise, he might even swallow that nipple. Francie held her crayon above her paper and turned to stare at Teddie. She could see the soother floating around and around in his stomach, trying to get out, but only shrinking smaller and smaller until it became just a wee doll nipple. Teddie caught Francie's eye and grinned foolishly, the nipple plugged in the middle of his face. Disgusted, she turned back to her butterflies.

They wasted no time in getting home. At first they raced Prosvigs, but as they neared the shelterbelt, the teams parted. Prosvigs hung over the sides of their open sleigh, running the horses hard.

"See you tomorrow, Francie," Rosy called. Jackie Prosvig put his cold leather mitten on her face, pushed her down into the sled and sat on her. The boys thought it was funny, but Francie knew that Rosy would be real mad.

The Polanskis raced into their yard as long blue shadows slanted across the snow.

CHAPTER THREE

After supper they gathered again under the gas lamp. The pile of feathers in the center of the table was much smaller. Francie shivered as she heard the wind snuffling at the corner of the old house. In the black window she could see herself. Something could be out there, looking at her. She moved to a place from where she could not see the window, even though she sat nearer to her mother and would have to work harder tonight. It was better than being near a window, and her mother would be in a good mood because the work was nearly finished.

In the corner Dad carded wool into fluffs. After he had combed enough, he put one foot on the pedal of the spinning wheel and picked up a handful of wool. Carefully he fed it to the spool, pulling the strand just so. When Dad spun wool, there were hardly ever any lumps in the yarn. Francie had tried it, but her yarn turned out lumpy every time. The spinner had to work his foot slowly and carefully and ply the wool evenly. That was the secret, but Francie's foot worked too independently. She was sorry that she couldn't do better, because if she could she wouldn't have to strip feathers or embroider in the evenings. Best of all, her father would be proud of her and maybe tell Mr. Chorney or Mr. Szoda about how good she was. Then the men would see that girls were useful on a farm too, just as boys were.

"Tell us more about the olden days," Joe urged.

Dad had left his mother and father and all of his brothers in the Old Country. He had been the first one to leave home, and he had known, when he said good-by to his mother with the long yellow braids, that he would likely never see them again. But to Canada he came because there was not enough land in the Old Country, and there was a war going on there someplace. The soldiers would have come soon and taken Dad away to fight, but he didn't want to kill; he wanted to farm and not do foolish things.

So he had put on his cap, put a few clothes in a bag and bought a ticket to Canada. The family had just enough money to buy one ticket. The oldest boy got the first chance to come to Canada. When he made enough money, he would send for his brothers, one by one.

Francie looked at her father patiently whirring the spinning wheel as her mother talked. What had his mother with the long yellow braids said when he had gone away forever? Had she cried? Her father would not have cried. He would have just thrown the bag over his shoulder and walked away, tall, into the ship, without turning around, because he had to go.

The little grandma who lived to the west wouldn't have cried either. She would just say, "Good-by, good-by," and start cooking another supper.

"Was it hard in the early days, Dad?" Eddie asked.

"Eet sure was hard times. Een Poplar Valley dere was many Ukrainian and German farmers. Nobody was rich. Eef your cow have de calf and dey both live, they have a party."

Mr. Polanski described the homestead. "De neighbors come and help us build de sod house. Een two days eet was finished.

"Dat was a good house. Een de winter eet was warm and no drafts. Een de summer eet was cool. Harry and Joe and Eddie and Nick all born dere."

Harry could not remember the house of his early years. "Were the walls made of dirt, like our cellar?"

"Ya, dey was much de same. Only de Mother put de whitewash on de walls. Sometimes when we get old newspapers she paste dem on.

"But you must understand. Eet beeg t'ing to break a window een de middle of de winter. Ma can only stick some rags een dere, and eet stay like dat until da spring come.

"Den I heetch up de oxen an' drive to Luouw, dat's forty-five miles away, for de glass. Eet take me two days to go to Luouw and back. Not like now. Now we can go to Field and back een one day."

"Francie, go downstairs and get some apples." Mrs. Polanski regarded the small pile of feathers on the table. "Nobody have an apple yet today."

Slowly Francie went to the cellar door. Where was Joe? He liked to close the door when someone was down there. In the dark.

Dad was showing Joe how to spin. If she hurried, she could get the apples and be back before he noticed. If she hurried.

She propped the door open and pattered down the steps. The light reached only to the bottom of the stairs. The apple barrel stood in a corner, its fat sides bulging. She would have to be fast.

Something moved under her foot and she jumped with horror. A spider web clutched at her face. It was awful, awful with live things in the cellar.

And with Joe up there ready to drop the door and to laugh while she screamed with terror.

Balancing herself on the rim, she grabbed for the apples. Hurry, hurry, make it fast. She darted to the bottom of the steps. Up and into the warm kitchen. This time she had made it. Joe was still at the spinning wheel.

"Apples, you guys," Eddie called. They attacked from all directions and emptied the basin fast. Under the dish Francie held on to the biggest apple for herself.

Joe reached under the basin and took the big apple easily. His eyes danced as he bit into it, the juice trickling down his chin.

She hated Joe. He was always like that, wanting to spoil it for everybody.

"Stop that fighting," Mrs. Polanski warned Bennie and Nick who were wrestling on the floor. "I will finish up these feathers. Thanks God. You boys find something to do or yous will go to bed."

The younger boys fished out their wooden tops made from their mother's sewing spools. Eddie, who liked to work with his hands, had carved two tops from one spool, whittling down the shanks to fine points. Short, pointed sticks served as pivots. Danny and Stanley sat with their feet touching, enclosing a space with their legs so that the tops would not twirl under the stove.

"See who can turn the longest."

Eddie bent his head over another spool. This winter he had made ten spool tractors.

"Francie, you doing nothing. Go iron dose flour bags and do some embroidery."

Francie dragged the wooden box holding the embroidery supplies toward the table where the light was better. She began looking through the stencils that had not yet been used.

The older boys embroidered too, until they had to do the barn work. Eddie did the best of all, with his small, even stiches. Joe hated it. He jabbed the needle any old way into the cloth so that his mother would say, "Dat's enough. Go and do something else." As long as the younger boys kept quiet in the evenings they were safe.

With Francie it was different. Girls weren't to waste their time doing nothing. Often she and Eddie and their mother sat embroidering around the heater in the Other Room, toasting their toes, while Harry helped Dad with the harnesses and Joe played solitaire. Not a single tea towel or pillowcase in the Polanski household was blank.

"Some peoples," Mrs. Polanski would say, and Francie knew that she meant Prosvigs, "they don' do nothing een da evenings. They don' embroidery; they don' sew, they don' strip feathers. I don' know how they can live like dat. They don' haf nothing nice in da house."

16

Rosy was lucky that her mother didn't care about embroidery. All of Prosvigs' tea towels were plain. Yet Francie was sure that their towels wiped just as dry as anyone else's. Prosvigs had a lot of fun on winter evenings. They played cards and other games. Some days Rosy came to school sleepy because she went to bed whenever she got tired.

When Francie lay in bed that night she thought of the next day. Her father would go to town and get the papers. There would be the funnies, maybe an almanac with new jokes and riddles and the page in the centre of *The Western Producer* with all those letters written by young people.

CHAPTER FOUR

The morning came, bitterly cold. Snow had blown in between the windows, and now they wouldn't be able to see out until spring. That didn't matter very much, because all there was to see was a solid wall of snow as high as the house.

In the bleak light that filtered into the Other Room, Francie stuffed her skirt into her overalls. Maybe she should put on another pair for that long walk home. She and Rosy wore their brothers' old clothes cheerfully because boys' clothes were so much warmer than girls' clothes. It was always warmer on the knee that had the patch.

During recess all the kids played blackboard games. Mrs. Kyraniak didn't mind, although the air hung close with the smell of chalk dust. They played tic-tac-toe and hangman and X's and O's. Everybody watched what everyone else was doing so that if a new game was started, they could copy.

"Rosy, you're not spelling that right. It's f-r . . . ."

Francie felt a sudden, sharp sting on her cheek. A small, pointed piece of chalk fell to the floor. She spun around swiftly, sure that she would catch Joe. But he was beside the furnace, playing marbles with Johnny Szoda, who was not smart enough to win anything.

Something in the look of Outlaw Turner's back raised suspicion in Francie. He stood at the blackboard, his back too rigid, too still. He was mean and smart. He could have thrown that chalk, but he would never let on.

He wasn't really an outlaw, and his real name was Jesse. But no one except the teacher called him by his real name. Everybody called him Outlaw because he had been expelled twice. He had sworn at the teacher and broken a desk top with an axe that he had been chasing the girls with. He was the worst boy in the school, and every day he took a chance at being expelled again.

Francie walked up behind him. He knew that she was there.

"Tic-tac-toe-round-I-go-if-I-miss-this-I-will-get-this." He opened his eyes and saw that he had landed on a ten.

"You're cheating," Francie said loudly. "Your eyes were open."

Outlaw calmly chalked a ten under his name. Every number was a ten.

"Mind yer own business, skinny. You can't even count up to ten."

She stood her ground. "You threw that chalk." Outlaw would never dare to hit her with the teacher in the room. But if she kept after him long enough he might swear out loud.

"Prove it."

He said something to the Miller boy behind his hand, and they both snickered. He had her, and they both knew it.

"Children," Mrs. Kyraniak said. "I would like you all to go outside and get some exercise. You have been inside all morning. Before you go, there is something that I want to talk about.

"When you are playing, some of you call each other names. That's not right.

"I don't want that to happen again. The next time it happens, I will have to punish whoever does that."

She looked right at Outlaw Turner when she said it. Mrs. Kyraniak was kind, but she meant it. Either Outlaw or Joe would get caught calling names. They had names for everyone.

"Let's play Fox and Goose," Joe suggested when they trooped outside. "We'll tramp a big pie in the snow, then cut it up into eights. All the geese stay on the trails. The fox tries to catch one. If you run to the center, you're safe. But only one goose can be safe at one time."

Rosy chugged along at the end of the line, her breath making a fog around her face. Joe swatted her over the bottom.

"Rosy's It! Everybody scatter!"

The only way Rosy could catch anyone was to get several geese bunched up on one section of the pie. Especially if a Miller was in the lead. Millers couldn't move fast, and they slowed everyone down behind them.

Rosy stopped in the middle of the pie, looking them over, her cheeks flaming.

"Yah!" Outlaw hooted. "You couldn't catch a casterated turtle!"

Rosy went for him then. Outlaw ran toward Francie.

Dismayed, Francie took off, trying to get to the outside of the pie. But Rosy changed direction and came around the other way. Now Francie found herself right behind Outlaw.

"Hurry up!" She crowded his heels. "Move!"

"Go chase yourself." He slowed deliberately.

No one could run past another goose. She was trapped. Rosy pelted her joyfully on the back.

"Francie's It!" Outlaw guffawed.

"You old — bugger!"

Everyone stopped dead. Outlaw's eyebrows shot up with delight. "Francie called me a name! You guys heard her!"

"Now you're going to get it! I'm telling on you." Joe ran to the school.

"Ha, ha, Francie. Now you're going to get it."

She stood there, unbelieving. A contrite Rosy put an arm around her shoulders.

"Sorry, old pal. I shouldna done that. Don't be mad at me, huh?"

Joe skipped down the steps. "You're to go in, Francie. Teacher wants to see you."

They walked toward the school together, arm in arm. At the door Rosy said earnestly, "I'm going to wait out here. It was my fault."

Francie looked at her friend. Rosy looked like a miniature Russian, with felt helmet pulled down part way on her head. The laughter was gone.

Mrs. Kyraniak was checking exercise books. She did not look up.

Francie waited, her knees trembling. She leaned against a front desk so that her knees would stop shaking. Mrs. Kyraniak's hair was waved neatly and pinned down.

"Well, Francie." The tone was sad. "What did you do?"

"I called Outlaw a name." Shame choked her.

"After I warned you all?"

Francie swallowed.

"What name did you call him?"

Francie whispered the word, "Bugger".

"That wasn't nice."

"I didn't mean to. It just happened."

Mrs. Kyraniak still hadn't looked up. Francie brushed a hot tear from her cheek and waited. The red pencil flicked over a page.

I wish she'd hurry up, she thought. I wish she'd just give me the licking so that I could be stopped crying when the others come in.

Mrs. Kyraniak began to pile the exercise books. Francie grew faint.

"Go and ring the bell." Mrs. Kyraniak smiled at her.

She managed to pick up the bell, to swing it weakly. Feet began to pound around the corner.

She scuttled to her desk, preparing herself for the onslaught of eyes.

She swung her legs carelessly when they trooped in, their eyes searching out her shame. Mrs. Kyraniak adjusted the blinds on the south windows.

20

"She didn't do anything," Francie whispered to Rosy. "Nothing at all."

She wished she could shout it to the whole room.

Suddenly she loved Mrs. Kyraniak very much. Dad had always said that she was a good teacher.

As soon as Mrs. Kyraniak left for dinner the other children gathered around Francie.

"What did she do?"

"Did you get a licking?"

"Ha, ha, Francie."

"Serves you right."

They would never believe her. They would say that she was just lying if she told them. Or call her the teacher's pet. She wouldn't tell on Mrs. Kyraniak, ever.

During the last recess a shout from the road checked them in their play. Mr. Polanski held his team and gestured with a big, mittened arm. They stood uncertainly. He was the secretary of the school board. Even Prosvigs knew that he was not to be fooled with.

"Hoi!" he called. "Come on over!"

They moved forward slowly. The big man climbed over the coal heaped in the front of the bobsleigh, reached down and tossed aside the horsehide rugs. With a swift underhand motion he flung something round and red at them.

Apples! They must have been sent out for the school children! A mad scramble began.

Mr. Polanski was in a rare good mood. Again and again he threw the apples, first this way, then that. They clambered over each over, grabbing and shouting. Francie saw her father's white teeth flash under the dark moustache. He liked giving to people. Icicles hung from each end of his moustache, giving him a sinister, Mongolian look.

He clucked to the horses and moved on. As the bell called gently, they ran to the school, rich beyond measure. Almost everybody had two apples.

"Here, Francie." Rosy handed over a large apple. "I got three, and you just got one. You have this."

Teddie offered an apple to his mother.

"Eat the apples now if you want to," she smiled. "Just as long as you do your work."

They bit into the sweet flesh with relish. The fruit was very cold, and the juice ran down their chins.

In spite of the cold, Francie danced home after school. No one had to embroider or do any work when the papers came. After the dishes were done, their mother brought the papers to the table.

"Leave for me da *Home Loving Hearts* in da *Free Press*," she said, doling out the funnies to reaching hands. "Daddy brings you some cheese from da municipality. I cut you some an' you can eat it for lunch. Iss rich and wery good for you."

The children tore their eyes from the papers and looked at the big disc of yellow cheese. They did not grab. To them, cheese was cottage cheese, which was made into perogies. This yellow stuff was the cheese that the English people ate. No one cared for it. It tasted dry and had a moldy smell.

"It is heavy, that cheese. I t'ink it wery good for you. Take it and put it under da big bed upstairs, Harry. Nobody will step on it there, and it iss wery cold on da floor. It will keep good and not freeze."

She was right. The cheese would keep forever up there. It was safe — safe as anything because nobody liked it.

CHAPTER FIVE

Francie awoke Sunday morning with a singing in her heart.

Now I am eight, she thought. It's the last year that I can still get a doll. They must have gotten the doll from Eaton's because they got the parcel last week.

She dressed with haste. Her parents were already up. Francie could hear her father blowing on his coffee in the kitchen.

"Happy birthday, Frynca." Her mother smiled above her brown apron. "Eat some porridge so you'll grow bigger. You so small you never make da good farmer's wife."

Francie helped herself to the porridge in the gray pot. She took a spoonful less than usual. Her mother saw, but said nothing.

The floor was drafty, so she sat on her legs on the bench. The boys came into the kitchen, yawning. None of them said anything to Francie until Danny wandered in, one shoe off and hunting for his remaining sock.

"Fwancie," he yawned. "Is today your birthday?"

The boys perked up.

"Oh, boy!" Joe grinned. "Wait till we catch you and give you the royal bumps."

"Ya." Their mother smiled. "She need something to help make her grow."

She tried to get out of the kitchen while they were still eating. But they had been waiting for her all the time.

"Her legs! Grab her legs!" Eddie yelled as Joe caught one arm and Nick the other. Francie kicked wildly but uselessly.

"Okay. Bump her!" Joe counted as they lowered her. "One!"

She stiffened her back.

"Two!" They bumped her whole body on the floor.

"Three!" Joe leaned over and jabbed a cruel finger under her arm. Francie relaxed immediately.

"... seven, eight! Give her one more to make her grow!"

Francie struggled to her feet, glad that it was over. Now she wouldn't have to dodge them all day.

"Go and look what's there on da writing desk," said her mother.

The doll. She flew into the Other Room. An oblong brown paper package lay on the desk.

It couldn't be the Eaton's Beauty. The package was too soft. Maybe they had bought her another rag doll.

As her fingers tugged at the flour bag string, she knew, with a sudden constriction in her throat, that it wasn't going to be a doll at all.

She stared at the navy bloomers and two bright red ribbons for her braids. She turned over a pant leg. Fleece-lined. Nice and warm for school and just awful because dark bloomers showed up so much under dresses.

Joe came into the kitchen and dumped something hard on the floor. "Where's Francie?" he asked. "Here's something Dad made for her."

Francie moved under a shadow to the kitchen. On the floor sat a sled, a gay, little red sled made just for her.

"Now you can hitch it to the bobsleigh and ride behind," Eddie said, looking at Francie curiously. "Don't you like it?"

Francie picked up the rope and pulled the sled to the Other Room where she could be alone.

She stood beside the heater, looking from the sled to the bloomers, from the bloomers to the sled. She could wear the bloomers when she rode on the sled. Everybody had to have warm clothes for winter. But there was something growing in her throat.

"Fwancie," Danny sang, tucking a bare foot under as he straddled the sled. "Pull me. Gimmee a wide."

"No, not on da floor," their mother warned. "you wear out da floor with dat. Yous dress up and go play outside. There's lots of snowbanks outside."

Francie helped Danny find his lost shoe. It was hard to pull his rubbers on over his shoes.

"Danny, hold your leg straight." The tears were very close.

"Okay," he sighed, leaning back along one elbow. The rubber boot finally slipped on.

Francie was glad to get outside. The cold wind made their eyes water, and she could cry without anyone knowing. Her plaid scarf turned soggy, then began to freeze over her cheeks.

She pulled the sled up to the higher snowbanks, Danny ploughing behind. They sat on the sled together, Danny in the front with his knees up. The sled took the banks well. Dad always built things to last. He had nailed narrow strips of tin to the bottoms of the runners to make them slide easily.

The day was long. They tired of riding in the sled and went back into the house. They colored in their coloring books and listened to the bigger boys playing Durack. Francie could not be coaxed into joining the card games.

"Thinks she's too big for us now," Joe jeered after she refused for the third time. "Just because she's eight years old."

No one came visiting because the weather was too cold. It seemed like a long time until night.

That night Francie lay in bed, watching the firelight leaping on the far wall. Sometimes she could see in it the form of a jester, mocking and dancing.

She would never get a doll now. She was eight years old.

CHAPTER SIX

By the first of December, the business of getting the Christmas concert together became serious at Westfield School. Lessons were held in the mornings only, and the entire afternoon was spent in practicing and making costumes by hand.

First, all of the children stood on the stage in rows and sang carols. They had to know the words by heart because it wouldn't be polite to hold books in front of people. Anyway, they would show the people who came from Field that they could sing any of the English carols just as well as the school children of Field.

Outlaw was tall and so was Joe, so Mrs. Kyraniak put them in the back row. That was what they wanted, because when everybody else was singing a high note, they would suddenly poke someone near mean and hard in the ribs. The one who got the poke stopped singing with a yelp, and Joe and Outlaw would laugh like crazy. They never laughed out loud, but just in quiet explosions. Everyone would start wondering who got poked this time and then they would start to forget lines. Mrs. Kyraniak didn't seem to notice. She watched the words and the music and used her arm to remind them when to sing right out and when to sing softly.

Then the kids would file off the stage, and Francie would stay on for the welcome recitation. She had to dip her head a little and hold out the sides of her skirt at the beginning and end. She would not be wearing a dress until concert night. Outlaw snickered whenever she pulled her overalls sideways. During some of the noon hours, he followed Francie around the room, bowing and pretending that she was royalty, "Make way for the queen," he'd say solemnly. Then, as if he were calling his dog, "Here, Queenie, here, Queenie."

One blustery noon hour she had had enough. She whirled and chopped at him with the yardstick. She missed Outlaw and broke the stick neatly on a desk top. Outlaw guffawed for the rest of the noon hour.

Every afternoon they went through the concert, following the correct order so that they would learn the program automatically. Then they went back over the things that gave them the most trouble.

Mrs. Kyraniak prompted with infinite patience.

"All right, Rosy," she said as the girl clumped onto the stage, holding an imaginary wand in her hand. "You're a fairy. Try to walk like one."

The big boys snorted. Rosy turned red and tried her entrance again. But she was still Rosy. She came down hard on her heels — ka-lump, ka-lump.

"No, no, Rosy." Mrs. Kyraniak tried to make her understand. "A fairy is as light as a feather. So light that the wind can blow her away. Imagine yourself drifting like a feather."

Rosy tried again. She started to tiptoe. Too late she realized what flexing her calves would mean. Both of her stockings wilted, then settled halfway down her legs.

Rosy giggled while the boys howled. The teacher rolled her eyes to the ceiling.

"Just say your part."

Between suppressed giggles, Rosy began. "I am ... the ... the ... Christmus ... fairy ...."

". . . and I bring . . . ." Mrs. Kyraniak prompted.

"And I bring . . . bring . . . ."

Mrs. Kyraniak sighed. "Better study your part harder, Rosy. I don't want you back on the stage until you know it perfectly." Rosy clumped off the stage, giggling, holding up the tops of her stockings.

Prosvigs didn't care much about concerts. They didn't care much about anything. Mrs. Kyraniak had a hard time getting them to learn their parts. That was why she started the practicing so soon. All of the Westfield people would be at the concert, whether they had children going to school or not, and part of Prosvigs' district and, of course, the Board.

If the concert turned out well, then the teacher was good. And because they liked Mrs. Kyraniak, most of the kids tried hard to learn their parts.

Three more sleeps until the concert! Then there were two, and all at once it was the night before.

Francie climbed into bed, her head spinning with lines from the plays. She had memorized not only her own part, but almost everyone else's part as well. She was so excited that she felt hungry, even though they had stuffed themselves with perogies at supper.

Everyone made mistakes at the last practice the following morning. Perspiration beaded Mrs. Kyraniak's high forehead. It was a full dress rehearsal, with Joe and Outlaw drawing the bedsheets after every item. The bedsheets had been hung from the wires above the stage. They slid easily by means of large safety pins. With the hanging of the sheets, the concert

27

changed from a dream to a reality. The impersonal white cloth enclosed a rectangular world of wonder.

The horses were surprised to find themselves going home at noon. They never went home from school that early except on concert days, or if a blizzard was coming. That afternoon would be long, long; the night would never come. Francie ran from the kitchen to the Other Room and back in anguish.

But then it took a long time for everyone to have a bath and to put on clean underwear. The big boys couldn't do that until after chores, so the little ones were scrubbed first in the Other Room behind the heater.

"Put your head down." Francie obediently lowered her lathered head and squeezed her eyes shut. The soap got into them anyway and burned hard. She wished that she had shorter hair like the boys. They didn't get knots that filled up the comb, and no one could pull their hair. And they never had to curl it.

Curling was awful. After her hair had dried, and Francie stood forlorn in her white petticoat, her mother lit the kerosene lamp. In its glass chimney she hung the long black curling tongs. After they became hot she took them out of the chimney and quickly clamped the tongs around small bunches of Francie's lank hair. There was an immediate transformation.

"Turn." And Francie turned, just a little. "Da oder way! No so *much!*"

The ordeal always wore her mother down. The tongs were returned to the lamp when they no longer inspired a tight curl. They were sure to be too hot when her mother first took them out again, and Francie jumped when the hot iron touched her scalp. "Keep still!" The acrid smell of burnt hair tingled Francie's nostrils.

At last she stood looking like a white lamb, her hair in tight unnatural curls, her neck warm and unhappy, her scalp sore in several places. Her mother slipped the clean, pressed satin ribbon under her hair and up over her ears and tied it in a blue bow at the top of her head.

Francie looked at her reflection secretly after she had put on her dress. She was the only one with light-colored hair in the Polanski family. She wished tonight that her hair could be dark and shiny like that of her brothers. Every single one of them was lucky, and she had to be different.

Francie shrank from the picture she saw of herself standing on the stage tonight, singing with everyone else who had dark hair. If she were tall like Joe, she could stand at the back and not be seen by all the people, but Mrs. Kyraniak had put Francie and Rosy side by side in the very front row.

Dad brought the bobsleigh to the kitchen door, and the boys carried out the feather ticks and laid them from the front to the back. Mum and Francie and the younger ones sat on the first ticks and were covered with a second layer. Francie fought her way out of the soft mass so that she could see the stars spangled in the black sky. From where she sat she could not see over the edge of the box, but she could make out the white cloud of the horses' breath rising in the quiet air and the big, dark outline of her father at the front.

The branches of the shelterbelt passed by, and they were out in the open. The bigger boys clung to the outside of the wooden box; they never got cold. Francie inhaled the fresh night air filled with the smell of horse. She was so happy that she could die.

And oh, what a wonderful place the school had become with the night. The air was pungent with the scent of spruce, and the big tree glimmered faintly in the moonlight coming through the windows.

Then the panic began. Coats had to be put away with care, or they would be lost in the stampede after the concert. It was so very hard to do the right things because they all felt that they were ready to fly to pieces with excitement. The children raced in and out of the girls' cloakroom, which would serve as the dressing room for everyone tonight. They gazed hungrily at the small pile of gifts beneath the tree. Francie's godmother, Mrs. Wilk, sat in a front seat beside Mrs. Polanski. Mrs. Wilk would have a present for Francie under the tree. All the mothers filled up the front rows, like so many brooding hens. The fathers and the boys who didn't go to school any more stood at the back, even though there were planks laid out across the desks for sitting. One solid row in the middle of the spectators was filled with people from Field.

"On the stage, everybody." Mrs. Kyraniak's face was white. Fear gripped them all. They lined up in proper rows, subdued. In the front row, right up against the white sheet, Francie felt her knees shake.

"Oh, Rosy, but I'm scared!"

"Me, too," Rosy said cheerfully.

They stood there while Mrs. Kyraniak stepped out in front of the sheets. Quiet descended upon the crowd. The teacher's voice sounded tiny. She welcomed all the people and wished them a merry Christmas. Then the sheets parted.

For one terrible instant they stood looking at the rows of uplifted faces in the crowd. But it wasn't an instant; it was a long time before Mrs. Kyraniak turned to face them and brought her arm down. Some of them began "O Canada" right away, with weak voices; the others joined in by the second line. Francie's lips began to move. At first she said the words, then the fear began to subside and she could feel the warm waves of happiness returning. It was going to be a good concert.

In the cloakroom sheer madness raged. The children had completely forgotten the order of the program. They kept referring to the lists tacked up in several places to see what came next or after that. The only light available bobbed from a kerosene lamp on the windowsill.

Francie struggled to pull her mother's old purple crepe dress over her curly mop. It went on crooked; the fabric stretched and the front pleats ended up on her side. When she tried to straighten the front, the pleats pulled over crazily in an S pattern. It was the clothes underneath that kept the dress from falling smooth. She grabbed a cushion and stuffed it into the top part of the dress through the V-neck. She took a second cushion and tried to stuff it up to her front from underneath, but the first cushion prevented her from seeing exactly where to push. The dress stretched, and Francie hurriedly pulled a belt around her grotesque body. Applause drifted into the frantic cloakroom, and the children dressing there re-doubled their efforts. The first drill was over, and the mother play was next.

"Hurry up, hurry up," hissed the others.

Francie snatched a stick pin, the only thing she could find, off the windowsill and jabbed it into the belt which she could not see. The belt held, and she was propelled by Mrs. Kyraniak out of the cloakroom, because other children had to get ready for the pageant. Francie grabbed the mother's broom and dashed onstage.

There wasn't any time to think. The sheets parted, and Francie began to pretend-sweep the floor. She was on stage alone. She felt the awful hush as the audience waited for her words. She stopped sweeping as the teacher had told her to, leaned on the broom and said in a sing-song voice, "Oh, dear me. Whatever will I do, poor widow and all? Here it is, Christmas again, and I have no gifts for my children. I wish that I could give them something to make them good."

Four terrible children ran shrieking onto the stage. They raced around her, through the litter that she was supposed to be sweeping, over the chairs. Francie put her hand up to her eyes to show her suffering, and then she went into her mad act.

Johnny Szoda was one of the terrible children. He could act his part better than anyone else. Francie raised the broom and smacked him on the behind as he lowered his head to dash under the table.

Startled, he jerked up and cracked his forehead on the edge of the table. A vase of crepe paper roses fell to the floor.

"Children! Children!" Francie yelled over the bedlam. That was when it happened. The belt parted from around her middle. Francie felt the sudden list of the belly cushion.

She dropped her broom and grabbed at her middle, giving the cushion a hitch. Someone in the wings snickered; she knew it was Outlaw. People started to laugh.

In came Rosy, bumbling over the long crepe paper dress, her fat face flushed and the silver foil star perched crookedly to one side over an eye. She came on strong, smiling, then forgot her lines.

Mrs. Kyraniak prompted once, twice, three times. Rosy stood there turning red. Francie tugged at her sagging middle, leaned down awkwardly and rescued her broom.

"Children! Children!" she yelled again, only this time they were not doing anything bad. The were all standing and looking at Rosy. Francie swung the broom clumsily. It jabbed Johnny Szoda in the corner of his eye.

"Ow-w-w," he said audibly.

Rosy woke from her trance. "I-am-the-Christmus-fairy," she droned. "All-who-come-under-my-spell-are-filled-with-the-spirit-of-love-and-goodwill."

It was Rosy's biggest speech. She tapped all the wicked children on their heads. Johnny was wiping his weeping eye with his sleeve. The star fell off the end of the wand when Rosy tapped him.

Then all the children ran to their mother. They were supposed to put their arms around Francie and beg forgiveness, and she was supposed to hug them all. But she couldn't do it right because the bottom cushion had slipped down to her knees and she was having trouble keeping her feet together and the cushion in place. She gave the lower cushion a big hitch. It jerked toward her middle at the same time that the contrite children pressed close to her for forgiveness. She had her hands too full to hug them. "Quit pushing!" she whispered savagely.

The onlookers laughed and clapped when the bedsheets were drawn, but they weren't supposed to laugh. The ending was really a bit sad.

Johnny wasn't mad at Francie when they changed in the cloakroom. He never got mad at anyone but himself. Still, Francie was sorry that she had hit him like that. He was older than she was, but he was never mean.

They noticed the smell when they were dressing for the tramp drill.

"What's that?" Rosy sniffed, pulling on ragged overalls. "Francie, do you smell something funny?"

They looked toward the lamp framed in the black window. "Smells like chicken feathers burning." Francie pinned one of her suspenders with a safety pin.

Mrs. Kyraniak hurried out to check the stage. They heard her outraged whisper.

"Jesse! Quick, put the fire out! Have you been smoking?"

They wanted awfully to get out of the cloakroom and see what was going on, but they had to get ready for the drill first. Smoke floated into the cloakroom, making their eyes water.

"Wind up the gramophone, Betty," the teacher ordered. And to the tramps, "Get in line. Those who are supposed to come in from the other side, get over there. Remember, don't march out until the fourth beat."

Francie and three boys scurried across the stage to wait behind the side

31

curtain. But there was no side curtain. There was about half of one. The lower half had been burned off and was still smoking.

Left-right-left-right they clomped across the stage in men's big boots, carrying sticks with red spotted handkerchiefs hanging from the ends. Shapeless felt hats were pulled down over their heads, with strings of grey wool hanging around their ears. All of their shirttails hung out. Even though the onlookers laughed as they recognized each tramp in turn, Francie thought that the drill wasn't so far from the truth. Nobody had much money; everybody wore old clothes every day; the people were laughing at themselves.

After the first drill, the older children put on a play. It was about a girl whose lover had left her to make a fortune, but he had forgotten to write, and she thought that he had forgotten her. The banker, who was Francie's cousin Bill, came to foreclose the mortgage. The girl cried and cried.

"Alas, take pity on me."

The banker remained heartless. He rubbed his hands together with joy.

"There is only one way left to you," he chortled. "Marry me and you shall be well off for the rest of your life."

"Never, never," the girl wept.

"At midnight, then," warned cousin Bill, twisting his black moustache. It came off in his hand, and he had to hold it under his nose.

"At midnight I shall return. And then, my fair beauty, if you do not consent to be mine, you will be turned out of this house into the cold, cruel world to fend for yourself."

He strode offstage, holding up the moustache, and the girl squeezed water out of a wet cloth that she kept hidden in her hand, to show how bitter her grief was.

They couldn't watch the end of the play because they had to get ready for the next drill. Great, grinning faces had been crayoned on the bags, and the children put them over their heads backwards. They could see a little through small slots cut in the backs of the bags.

Mrs. Kyraniak began to play the funny, clumsy music for the drill; the children clumped onstage. People began to laugh right away because the children had their clothes on backwards. When they turned their backs to the crowd, their funny faces grinned. Then the people laughed louder because it looked as if the children had their feet on backwards.

It was hot inside a bag, with trying to see ahead and with the warmth onstage. One more circle and then they could file off. Teddie stepped on her shoe and pulled it off. Francie kept on walking. Stupid Teddie, she thought. Bet he's sucking that nipple under his bag.

She heard the bump behind her and the roar of merriment that followed. But she kept right on walking, as Mrs. Kyraniak had told them to in case anything happened.

"What happened?" she asked Rosy as they pulled off the bags.

"Johnny walked right off the stage," Rosy giggled. "He fell on top of Mrs. Chorney."

Johnny came into the cloakroom, smiling broadly. He had done something to make the people laugh. He felt good.

In no time they were back on the stage, singing carols. Just as they were finishing the last song, they heard a commotion out on the porch.

"Ho-ho-ho! Merry Christmas!" There was a stamping of boots and the mad jangling of the hand bell. No one sang the last lines of the carols. Santa bounded in, making a lot of racket and carrying a big, lop-sided gunny sack over his shoulder. He was wearing a coat that looked like Dad's, and big leather mitts. On his head perched a gay red toque. He had a hard time seeing out of the little slits cut into the eyes of the mask.

He fooled around with the little kids first.

"Hello, little man!" he shouted at Danny, who was staring open-mouthed from between his mother's knees. "Have you been a good boy this year?"

Danny hid his face.

"Has he?" Santa asked Mrs. Polanski.

"Yah . . . oh, sometimes." A ripple of laughter ran through the schoolroom. Onstage, the children trembled with hope.

Santa pumped the teacher's hand. "How about a kiss for old Santa?" And everyone roared as Mrs. Kyraniak, her face a bright pink, kissed the paper face.

"O-ho-ho!" Santa cheered, rubbing his mitts together and looking around for someone else. He caught sight of Francie giggling, her hand stuck in her mouth.

"How about you, little girl? "Santa shouted at her. "Have you been a good girl?"

"Yes!" Francie squeaked in terror. The big man reached up and plucked her off the stage and swung her around. She wriggled unhappily out of his arms.

"How about a kiss for Santa?" her tormentor continued. "Give me a kiss, and I'll give you a present."

Francie pressed her mouth against the funny paper face and caught the strong scent of whiskey on the man's breath. Her reward was the first brown paper bag full of treats.

Everyone got a bag. The paper was smooth and shiny, and the bag was rolled tightly. Nestling on top of the nuts and the delicious ribbon candy inside was a fragrant Christmas orange and a dark red apple with a winey scent. They would eat for a week out of that bag, carefully hoarding and setting aside so much a day to make it last.

All the children were given a small, thin gift wrapped in white tissue paper containing two pencils from the teacher. Francie tore apart the gift from her godmother. She was delighted to find an incredibly clean, soft red scarf. It could be wound around and around her head on cold mornings.

"Feel it, Rosy. It's like kitten fur." She climbed off the stage in the melee and ran with the gift to her mother.

"Say tank-you to Mrs. Wilk for such a nice present," her mother instructed.

Francie's shy thanks pleased the woman. At that very moment she heard someone call her name.

Over and over the heads it came, passing from one hand to another. Francie stood speechless, looking at the shoebox in her hands.

"Open it, open it," urged the old women around her. She felt their gladness coming at her from under their heavy, black babushkas. She pulled off the flour bag string.

A fold of brown paper covered the contents. She turned it over and looked into the painted blue eyes of Rosy's best doll.

"For me? You want me to have your doll? Don't you want to keep it?"

"I want you to have it, pal. I'm nine now and I don't need her anymore."

"Oh, Rosy ... I'll take very good care of her." Francie hugged her sturdy friend joyfully. If only she could have given Rosy something, like a bottle of hand lotion or a box of fine handkerchiefs.

Joe came up to see her prize. He was chewing a whole package of gum at once. He looked at the doll and then did the Bad Thing. He reached out and flipped the doll's skirt to see if it had any pants. Francie pulled the box away.

During the ride home Francie curled her legs under and nodded in the warm cocoon of feather ticks. In her arms she cradled the shoebox, feeling rich, rich beyond words. She had a real doll and a bag of treats and tomorrow was Christmas Eve.

CHAPTER SEVEN

Christmas Eve was very special. People worked in the morning, but the late afternoon became a holy time, so the boys did the chores early. Mum helped Francie and the little ones clean the wheat for supper. All the wheat was poured on the big table and divided into small areas with their fingers. Then the grasshopper heads and chaff were removed. The wheat was very important. It was the Life, and it would be the first thing they ate that night.

In the Christmas Eve twilight a knock sounded on the door.

"Come in," Mum called in a soft, respectful voice. Harry, the oldest son, carried in an oat sheaf and spoke for it.

"*Dobra vachi*," he said to them all.

"*Die Boza zdrowla*," their mother replied.

"*Dobra vachi*," the sheaf repeated.

"*Die Boza zdrowla*."

After the sheaf had spoken for the third time and received the proper greeting, Harry carried him to the corner of the kitchen and set him on a chair. No one could move him until New Year's Day when he would be carried to the barn and spread for the cows to eat, the old year no longer of any use.

"Go feed the old *jeedo*," their mother directed. They hid apples and nuts and candies in the sheaf's beard. The old year had to have his supper first. Old people always ate first.

Then Joe came in with the hay. With the proper words he greeted his mother, and she replied again. She took the hay from him and lifted the tattered oilcloth off the table. Over the scarred wood she spread the scented grass in thin wisps, then replaced the cover. Jesus had been born in a barn with hay all around Him. Could little babies smell? Francie thought that she would have liked to be born in a barn too, where the hay smelled so fresh and clean.

Some of the hay clung to her feet as she scurried around with the plates.

But she just walked on. Dad never let anyone sweep on Christmas Eve after sunset. No matter how messy the floor got. To work on the Holy Night would be a big sin.

The plates didn't stand straight on the table, but it didn't matter. Dad came into the kitchen with the little envelope that the priest had mailed them. He sat down heavily at the head of the table, and the children became very quiet.

Francie had to walk around him as she laid the knives and forks. She didn't like to see him sitting there looking away from them all. Her mother bustled around the stove, putting the food into big dishes.

They gathered around the table, soft candlelight playing over their faces. Behind them the shadows crept closer. No one grabbed tonight. They kept their hands in their laps and waited for their father.

Looking into the candlelight, he made the sign of the cross three times, according to his church, then prayed aloud in Ukrainian. Motionless, their heads bowed, the children sat listening to the rich baritone voice of their father as he spoke simply to his God.

Slowly and deliberately, he removed the Host from the envelope. He broke a small piece, put a bit of honey on it, closed his eyes and partook of the Holy Bread.

Their mother was whispering a prayer in Polish, the light brushing her high Slavic cheekbones with shadow. Dad broke the bread again, touched it with honey and gave it to her. Then it was Harry's turn, then Joe's, and so it went, from the oldest to the youngest all around the table.

When Francie's turn came, she closed her eyes tight to be worthy and held the Host in her mouth until the honey melted with a sweet burn. It slipped down before she knew it. She was glad it had not touched her teeth; no one could ever chew the Host.

The first dish to go around the table was the wheat. It had cooked slowly for hours and lay plump and sweet in the blue bowl. Some of the kernels had burst with fatness, and the good white inside peeped out.

Tomorrow was Christmas Day, and then everyone could eat meat. But tonight, on the Holy Night, the meal was meatless, even though there were twelve dishes. The second dish was a clear, salty fish soup. It made them hungrier. They stuffed themselves on meatless cabbage rolls, perohi, fried fish and pie.

People like the Millers and the Turners and those living in Field didn't have any fun on Christmas Eve. They ate and washed dishes and went to bed just as they did on any other night. But the Polanskis and the Wilks and the Prosvigs knew that it was not Christmas Day on which Jesus had been born. He had come in the night, when there had been a star. Even the cattle knew it. If anyone wanted to, he could go out to the barn at midnight and hear the cows talking about the Baby. That was the only time when animals talked.

After supper was over, Dad sat at the table for a long time. Mrs. Polanski and Francie walked around him as they cleared the table and carried the dishes to the pan of hot water on the stove. After a while he began to sing. At first he sang just to himself, but soon the old words came back and he sang as if he were in a church. Francie didn't understand the words, but they made tears come. When she looked at the candle flames, they turned into crosses. Francie felt ashamed of herself and wiped her nose on the tea towel when her mother wasn't looking.

After the dishes were done, Francie crept into the dark nook behind the stove, holding Rosy's doll and watching her father. He gazed into the candlelight. When one song was finished, he thought for a while and then started another. Her mother continued to move between the cupboard and the stove, praying to herself.

A jingle of harnesses announced the arrival of visitors. The dogs greeted them with half-ashamed hough-houghs, because they knew that those who came were friends.

It was Mr. and Mrs. Chorney, who had no children. They always came over on Christmas Eve. Francie left the dim corner to itself. She did not like Mrs. Chorney because she laughed so hard whenever she trapped the girl into speaking Ukrainian. Mrs. Chorney could speak English well enough; she chose to address the children in Ukrainian because she knew that they felt obliged to answer in their father's tongue. And then, her rosy cheeks and fat, round face did not meet with Francie's approval.

"*Scho ti robiss?*" she teased Francie as the child tried to slip into the Other Room where all the boys were playing coyotes.

"*Neech,*" Francie denied, trying to be polite.

"*Scho ti tum miyis?*" continued her good-natured torturer, knowing full well about the new doll.

The trap sprang. Francie came to her in a rush, holding out her prize.

"*Lilka,*" she exclaimed.

Mrs. Chorney burst into a peal of laughter at the display of eagerness. Francie stood scratching her elbow, feeling foolish and confused. Too late she realized that Mrs. Chorney had been waiting to hear the word mispronounced.

In the flurry of removing coats and boots, Francie slipped thankfully into the Other Room. The boys greeted her with enthusiasm.

"Hey, Francie, we need another coyote!"

"Ya, Francie, make yourself a coyote hole."

Each boy except one had a coyote hole under an over-turned chair. One boy was the hunter. He shot at the coyotes with the poker. All of the coyotes had been shot several times. They wanted Francie to get shot too so that they could scuttle around on their hands and knees a longer time before they were shot again.

When the hunter saw the coyote gamboling on the floor in the half-light and pointed the poker and said Bang! then Joe would have to fall dead. If the hunter said Pow! it was time for Harry to die. When he said P-s-s-s-h! like an explosion, Danny had to die. They all died in different ways, but Joe could die the best. He had helped Dad to shoot a dog that ate chickens, so he knew how they died.

Bang! went the hunter, and up jumped Joe, right off the floor on all fours, throwing his head back and coming down hard, legs thrashing. It was good, but he made a big noise when he came down, and Dad yelled from the kitchen for them to be quiet. Then they all began to laugh, trying to be quiet at the same time. But when Bennie grabbed a cushion off the couch and stuffed one corner of it into his mouth, they laughed all the harder, until they were too weak to stand up.

Francie liked the game, but the doll had to have her attention. She satisfied the boys by sitting cross-legged on the couch and being the hunter's wife.

"Sssshhh. Dad's coming."

Dad walked through the Other Room. He came back out of the bedroom with a bottle of whiskey. They sat watching him as he went back to the kitchen. For a moment they had been sure that he had gone into the bedroom for the strap.

The boys changed the game to wolves. That made the play rougher, because wolves sometimes chased the hunter and even bit him on the leg. No one wanted to be the hunter very often.

In the kitchen Dad and Mr. Chorney lifted their voices in song. Something about their singing pulled Francie from the Other Room. Men had nice voices for singing.

Mrs. Polanski saw Francie standing in the doorway.

"Frynca," she said above the noise that the grownups and boys were making. "Get a bowl and give to da boys an orange."

Francie filled the cracked mixing bowl with the wrapped fruit. The boys were getting so rough that Francie had reservations about entering the Other Room. She took one orange for herself, then poked the dish of soft-skinned mandarins around the corner. A chorus of wolf howls greeted her offering. She fled to the safety of the bench behind the table with her doll.

The grownups didn't dance on the Holy Night. They drank and told stories and laughed. Sometimes Dad told a joke; then all of them roared and slapped their thighs. They laughed in English, Francie thought. Even though she could not understand what they said, she knew it was funny by their laughter. No matter what language people talked in, they laughed in English, and everybody understood a laugh.

People laughed in different ways, though. Her dad threw back his head and made a big noise. Mr. Chorney laughed without making a sound. He crinkled up his eyes and sucked at his pipe. Mrs. Chorney laughed all over, her face turning red as if she couldn't get enough air. And when her mother laughed, her two front teeth stuck out a little and she made just a little noise.

Silence fell on the group around the table. Dad filled everyone's glass, then his own. They lifted the glasses, a longing upon their faces that Francie could not understand.

"Die Boza zdrowla." They toasted one another.

One gulp and the drinks were gone. A cloud of blue smoke wreathed Mr. Chorney's face. Dad looked away into himself and began the sad, old Christmas carol.

It was funny. They were having a good time, joking and singing and laughing, but all of them had tears in their eyes.

CHAPTER EIGHT

It was still dark on the morning of the New Year when Francie awoke to hear Harry and Joe come tiptoeing down the stairs. She heard the rustle of their overalls as they pulled on their felt socks beside the heater. Her younger brothers dreamed peacefully; from the partition where her parents slept came no sound. But Francie knew that Mum and Dad were waiting, as she was.

The boys crept out of the house, their boots squeaking on the snow. When all became quiet, Francie lay in tense expectation. Cold, grey morning light stole miserably into the Other Room.

They burst into the kitchen. Then came the assault; together the brothers swept into the Other Room, chanting the wheat blessing as they flung the ice-cold grain over the floors and walls: "Sheesha, rodisha, shilaka spinicha . . ."

They moved to the curtained partition, throwing handfuls of wheat over their father who thanked them courteously. Francie ducked as the grain stung her face, but not soon enough. Her sleeping brothers wakened suddenly; she could hear their protests under the covers. The rattle of wheat striking the floor ceased, and away went Harry and Joe, riding hard past the house, beyond the shelterbelt, because they wanted to catch the Chorneys and Szodas in bed. At each house they would receive thanks and a pocketful of small change. The Chorneys would be especially grateful because they had no sons to wish them a good harvest. Szodas had Johnny; the trick would be to get there before Johnny woke up and threw the grain himself.

Today they would all stay at home while Mum and Dad went visiting in the closed-in cutter. Excitement rose high in Francie at the thought of the fun they would have when evening came. They would play cards in the afternoon, but after supper they would play the games that were really fun. She hoped that her mother and father would not come home too early and spoil it all. Joe got real crazy whenever their parents were gone. He could think up new games for the rest of them.

Their parents were hardly out of the yard when it was agreed that they would all play cards.

"Durack!" Joe yelled. "Where's the cards?"

There was a mad rush for the bench behind the table and for chairs. They divided themselves into two groups, one at each end of the table. Francie sat away from Joe. He always knew what her cards were, and he could always make her a Durack. She didn't like being called the crazy fool any more than the rest did. It felt awful to be the crazy fool over and over again.

Danny hung around the fringes of the two groups, blowing softly into his new harmonica. He watched from between the chairs, almost catching on. Danny couldn't read yet, but he knew that faces were big cards.

Pow! Joe first crashed down at the other end of the table. He laid two jacks for Harry to kill. Kings or queens or aces killed jacks; trumps killed everything except higher trumps.

Francie looked at Joe with awe. Most of them started the game with low cards. Jacks were hoarded until the end.

Harry picked up the jacks because his cards were too low to kill them. So his hand grew bigger, and at the same time he lost his turn to pass a card to the next player. That was the way Durack was played. The one who was left with cards at the end of the game was the crazy fool.

Smash! Francie jumped. Eddie had just killed a four of hearts with a five. Francie clumsily pulled a black five from between her sticky cards and tried to stop Eddie with it. He had a trump, though, and polished off her card with gusto.

Making a big noise meant that a person was a good player and that he could kill. He pounded the table hard when he laid down a high card. When someone passed an ace to be killed, he hit the table as hard as he could. Aces could be killed only by trumps. Most of them kept the aces for the final, bitter, telling round.

Francie pounded the table hard whenever she passed a big card, but in a short time her hand got sore and she couldn't keep pounding. Danny wandered back and forth, attracted by the blows that shook the table.

"I wanna eat," Danny stated to nobody in particular. All at once everyone was hungry. And all at once they saw that while they had been playing, the grey half-light of a January twilight had crept unobserved into the kitchen. No one had remembered to put coal on the fire either. A sudden menace threatened them all.

Joe threw chunks of coal into the heater in the Other Room. Eddie opened the kitchen stove with a clatter of lids. The fire was too low for coal. He arranged split wood over it and placed small chunks of good coal over the wood. Good coal was black and shiny; it caught fire quickly. The poor coal, grey and lifeless, waited at the back of the coal box to be used later when there was a good fire going.

The remaining children shivered and watched Harry light the lamp — the lamp that only Mum and Dad or Harry could light. It was too dangerous for the younger ones to fool around with. They could light the kerosene lamp if they ever had to, because it was safer. But then, the kerosene lamp gave off such a sad, soft light. The gas lamp turned night into day.

Reassured by the cheery hiss of the lamp swinging over the table, they dove into the cold cabbage rolls waiting in the speckled blue roaster. When Mum was going to visit, she always made sure that easy things were left ready for them to eat. *Holopchi* were tasty warm or cold. With them around, no one had to dirty any cooking pots.

"Let's slide down the stairs."

They rushed for the feather ticks. They had to double up on them because there weren't enough for everyone. The ones sitting behind always fell over the one guiding the tick at the front.

Francie and Bennie and Eddie landed on top of each other at the bottom of the stairs.

"Look out!" They heard Joe's yell before they could disentangle themselves. Then there were six of them, smothering and thrashing at the bottom of the stairs.

"Let's play war."

The ticks were thrown onto the beds and they made for the kitchen to set up the battlefield. A scuffle for chairs followed. By tacit agreement, Harry and Joe went on opposite sides. They were the captains.

"Count the 'lastics."

Inch-wide rubber bands, cut from discarded tire tubes, were carefully apportioned.

"Wanna play, Francie?"

She shook her head, remembering the awful splat of a rubber band in her forehead the last time.

"Okay. Stay in the middle and pick up the 'lastics that fall between."

She was in charge of no man's land, then. Joe and Harry laid all the sheepskins and coats they could find over the chairs so that the opposing armies could shoot from behind blinds.

The two armies crouched, each waiting for the other to make the first move. Francie lay low at one end of the space between the two rows of chairs. She knew better than to stick her head up. Even the water pail had been covered. Nothing was safe when they played war.

Splat! Splat! Harry and Joe had poked their heads up at the same time and shot wildly. Now they knew where the captains were. Francie saw Joe sneaking down the line to a new position so that he could catch Harry off guard.

Two more elastics struck the walls. Only the biggest boys could shoot straight and hard. Francie couldn't shoot at all. Whenever she tried, she shot herself in the back of the thumb, and it hurt like crazy. She'd hop about, her thumb in her mouth, feeling silly and useless. It looked so easy for the boys.

Rubber bands began to fly in earnest. A yelp of pain was followed by a guffaw. The fusillade had begun.

Playing war was hard work. The boys sweated behind their protective blinds, creeping about and popping up to fire telling shots. Some shots went wild, and the bands struck the ceiling. Then it was Francie's job to wiggle forward and retrieve them. She'd creep backward, keeping as low to the floor as she could, then fire a thumb-numbing shot straight up above her. After several such attempts, she would succeed in replenishing the rubber band supply behind one of the lines. Francie played no favorites: first Harry's side got the elastic, then Joe's side.

"Hold it! Time for a drink!" called Harry, and they stood up warily, hot and thirsty. By mutual agreement they rushed to the water pail and grabbed the dipper in turn. Francie had to wait until everyone else had drunk because she was not a soldier. But Joe got back to his refuge before Eddie got to his. Gleefully, he stretched back the rubber band as far as he could and fired a powerful shot right at Eddie's wet mouth. At the same instant, they heard Joe's shout of triumph and Eddie's cry of pain.

Eddie's tears left them stricken. He couldn't help it. Joe tried to make a joke out of it, but it was no good. The fun had gone out of the game. It was always like that when somebody got hurt. And somebody always got hurt when they played war. That was why they never played it when Mum and Dad were home.

All the mess had to be cleaned up. Eddie went straight to bed and let them do it. Danny had fallen asleep behind one of the lines under a chair. He didn't even wake up when Harry pulled off his pants. As if it were signalling that it was time for bed, the gas lamp began to expire. A whole tankful of gas had been used up; Dad would know when he came home that they had stayed up late.

Francie crept to bed, tired beyond feeling. She hoped that Eddie's mouth wouldn't show a sore in the morning, or they all might get it the next day.

CHAPTER NINE

On the Feast of the Epiphany, January the sixth, a blizzard stormed in out of the west. Although the base of the house had been banked high with horse manure before the snows came, the floors remained bathed in an icy draft and the children stayed up on the chairs. The west wall of the kitchen allowed the frost to creep through, and the whole family migrated to the Other Room.

Only the bigger boys were allowed to go outdoors to feed and water the stock and to carry in a fresh supply of coal. Francie stood at the kitchen door, opening it whenever she heard the soft thump of an elbow demanding entrance.

At last the boys struggled in, their eyebrows crusted over with frost. With relief they pulled off their sodden sheepskins.

"Did you give the cattles water?" Mrs. Polanski worried about the stock as she worried about the children.

"Yep. Snow melter burned pretty good today. We dug out the dry wood, and Joe carried some to the barn so that it will keep dry until tomorrow."

The snow melter crouched somewhere out in the furious storm. Under it the boys stuffed wood and coal to melt ice and snow for the cattle. When rainfall was scanty the summer before, the water in the shallow dugout froze clear through. Then they had to chop out chunks of ice and snow to melt down for water. But it was hard to ever have enough water for all the thirsty animals, especially when they ate a lot of straw.

Mrs. Polanski looked into the water barrel that stood beside the kitchen stove.

"Eddie and Bennie, you have to go out yet an' cut some clean snow for da drinking water. We don' know how long da storm gonna last."

In came Eddie, his cheeks red, his arms around a huge chunk of snow. Slowly he eased it into the water barrel. The chunk was too large, so his mother sawed it in half with the butcher knife, and then the pieces sank slowly into the water barrel.

It took several trips, the boys packing an extra boiler full. At last all the necessary work was done. They could settle in for the night.

Danny puffed mournful little sounds into his harmonica, leaning on one arm to watch Francie coloring. She lay flat on her belly beside the heater while Joe and Eddie played cards. The younger boys wound up their spool tractors and made them climb over the backs of their leather mittens. Once Dad came in and the group around the heater parted, allowing him to toss the glossy black coal into its fiery throat. There would be a lot of ashes to carry out in the morning.

"Harry." Their father rolled his r's. "Ve make de wheeskey tonight."

Harry understood. The only time it was really safe to make whiskey was on a blizzardy night. Mounties didn't ever go out in a snowstorm.

From the doorway of the Other Room, Francie saw the copper pipes brought from the granary where they had been buried in the wheat. The copper boiler was slid onto the stove. Like priests performing some secret rite, Dad and the two older boys moved mysteriously around the kitchen, their voices low. The younger children were discouraged from entering the room. The less they knew about the operation the better.

In some way the act was wrong. Francie didn't understand how that could be, because her dad wouldn't do anything bad. Of that she was very sure. Yet if the Mounties found her dad making whiskey, they would take him away or maybe hurt him. Mounties didn't like people to make whiskey. Francie wondered why. Her dad sold it to get money to buy things they needed. Like all their winter clothes. And like sugar and raisins.

Her mother hummed as she looked through the bulky Christmas issues of the farm papers. Snatches of conversation came from the kitchen.

"What's in the mash?" she heard Joe ask.

"Datsa da mixture of sugar and yeast and potatoes. Dere's some raisins een dere too, and rye."

"How come you mix it in a barrel on the manure pile?" Joe knew less about the business than Harry.

"It take too long to make eet een de house. De poleece like to come anytime and dere's big fine eef dey find some mash on de place."

"But why do you put the barrel in the manure?" Joe was persistent.

There was a silence while Dad adjusted something.

Danny began to roar as his spool tractor attempted to climb to the toe of a boot. "RrraaaoOOWWWWW!!!"

"Shut up, Danny," Francie said, trying to hear the answer in the kitchen.

"De fresh manure out dere make de heat for de mash to work," her father was explaining. "You haf to watch eet every day. Sometimes de manure gif off too much of da heat; sometimes too little. Dat's vy you can't be in de hurry to make de wheeskey. Eet takes seven to twelve days to make da barrel. Den you haf to cook eet."

Their mother smiled as she heard their father talking about making whiskey.

"Wun time," she said, rocking back and forth in the rocking chair, "Daddy gif da mash dat's left over to da peeg." She started to laugh. "Iss dat ever a funny peeg. It so greedy, it eat an' eat da mash. An' den da peeg gets drunk." She wiped her eyes with the corner of her apron.

"She just sits dere an' squeals. She can't move her feets, so she just sits an' squeals."

Francie was fascinated. A drunken pig?

"What happened to her afterward?"

"Oh, she came all right. But Daddy never gif da mash to da peegs no more. Dey act so silly. Sometimes he gif da chickens some, an' dey get silly too. Dey run dis way an' dat, an' dey iss falling over."

Much later in the night Francie awoke to see her father and Harry standing beside the heater. By the light of the flames flickering through the slots in the door, they poured something into a spoon. A match scratched; the masculine smell of sulphur filled her nostrils. Dad touched the match to the spoon. A blue, unholy light hovered over the spoon. Francie could make out her father's tired face as he watched it burn. If it burned like that, it was good whiskey.

In the morning a strong, yeasty smell awakened them. Outside, the blizzard raged all day without let-up. When night crept down invisibly, Dad got ready to make another batch. The neighbors would be wanting some whiskey soon for the Easter season. Then the Polanskis would be able to buy new mattresses, rubber boots for the spring, more salt for the cows.

Francie remembered what people said. "John makes good whiskey," they'd nod to one another. Francie didn't care much for it. Once when she had been sick, her mother had given her some in a little glass. The whiskey had caught her by the throat when she swallowed it. She had coughed, and tears had sprung to her eyes. She wondered how her dad and other men could drink one glass with a single gulp.

She stood beside the heater and practiced it.

"Look, Danny, I'm Dad." She placed her feet apart and pretended to shake the pepper shaker into a glass. She raised the pretend glass to her mouth, threw back her head and downed the burning liquid with one swallow.

"Ah-h-h!" she spat out, wiping her mouth with the back of one hand and stamping her foot. "Good! Good!"

Just as she pronounced the words, her father walked into the room. Something like a growl came from his throat. He thought she was making a noise just for the heck of it. Anger wakened in him. Two nights of making whiskey had exhausted his patience.

Before Francie could move, he struck her on the side of the head. She and Danny ran into the kitchen and ducked under the table. They would stay there awhile until it was safe to come out again. They knew that they had to watch it today.

Their mother kneaded dough wearily in the speckled blue pan on a chair. "Oi, Boza," she invoked God softly, telling Him what hard work it was. She prayed in Polish as her round fists punished the dough.

Francie could never understand her mother's language. Though it sounded a bit like Ukrainian, the funny twists of the tongue puzzled her. Sometimes, when her mother told her in Polish to carry out some errand, the girl stood hesitating, struggling to understand, trying to get some hint from her mother's tone. Then her mother lost patience.

"Oh, you stupid," she would say in exasperation. "How you don't know Polish. When it so much easier dan Ukrainian?"

Francie didn't know why she didn't understand. She thought that maybe she was a very stupid child.

The morning came in at forty-five below. Only the tops of the shelterbelt showed above the snow.

"Today too cold for yous to go to da school," their mother said. "Tomorrow yous can go eef eet get warmer."

Francie resigned herself to embroidering beside the heater. She thought of all the dreary work that awaited them at school. They would have to take down all the Christmas decorations and clean up the mess from the concert. And then they would just have to wait for spring to come.

CHAPTER TEN

Spring came to the prairie. Overnight the clean-washed sky turned an incredible blue. A few ragged remnants of snow clung to the gaping ditches. Grey brushmarks of poplars etched the horizon. The blackened drifts still leaning against the fence posts shrank away to nothing.

A great joy woke in the children. They could not get enough of the wine-scented air. They walked out of their way to run and slide over rotten icy patches. One big slough formed in a depression surrounded by red willows. They all ran until they got there, so that they could play a little before having to go on to school.

"Look out! Look out!" Francie screamed as Eddie galloped over the ice, pulling up his legs as fast as he could. The minute he slowed down or stopped, the ice would break and he would get a boot full.

Laughing, they watched as she took her turn. Some of the boys had broken through in different places, and it was hard to see where to run without stepping into a hole. She had to hurry up or they would all leave her behind, and then the coyotes might get her. Francie took a deep breath and darted forward.

The ice crinkled in all directions. Oh, but it was dangerous. Oops! One toe broke through, and the sudden pull of the broken ice unbalanced her. Francie jerked her rear leg. Her foot came free, but the little red rubber boot stayed, tilted, in the ice.

From the shore the boys whooped with laughter. But Francie didn't have time to enjoy herself. She had to keep moving, always moving, or the treacherous ice would grab at her other foot. She veered in a large circle, running lightly on one rubber boot and one sock foot. Out of the corner of her eye she could see that the boys were leaving, and panic ran with her. They might just leave her running around and around on one boot, with the coyotes waiting in the buckbrush.

Fresh energy poured into her legs. As she flew past the lonely boot, she reached down and plucked it out of the ice. When she made it to shore, exhilarated by her success, she tugged the boot over her wet sock and ran madly to catch up with the boys.

"Look, there's a patch of ground!" someone yelled, and they all tore toward it to find out again how plain ground felt under their feet after months of slipping about in the unsteady snow. It seemed as if they could run almost without touching the ground. It always felt like that in the spring.

These were the days when they ran and ran — to school, during recess, on the way home. They filled their lungs with great gasps of the keen air and pumped legs until thigh muscles got a good sore feeling toward evening. Never had food tasted so delicious. Lunch pails came home empty; even the crusts were devoured. At night they barely made it into bed. The storm windows were taken down, and at night the sweet air drugged them with deep dreams.

"Frynca, take Danny and Stanley and go find me a crocus," Mrs. Polanski said one windy spring afternoon. "I go lay down and have me a rest."

Always in the spring, their mother liked to see the first crocus, the earliest buttercup. They wound behind the barn, past the dugout half full of dirty ice, out into the pasture. Somewhere in the scented, brown grass were hidden the small cool flowers of spring.

They searched diligently, for it was important, the first crocus. Mum would put it in a whiskey glass and set it on the writing desk and go to look at it once in a while. It brought her pleasure, and they wanted to please her.

Danny found the clump on a knoll. They came running at his excited call and knelt in the grass to see the miracle. Four blue-purple crocuses stood staunchly in the shelter of a spotted brown rock. Gently, Francie picked two of the flowers as close to the ground as possible. The others must be left for seed.

Then it was gopher time. Fat, cheeky rascals stood up very straight all over the prairie, squeaking insolent questions at the children. Baby gophers started creeping out of the holes in May. They were clean and soft and ever so nice to hold.

Francie knew how to get one. She made Danny sit down so that the gophers underground wouldn't hear his feet walking. Then she stretched herself out on her belly behind a hole into which a clumsy little gopher had stumbled.

She cupped her hand around the hole and began to make small, kissing sounds. That teased the gophers and made them very curious. They just had to come out and see where the sounds were coming from.

Francie's ear, next to the ground, caught the scraping of little gopher

49

feet somewhere in the depths below her. She tensed, holding her breath. Something soft tickled her fingers; she closed her hand and had him before he knew what was happening.

They sat in the soft sunlight and marvelled at the wee thing.

"He's got four feets, Francie," Danny said. "Why for he's got four feets, Francie?" He screwed up his nose as he squinted at her.

"That's what all gophers got to have," Francie answered.

"Whatcha gonna do with him?"

"You can play with him for awhile. Then we have to let him go so that he can find his mother again. If we keep him too long, he will die."

Danny nodded. Francie knew about gophers. He stroked the animal that lay contentedly in the sunlight, between his legs.

There were other things to touch beside the baby gophers. Mum had hens sitting on all kinds of eggs — duck eggs, chicken eggs, even big goose eggs. The hens were awful mad. They pecked hard at anyone who came too close. Only Mum knew how to handle them. She walked up to the hens fast and had her hand under them before they knew it.

They would let her take out the floppy, newly hatched things without making a fuss, using chicken talk to tell her to take good care of their babies.

The first thing Francie did when she got home from school was to look in the chicken box. Into it Mum put the weak ducks and chicks as soon as they hatched. They needed time to dry off and not get stepped on by the hen. The box stood on the reservoir of the kitchen stove, where it was just warm enough.

"Ooh, ducks!" she exclaimed one day when she pulled back the covering rag. Two yellow ducklings and one black one tumbled over, blinking at the light. Francie's heart went out to them. They were so clean, so soft. She picked up the black duckling and let its feet go pitter-pat on her palm. Its feet were so new that they looked waxed. Black ducks always came with black feet; yellow ducks came with orangey feet like the yellow chicks.

A mosquito hummed past her head. It landed on the window pane, showing off to Francie. She carried the duck to the window, holding it so that its eye could see the insect. Suddenly the duckling turned its head and scribbled its waxy little bill over the glass. The mosquito was gone.

Some of the hens got the time mixed up in their heads. They wanted to keep sitting on eggs after it was too late for chicks to hatch.

"Did you t'row out any hens today?" Her mother asked the dreaded question after Francie gathered the eggs. "Go, den, an' t'row dem out. Dey makin' me mad, dem hens."

The hens knew that Francie was afraid of them. She could see it in their eyes when she came close. They ruffled their feathers, uttering shrill warnings. She plunged an arm into a nest and bopped out a hen, feathers flying in a small cloud. Amazed, outraged, the hen walked in circles, cackling to the whole barnyard. Francie made a rush at her.

"Shut up," she gritted through her teeth. It was enough that the hens made her go into a smelly chicken house. That they should make so much noise about their eviction irritated her.

"How many?" her mother asked when Francie returned to the house. "How many hens sitting today?"

"Nine." Francie fingered the peck marks on her wrists.

"Tomorrow we haf to put dem in bags," Mrs. Polanski said. "Dey won't stop sitting until we scare dem."

Good, thought Francie. Then I'll get even with them.

The following afternoon Mrs. Polanski came to the hen house with the girl. Francie held a gunny sack open as her mother popped in a squawking hen.

"*Geetchie coorka,*" her mother muttered, stuffing in a second indignant hen. This one had pecked her, hard.

They put two hens in each bag, then hung the sacks on the clothesline. The wind blew the bags to and fro, and the bewildered hens raised cries of alarm. They would swing and cackle like that for two days, and by then they would be scared enough to stop sitting. They would get back to the serious business of laying eggs.

And then the lambs started coming. Harry stayed up all night in the barn. Sheep didn't have babies easily, and if Dad or Harry weren't around sometimes the babies died. Sometimes even the mother died, so sheep had to be helped to have their young.

On cold nights the shivering new lambs were brought to the house to dry off. They were placed in an apple box that stood on the door of the oven. Even though they were so young, they opened their black lips and bleated shrill questions about their mothers.

Their tongues vibrated between their jaws when they cried. No one liked them when they were wet, but after they dried, the children petted them and looked at the tight little curls all over them. The lambs had black noses and knobby black knees. Harry took them to the barn as soon as they dried, because if he didn't, the mothers would forget their children and refuse them. Sometimes they even bunted their own babies to death. Sheep were funny. They didn't remember things long.

"Here's an orphan," Joe announced one evening, carrying in a spent, wet animal. Its black ears drooped over a delicate nose. Its eyes had a merry sheep look.

"Ya?" Their mother looked at the lamb. "We will haf to gif it da bottle."

From the cellar an old baby bottle was resurrected. Dad had bought a supply of brown rubber nipples for the spring. This was the first lamb they would have to feed, but there would be more orphan sheep and even baby pigs later on.

Something tingled in Francie as she guided the lamb's mouth to the dripping nipple. It tasted the milk and shook its tail merrily. The children laughed at its vigor. The lamb kept on shaking its tail and smacking away at the milk. Foam squeezed out of the sides of its mouth.

"Not too much," their mother warned. "Wait a little and den gif it some more."

Francie was never allowed to watch things being born. No one said anything if Stanley or Danny went into the barn when the baby pigs or calves were being born, but whenever Francie tried to get in to watch, her father or one of the bigger boys immediately chased her out.

"You go back to the house," they would say. "The barn is no place for girls."

"You let Danny in, and he's a lot younger than I am," she countered.

"Danny's a *boy*."

Danny's a boy, Danny's a boy, she thought, her cheeks hot. So what if he was a boy? Couldn't she ever have the fun of seeing things being born, just because she was a girl? What did it matter what she was? She dressed like a boy and caught mice and gophers like one. If she could do the same things they did, then why did they shut her out of that wonderful, secret baby time in the barn?

One day she ate her dinner early, then after her father and the boys sat down to eat, she slipped out and made a wide circle around the shelterbelt. Approaching the barn from the rear, she kicked the prop that braced the door and squeezed inside by pulling the bottom of the door away from the barn.

For a time she could see nothing. Horses munched on hay in the dimness. Fat baby piglets grunted in one stall where they rooted in the straw. To her left Francie could see the ladder that led to the loft. Behind it she saw the door of the lean-to.

Cows that were ready to have calves were kept in there. Francie knew that a cow was in there now. She lifted the latch and stepped inside.

A cow lifted her white face to the girl. She did not stand like any other cow that Francie had seen. This cow stood hunched over, as if in pain.

Francie decided to take no chances. She climbed into the long manger and watched the cow from there. If it ran at her, as young cows sometimes did, she would be safe.

The cow knew that she was not alone. From time to time she looked at Francie, mooing in a very soft way, telling the girl to go away. But Francie stayed.

They will be finished with the soup now, she thought. They will take longer to eat the meat and the potatoes. And after that still longer to eat the canned peaches her mother had opened for dessert. She had plenty of time to see a calf being born.

The cow spread apart her back legs suddenly and a lot of water came out. Then it happened.

The cow stiffened on all four legs and put her head way down. A slimy, grey thing was coming slowly from under her tail. The thing took a long time to come, growing bigger every minute.

All at once a grey bag slipped out and landed with a plop on the ground. A calf was inside it. Francie watched, horrified, as the cow turned anxiously and began eating the bag off the calf.

How could a calf fall like that and not get hurt? What was it doing in a bag? Were people babies born in a bag too? And why did the cow eat that awful thing?

Francie crouched in the manger, shuddering. She had seen a calf being born, and she didn't like it one bit. She thought of her brothers eating meat and potatoes, while all the time the cow was eating something that came from inside her. They had all been in the barn just before dinner. How could they watch things being born and then just sit down and eat as if nothing had happened?

She wouldn't ask any more to go inside the barn where babies were being born. Girls were lucky to have houses to work in.

CHAPTER ELEVEN

The boys stayed home from school to put in the crop. From the blacksmith shop the pounding of iron upon iron could be heard by the younger children as they turned into the home lane after school. Dad worked until late every night sharpening ploughshares and reshaping the tired bones of old machinery so that things could last for yet another year.

Francie liked the mystery of the blacksmith shop. It was unlike any other building on the farm. The wide door slid open on quiet wheels, and the blue-grey tin roof shot rays of sun back into the mild spring sky. It was always dark in the shop, because the only light there came in through the open door or two small, very dirty windows. The packed dirt floor met her bare brown feet silently. Always in the shop there hung rich smells: the pungent scent of the naked earth, the homey aroma of her dad's tobacco, the sweaty smell of yellowed horse collars. Even the iron things, which she could not identify but which were very important to her dad, gave off a peculiar, almost visible essence.

Along the west wall ran a long workbench piled with tools. Saws grinned crazily next to hammers with round heads and flat short noses. Wrenches hung in the correct order on the wall above the bench, ranging from the baby wrenches to the grandpas. Things that needed fixing lay or leaned along the back of the shop. To her right squatted the black forge.

The forge was the heart of the shop, because in it all things underwent a transformation. Fat briquets shaped like perogies always covered the bed of the forge. The hottest part was right in the center, and to encourage the coals there to burn, someone stood at the end of the forge and turned a handle around and around. As the wheel whirred, the coals in the center leaped into life.

"Not so fast! Slower!" her dad would shout at her when she became mesmerized by the whirring of the wheel and the glowing of the coals that held her like an eye in that dim place. He had no time to fool around in the shop. It was the place where everything went to be fixed. Even the kitchen pots went there when their handles fell off.

When she wasn't needed to do the whirring, Francie stood by uncertainly; she dared touch nothing. Still, she couldn't keep away from the shop.

It was the blackness of everything there that held her. The dirt floor, the sooty forge, the great anvil, her father's smeared face and hands — all these things pulled her against her will to the place of fire and loud noises. She made herself small and stood watching Harry and Dad welding.

Dad put the ends of two long bars into the heart of the forge. Harry whirred the wheel slowly.

"Take dem out." They laid the bars end to end on the anvil. The tips of the bars glowed in the dimness.

Their father picked up the heavy hammer with both hands and raised it high over his head for each stroke.

Old Tubal Cain was a man of might
In the days when the earth was young.

The blacksmith poem that Mrs. Kyraniak had taught the older children ran through Francie's mind. Her dad was like Tubal Cain. He wouldn't care to make spears and swords on his anvil either. He'd make the first ploughshare too. He always said that there was enough fighting in the world already.

The heavy hammer flattened the glowing ends, compressed the metal, welded the bars. The glow began to fade.

"Put dem back."

Harry lifted the long bar and placed the middle of it over the glowing fire.

"Ve pound some more."

The anvil rang with joy.

"Turn," their father instructed, and Harry turned the bar ever so little. He kept turning the bar as Dad pounded, and the weld hardened.

It takes an awful licking, Francie thought. That's why it gets strong. Men have to do heavy work and hard work too.

Their father straightened, wiping the sweat from his brow. He saw Francie dreaming there.

"Yidi, prodeesch menee woda."

Francie scampered to the house. She liked to carry the drinking water to the men. It was very important to carry water when men were thirsty.

Her father drank almost all the water. He threw the remainder on the floor behind him. A greasy, black thumbprint remained on the handle. Francie looked at it on the way back to the house. Men made messes no matter what they did. Sometimes they only had to touch something and it made a mess.

55

Her mother sat at the kitchen table, sorting out garden seeds. Every year she saved seeds so that she had to buy very few.

Mrs. Polanski sighed.

"Frynca, you come help planting da radish and maybe da lettuce. Monday we put in da rest."

She rose with an effort and tied her brown apron into a knot. Into the pouch she had made, she dropped the seeds. She looked like a plump hen when she leaned over and unhooked the garden gate.

Every spring Mum planted in the same way. She used her left foot to drag a little furrow across the garden. Francie watched the moist earth piling up in front of her mother's faded running shoe. The varicose veins stood out on that leg. It was her bad leg.

"You plant da seeds. You're young."

Francie wondered why her mother didn't bend over and plant a few seeds herself. She didn't seem to care either when the seeds slipped out of Francie's hand too fast. Instead, she took the rake from its leaning position against the fence and raked fine earth over the seeds. The old tea towel covering her head and knotted at the back of her neck brought to Francie's mind the picture of the gleaners that hung over the school blackboard. This spring there was something heavy and slow about her mother.

The following day Mrs. Polanski did not emerge from her bedroom.

"Edvard," John Polanski addressed his third son. "Heetch up de Polly and go bring de Grandma. Don' take Prince; he's too slow."

He returned to the Other Room. Subdued, the children helped themselves to thick slabs of homemade bread and strawberry jam. Their father did not eat with them. Once he came to the kitchen and made tea, which he carried back to the bedroom. He spoke to no one.

They were halfway through a cold noon meal when Joe burst into the kitchen.

"Hey, you guys. Where's Dad?"

Their father came into the kitchen. "Whatsa da matter?"

"A cow fell into the north well. Looks like she broke through the cover."

"Ees she still alive?"

"Yeah — she's trying to get out. We could help her with ropes, I think. It's not that deep."

"Which cow?"

"The black and white one."

She was one of their best milkers. But maybe she could be saved. The north well never had very much water in it.

Their father spoke.

"You can eat de dinner afterwards. Now you all go an' try to pull out de cow before she get too tired. Take de new ropes I make. In de shop."

"Gee, too bad Eddie ain't here to help."

Their father turned toward the Other Room. "I not go. Da Mother ees sick. I haf to stay here until de Grandma come. You go ahead. Eef you cannot pull de cow out, one of you go and get Uncle Paul and Bill."

They moved fast.

"Francie, you stay here with Stanley and Danny."

"I'll get the ropes."

"Bring 'em all, Joe. We might need quite a few."

"Hurry up, hurry up."

It was awful quiet after the older ones rushed out. The three youngest children sat at the silent table, chewing each mouthful more and more slowly. Francie heard Danny swallow, and his stomach make a rumble. But today it wasn't funny.

Nothing was funny. Chairs stood pushed back at crazy angles around the table. The door to the Other Room had never been closed in the summer before.

And then there were the noises. Stanley paused, his fork halfway to his mouth, when they heard the first noise. It was a low, moaning sound, and all of the pain of the world was in it.

Quick, hard steps rang in the Other Room, and Dad hurried outside, carrying the white chamber pot. In no time he rushed back in and closed the door to the Other Room again. But they heard the sound before the door closed: it was deeper, sadder and full of loneliness.

They toyed with the food on their plates, not looking at each other. Francie knew that her younger brothers were seeking comfort in her presence. She couldn't give them anything; she was afraid herself.

They all jumped when Dad burst out of the Other Room again, a bottle in his hand.

"*Frynca, die menee koleeshook.*"

She flew to the cupboard for the whiskey glass, glad to be useful. Dad closed the door behind him.

"Me ain't hungry." Danny pushed his bread around on his plate.

Francie wasn't listening. Her ear had caught the sound of suffering in the next room. They stared at one another as they listened to a voice that cried and moaned in a strange language.

It didn't sound at all like their mother, yet it couldn't be their dad. There was Something happening in the bedroom, and they couldn't stop it. She and Danny and Stanley and Dad all together couldn't stop it.

A sudden, sharp squall rang out in the Other Room.

They moved as one. In less than three seconds they flew under the table, backs to the wall, under the bench.

There they stayed, holding their breaths, listening. Something like a

57

rabbit snuffled and squalled in the next room. They eyed the door to the outside. If only it weren't so far, they could make a dash for it.

Francie wished that someone bigger was with them. Even if it were Joe, it would be better than having nobody. It wasn't so good to be the biggest.

Their father hurried through the kitchen with the chamber pot. "Shut up!" Francie hissed at Danny, who had begun to hiccup loudly.

Mr. Polanski stopped on his way to the Other Room and looked under the table at them. Solemn, wide-eyed, they gazed back at him from under the bench.

"Ha! Ha! Ha!" His laughs rang out. Striding into the bedroom, he could be heard talking. They could not hear their mother answering, but all of a sudden they knew that everything was all right again.

Just as they crawled out from under the table, Joe dashed in, his clothes muddy.

"Where's Dad?"

"What you want?" Dad stood in the doorway.

"It's the cow. We got her out of the well all right. But one of her front legs is broken."

"Broken! I sure hate to lose that cow."

"She can't even walk."

Buggy wheels clicked outside. Eddie and Grandma had come.

"You wait. I go with you. Go and bring de gun from de shop."

Their father pulled open the spoon drawer and selected a big knife. Slowly, methodically, he began to sharpen it.

They still didn't understand. Mum did not come out of the bedroom to greet Grandma. And Grandma brushed them aside as she hurried to the Other Room.

Francie wanted two things. She wanted to see the cow get shot, and she wanted to know what was going on in the Other Room. But she was a girl, and there were dishes to be done.

Later that evening Grandma told them. She placed the big, grey washtub on two chairs in front of the open oven door and poured just a small amount of water into it. She tested the water with one elbow to make sure that it was all right.

"Whatcha doin', Grandma?" Danny asked.

She did not answer but went to the bedroom. In a minute she was back, carrying a bundle.

"Myitis malinko bratko," she said. "Boh vam dyish."

She turned back the blanket flap and showed them the angry red face of a new baby.

A new brother, Francie thought. God had sent him, Grandma said. Why couldn't He have sent another girl? They had so many boys already. Now they would have nine! God was on Dad's side. He knew Dad liked boys better, because they could work hard on a farm.

They peered over the edge of the tub when Grandma lowered the baby into the water. He screwed up his eyes and bawled, small fists trembling with helplessness. Danny chewed on the lip of the tub with interest.

"What's that stickin' out of his belly button?" he asked.

"*Nas tak Boh zotrawiwh,*" came Grandma's quick retort. She was too busy right now to explain. Danny had to accept that it had to be; that was the way God wanted it.

Francie hung around the tub, wishing that her mother would get tired of staying in the bedroom and come out. Night was coming, and she felt lonesome.

CHAPTER TWELVE

The crop was in, and it was time to celebrate the birth of the new baby. People started coming for the party after supper on a Sunday evening.

The Chorneys were the first to arrive. Harry took their horse to the barn after Mrs. Chorney stepped down. She caught sight of Francie and Danny.

"Hallo, hallo," she laughed. "*Yak tum Mama?*"

"*Dobra,*" Francie answered uneasily. "She's in the house."

"*Dobra vachir!*" their father greeted the visitors from the doorway, whiskey glass in one hand and bottle in the other.

Mr. Chorney pulled his pipe from the side of his mouth. "*Die Boza schaschi na nawoho sinya!*" he congratulated. They were pleased that the Polanskis had another healthy son.

Their father thanked the visitors in the proper way.

"*Odequoyou,*" he answered, pouring each of them a glass of whiskey.

The Chorneys had not yet taken off their coats. Dad never waited until visitors sat down. He always poured them a drink as soon as they came in the door.

They raised their glasses to both of the Polanskis.

"*Die Boza zdrowla.*"

"*Odequoyou.*"

The guests downed their fiery drinks. They took off their coats and sat at the kitchen table. Mrs. Chorney's eyes twinkled. She was always jolly.

Mrs. Polanski took the baby from his homemade cradle and showed him to both of the Chorneys.

A foolish look appeared on Mrs. Chorney's face as she regarded the tiny sleeping child.

"*Oi, malinki.*" She did not know how to admire a baby. No one ever spoke about how small a baby was.

Mr. Chorney puffed at his pipe when the baby was brought to him. He knew the right thing to say about a son.

"*Finee hlopitz,*" he praised.

"Come on," John Polanski urged. "*Zno vipyumo poyidnomo.*"

He poured fresh drinks for the Chorneys and himself. Mrs. Polanski didn't drink anything. Francie knew that was because she was breast-feeding the baby and couldn't take strong drinks.

"Hiyam!"

"Shoolam!"

They roared with laughter and downed their drinks in one gulp. Danny edged closer to his sister behind the stove.

"What they sayin', Francie?"

"It's from one of Dad's stories. About the Old Country. Hiyam and Shoolam were two guys over there who had liquor stores. They just say their names for fun."

Danny didn't really understand, but too much was going on to allow him time to ask questions. The glasses were being lifted again, when buggy wheels rolled past the door. The two children tore out to see if any children had come.

Mrs. Prosvig had arrived, but no Rosy. Francie's spirits drooped. They didn't want any children at this party. It was just for the grownups.

Mrs. Prosvig greeted them all in her gravelly voice. Dad shouted his joy to her.

"*Dobranich!* Come een, come een! *Shiditi!*" He offered her a chair by the table and presented her with a drink.

After that the rest of the neighbors came all at once. There were Uncle Paul and Aunt Agnes, the Szodas and the Wilks. They crowded in, bringing the fresh scent of the evening on their clothes.

Moths flew into the open doorway and threatened the mantles on the gas lamp.

"Close de screen door," Mr. Polanski commanded. Francie pulled it shut and hurried back to the safety behind the stove. From there she and Danny could watch the grownups and not get in the way. The older boys slept in an empty granary in the summer. They did not hang around when company came.

"Hoi!" It was their father's signal for attention. "*Ya bedou shpewati.*"

And sing he did, the funny song about the Old Country, the *stara cryou.* Uncle Paul began to tune up his fiddle softly.

"*Stara cryou boula lepshi yak novou Canadou,*" Dad sang, tapping his foot. They all knew that he really didn't think that life in the Old Country had been better than life in Canada, that he was just singing the song for fun.

He sang that the girls back in the Old Country were prettier than the girls in Canada, because they didn't wear such painted faces.

Mrs. Chorney laughed so hard that her face turned pink. She laughed at just about anything, especially after she'd had a drink or two. But then, it was funny to hear Dad singing about young girls as if he were a young man still.

Dad came to the last part of the man's words. He asked in his song what there was to do in Canada, besides going to the hotel.

Over the merriment Danny asked Francie.

"What's a ho-tel?"

"I don't know. A place where men go to drink."

"Is there a ho-tel at Field?"

"I don't know. I don't think so."

"Whatfor the men go there and drink?"

"Listen," Francie shushed. "Mrs. Chorney is going to sing now."

In her song Mrs. Chorney did not agree with Dad. She claimed that the Old Country was far worse than the new land of Canada. In the old land she had worked as hard as an old mare. Besides, the men there drank too much and then beat their wives.

The grownups roared and pounded their approval on the table. The fiddle sang sweetly, following Mrs. Chorney's voice.

She'd had no fun, she sang, in the old land. She had just sat around there like an old hen. But here in Canada she had fun; she danced.

Francie thought that this was the best part of the song. Mrs. Chorney was round and soft and spread out like a hen.

"*Hodi, podamo kolomayki!*" Their father jumped to his feet, pulling at Mrs. Polanski's hand. "Dance!"

"No, no, *moyee nohee buleet*," she protested, showing the leg swollen with varicose veins. Francie knew that her leg hurt and that she was still tired from having the baby.

Dad wasn't to be stopped that easily. He grabbed Mrs. Chorney and away they went, around and around. Uncle Paul swayed over his fiddle, teasing out the sweet music that made Francie's feet go tap-tap against the side of the stove.

"Yeeaahooo!" Dad brought his foot down hard as he spun his partner. The watchers cheered and clapped. Francie tried to watch her father's feet. They hardly seemed to touch the floor because he danced on his toes.

The dancers bumped into the table, so they all scrambled up and pushed it against the wall. The women who were sitting looked sideways at the men who were not dancing.

Stamp! At the beginning of every twirl their father brought his foot down hard. Sweat stood under the dark curls clustered at his brow.

At last Uncle Paul stopped playing. He wiped his forehead with his shirt sleeve and tossed down the drink their father had ready for him.

Dad poured whiskey for everyone. The women protested, but not too much. They swallowed their drinks, made faces and giggled.

Dad and Mr. Chorney were the last to take a drink. Francie and Danny smothered their laughter as the two men placed their feet apart, threw back their heads and drained their glasses.

"Aaaahhhh!" Dad wiped his mouth with the back of his hand.

"Aaaahhhh!" Mr. Chorney coughed and choked.

The fiddle sang, wild and sweet. It was hard to listen to the music and sit still behind the stove. But there was more to watch now. All the grownups began to dance. There wasn't much room in the kitchen, so they bumped into each other and laughed as they twirled around, doing the *kolimayka.*

Over the children's heads the stovepipe trembled. The *kolimayka* was the fastest dance and the noisiest, because the men kept yelling "*Hoi!*" and stamping their feet as hard as they could.

Mrs. Wilk started squealing. She and Mr. Chorney had danced too close to the flypaper hanging near the west wall. The paper had wound itself around the two of them. The others shouted with laughter and pulled it off. Dad danced over to the stove and dropped it into the fire.

Mum had a hard time getting through the dancers to the table with the dill pickles and *kobasa.* The music stopped and Dad's eye fell on the tempting homemade sausage.

"*Yichee, yichee, kobasa,*" he roared, dancing by himself.

And he was off, dancing alone the way the men danced, the others clearing a space for him. The fiddle shrilled. He squatted and leapt up, his back very straight, his arms folded across his chest. Down, up. Down, up. He plucked Mrs. Szoda out of the group and turned her around before she knew that she was dancing. Down, up he went as she faced him and polkaed with one little foot in front of the other. At the right change in the music, he leaped upright and grabbed her waist. They spun around the kitchen while the onlookers clapped and shouted encouragement.

After several mad spins about the room, Mrs. Szoda fell into a chair, breathless. Dad danced by himself and sang to the rest: "*Yichee, yichee, kobasa.*"

It was another man-woman song, but this time all of the grownups sang.

"We have the eggs," the women sang.

"And we have the sausage," responded the men.

A burst of laughter followed. Francie couldn't see what was so funny.

"We have the frying pans," grinned the women.

"We'll be cooking then."

They stopped singing because a change came into the music. So for a few minutes they all danced very fast. When the dancing part was over, they picked up the song again.

The men sang first. They complained that they couldn't eat cooked beans or eggs; they had no teeth left; they could no longer chew.

Well, the women said, the old mare died just yesterday; go and take her teeth out and put them into your mouths. Then you'll be able to walk about the house whistling, and you will look ever so handsome, sweethearts, just like movie stars.

"*Hoi! Hoi!*" John Polanski leaped higher than ever and bumped the ceiling with his unruly dark head.

That started them off. All the men began to dance, jumping up every so often to thump their heads on the ceiling. But Mr. Szoda was short, and even though he tried very hard, he could not quite reach it.

Mr. Chorney and Mr. Wilk picked up Mr. Szoda and bumped his head on the ceiling, hard.

"They gonna have sore heads," Danny observed.

Francie looked at the beaming faces, the rising dust, the springing figures of the men.

"They can't feel it," she said.

Mrs. Polanski caught sight of them peeping out from behind the stove.

"Go to bed already," she exclaimed, dismayed to find them up so late.

Francie prodded Danny into the Other Room and up the stairs. Stanley lay fast asleep against the wall. She pulled the feather tick over herself and Danny.

Below them the fiddle played on. Francie listened to the thumping and wondered if they would have had a party if the new baby had been a girl. Did they dance when she was born, a wee girl with a red face and tiny tight fists? She didn't think so. A baby girl was not important to the farm.

When she was big and had children, she would have just girl babies. And she wouldn't have them on a farm. She would live in a town like Field and not make her girls do farm things like milking cows and throwing out mad hens. She would let them read just as much as they wanted to.

CHAPTER THIRTEEN

No matter how much porridge they ate for breakfast, the children felt hungry by the time they reached the school. Each child carried his own lunch pail, a discarded jam tin, in the crook of his arm. Sometimes at school they had a hard time getting the lids off. Lids stuck most whenever they were really hungry or in a great hurry to begin playing.

The school was cool in the summertime. It always smelled of skunks and toilets. The smell was especially strong on the days that the wind blew from the northwest, because both toilets were on the north side of the school. The skunks lived under the school during the summer holidays but left when school began because they didn't like to be around people. Still, their smell stayed.

Francie became used to the skunk and toilet smells, but she never could get used to the mice in the drinking water. The school well stood beside the teacherage. Every week someone was named to carry drinking water to school first thing in the morning. Sometimes it was her turn to get it.

She would jump up and grab the handle. It took four or five pumps to get the water coming; all the while the pump screeched in agony. The water gushed out cold and clear into the pail hung over the little bump on the spout. Sometimes there was mouse hair in it, and that was when Francie suffered thirst all day. She couldn't drink the awful water, especially after she had taken the small square wooden cover off the well and looked in.

She had to put her face up close to the opening. First she would see herself down there, looking back up at herself in the little square of light on the black water. After her eyes became used to the darkness, she could see the surface of the water. Often there would be a plump dark thing floating. It would be there the next day and the next. That was why she couldn't drink the water.

And then it was the spiders that stopped up her throat. On the weekends they spun beautiful webs from the water pail to the calcimined walls. Bits of web stuck to the lip of the pail when the boys brought it back from the well. Only if she was awful thirsty could she drink the water then.

They ate their lunch in the shade on the west side of the school. Outlaw Turner and the Millers had baloney sandwiches. Francie eyed the tempting pink slices of meat. She wished that her dad was rich enough to buy baloney for school. Mum bought it at threshing time. The only time they could have something special, like baloney or corn flakes, was when they were too sick to eat anything else.

The school chimney had been rebuilt over the holidays. Joe looked at the red bricks scattered over the ash pile.

"Hey! I got an idea! Let's make an oven out of those bricks and roast some live gophers in it!"

"Yeah!" Outlaw was always game for something new. "I wonder what they act like when they're roasting alive."

It was a good thing that they had all finished eating. A vision of gophers dancing horribly in flames flashed into Francie's mind. She closed her lunch pail in a hurry.

They caught the gophers in no time. Eddie had enough twine in his pocket to make two snares. He and Joe lay behind holes in the field next to the schoolyard. When the boys made kissing sounds, two curious gophers stuck out their sleek brown heads and became prisoners.

If only they knew! They'd never come out of their holes then, thought Francie. But who cared about gophers anyway? They ate gardens and crops of the farmers.

The girls watched, fascinated, as the big boys dug a hole behind the barn where the teacher couldn't see them if she happened to walk back from the teacherage early. They lined the bottom and the sides of the hole with bricks.

Outlaw ran into the barn to get a handful of straw.

"Hey, you guys!" he yelled. "There's some kittens in here!"

Sure enough, the old stray cat that had been hanging around the school that spring had hidden three tiny kittens in a manger. They mewed and screwed up their slanted eyes. They were all claws and ferocity.

Whatever would they do with so many cats? Everyone had cats at home, with kittens always being born. No one wanted more cats at school where there was nothing to eat.

"I'll fix them!" Outlaw pulled at an axe which stuck like a handle in a block of kindling. "Bring 'em here!"

Francie ran out, but she heard the axe come down. There was a triumphant yell from the boys, then another sharp blow.

They burst out of the barn, Outlaw holding the remaining kitten by the scruff of its neck. It twisted and spat. One thorny claw raked Outlaw's hairy wrist.

"Ow!! Son-of-a-bitchin' cat!" he yelled, jabbing the kitten against the middle of a fence post. He readied the axe.

This time Francie couldn't run. She stared at the kitten clawing its way to the top of the post. Its eyes were stuck tight and it couldn't see where it was going. It just kept on climbing.

The kitten reached the end of the post and clung there, its pointed little chin jutting over the top. Thunk! The head rolled off the post, but the furry body remained clinging to the wood. The boys roared as the body relaxed and fell helplessly.

Rosy faced Outlaw squarely. "You big bastard!" she shrieked. "Why do you have to kill everything? I'd like to see someone chop off *your* head!"

"Sure, sure," Outlaw sneered. "Little Goody Two-Shoes doesn't like good clean sport. Go and play with your dollies, girls. This is man's work."

Francie caught Rosy's eye and shook her head. Rosy had better not get in his way, or she would be sorry.

The fun was just starting. She hated what they were doing, but she couldn't help watching. They turned back to the gophers who were giving off loud stupid squeaks from the oven.

Joe twisted the end of a fine wire into the shape of the letter P.

"Let's brand the gophers first."

"Yeah." Outlaw dropped to his knees beside the oven. "You makin' yer old man's brand?"

"Yup." They built a small pile of straw and debris and lit it, then laid the end of the branding wire in the fire.

"How'll we hold 'em?"

"Put a noose around their front legs and I'll stretch out the back ones."

"You guys shouldn't do that," one of the big girls said. But she stayed to watch.

They stretched out one gopher and applied the brand. The acrid smell of singed gopher hair nauseated Francie. The gopher tried to wiggle but he couldn't do anything.

"It's not hot enough."

"Hell. Let's just roast the whole bloody works."

They threw the unhappy gopher back into the oven, dumping straw and dry grass on top. Outlaw struck a match and held it to the litter. He covered the oven with a piece of tin.

"Uncover the hole a little," Joe suggested. "So the air can get in for the fire."

Thick clouds of smoke billowed from under the tin. The boys turned their heads sideways and coughed. They heard the gophers begin to run around under the tin.

It was awful, awful. They were laughing, the boys, laughing like crazy, and all the time the gophers were running around and around under the tin, burning to death.

"Okay, let's have a look."

"Holy gee! They got fat!" Joe poked a stick through one of the animals and lifted a charred black object bloated out of all proportion.

For a long instant Francie stared at the plump form with its four legs sticking straight out. The big girls shrieked as Joe made a dive for them, the gopher held out on the stick. They ran for the school, Joe chasing them with ferocious yells.

"Jesus. Where's another stick?" Outlaw looked about him.

Francie waited no longer. Off she flew, avoiding the school, making for the teacherage. It wasn't safe to run into the school. The boys could corner the girls in there and push the gophers right into their faces, unless the girls made it to the cloakroom first and locked the door.

Shouts and hammerings followed Francie as she panted to a stop behind the teacherage and squatted in the tall dry grass. From the noise she could tell that the girls' door was already barricaded and that they would never open up to let her in. She was safer out in the yard.

It was Outlaw she feared more than Joe. She could always tell on Joe at home, but Outlaw would get her back if she told the teacher on him. She held her breath and listened for footsteps. She was sure that he would never follow her behind the teacherage, because the teacher might look out of the window, especially if Francie yelled. And she meant to yell. Nothing made Outlaw as mad as a girl who yelled.

In her flight Francie had deserted Rosy. Her friend chugged up to her now, and the two sat together in the scented yellow grass, listening to the pounding in the school.

A black bird flicked over them on its way to its nest; grasshoppers sang all around them. In that sun-filled solitude the ugly things that they had just witnessed took on the unreality of a dream.

Francie wondered uneasily what would happen when Joe and Outlaw realized that she and Rosy were not in the cloakroom.

"Keep your head down," she warned.

If they come for us, she thought, I'll run right into the porch of the teacherage. And I'll yell. Let them call me a sissy.

The door of the teacherage opened, and Teddie followed his mother down the trail to the school. Shouts and pounding made the teacher quicken her step. Francie and Rosy followed at a safe distance.

As soon as Mrs. Kyraniak hurried into the school, the noise stopped.

They could hear her high, nervous voice scolding. Out came Joe and Outlaw Turner, the bloated gophers dangling from their sticks.

The two girls poised for flight. But the fun was over. Outlaw gave his stick a wide swing in an effort to throw his gopher at the girls, but the carcass stuck to the stick and flew up over his head and landed on the roof. Joe flung his gopher onto the shingles also. Wiping their hands on their overalls, they returned to the school, laughing like two fiends.

Mrs. Kyraniak was mad, awful mad. The boys had broken the catch that held the bolt on the girls' door. The teacher had arrived just in time to see the boys rush into the girls' cloakroom with the gophers.

Boys weren't ever allowed in the girls' cloakroom, gophers or no gophers. And they had damaged school property besides.

Mrs. Kyraniak trembled beside her desk.

"First, I want you boys to understand . . . ," she began, only to be interrupted by a knock on the door.

She opened it and turned white. Of all days, Mr. Wheeler, the Inspector, had chosen this one to visit the school.

"Good afternoon, Mr. Wheeler," the teacher said in a small voice.

"Good afternoon, Mrs. Kyraniak, boys and girls," boomed Mr. Wheeler, shaking the teacher's hand vigorously.

Mrs. Kyraniak nodded to the children, and they all stood up as if pulled by invisible strings. A series of unintelligible mumbles came from their lips. Francie felt her lips move, but she didn't know what she said. But she was sure that she heard the words "Mr. Wheelie" come from Outlaw's corner of the room.

"Sit down, sit down, and carry on with your work," Mr. Wheeler smiled. "If you will kindly allow me to see your register," he said to Mrs. Kyraniak. She looked in all the wrong drawers before she found it.

Mrs. Kyraniak always went to pieces whenever Mr. Wheeler came. That was odd, because he was so very polite and pleasant. Not like Outlaw Turner. And yet Mrs. Kyraniak wasn't the least bit afraid of Outlaw.

Maybe she wasn't afraid of Outlaw because he had always been here in the district. Mr. Wheeler came from a different world — a world of big books, thick spectacles and shiny brown briefcases. Like the Mounties, he was not a man to be fooled with.

Mrs. Kyraniak would have to wait until the Inspector's visit was over before she gave the boys heck. Right now she pretended that it was just an ordinary school day. She passed notebooks out to the older students and called the grade twos up to her desk.

They stood in a row, the four of them. Francie looked down to see if her toes were in a straight line with the rest. Earl Miller looked down too, but not to see if he was standing right. He always looked down, a hank of hair falling over one eye. Earl was stubborn. Nobody could be as stubborn as a

Miller. When a Miller started school, he wouldn't look up at a teacher or answer until he felt like it. On some days Earl was all right, but with Mr. Wheeler in the room, Francie knew that Earl wouldn't read.

Francie began the reading. She liked the story of Snow White, and she felt sorry for Mrs. Kyraniak. The teacher had met with enough trouble for one day. Francie wanted to show that she was on Mrs. Kyraniak's side.

"All right, Francie. Rosy, let's hear you read the rest of the page."

Rosy had trouble reading. She had trouble with spelling too, and arithmetic blocked her completely. She was a year older than Francie but she found school very hard.

She stumbled through the passage, and the burden shifted to Teddie. He had hidden his nipple the minute Mr. Wheeler had appeared in the doorway. With a foolish grin at his mother, he ducked his head and began to read.

Teddie didn't like school. He cried easily, especially if the work was hard. When he read, he strung the words together and sang.

"The-old-w-witch-looked-at-at-herself-in-in-the-m-m . . . ."

"What's the word, Francie?"

"Mirror."

"M-mirror." Mr. Wheeler was listening dangerously near.

"Who-is-the-f-f-f . . . ." Teddie's voice trailed off. He blinked hard at the word.

"Yes, Jesse?" Outlaw Turner was waving a hand. It was funny to hear him being called Jesse.

"Please, Mrs. Kyraniak, can I leave the room?"

"Yes, Jesse, You *may.*"

Outlaw swaggered through the door and closed it behind him. The boys' cloakroom was in the porch.

"That's fine, Teddie. Earl can finish the page." Mrs. Kyraniak looked toward Earl, hopefully.

He just stood there. With Mr. Wheeler and all the children watching, he just stood, his hair falling over one eye and his head down, not even trying. Francie shuffled her feet.

"Earl?"

It was no use. The visitor had stopped his tongue.

Mr. Wheeler came to Earl's side.

"Come, come, young man. At least give it a try. I'd like to hear you read. Just a few lines."

Earl stood.

Outlaw came back into the room. Joe raised his hand.

"Yes, Joseph, you may go." Mrs. Kyraniak looked tired. She gave each of them a page of work to do and sent them to their desks. She and Mr. Wheeler held a whispered consultation at the side of the room.

The excitement of the day had drained the children. They plodded through their assignments quietly. At her desk Francie showed Rosy how to do the first question. She kept an ear tuned to what was going on in the rest of the room.

Mr. Wheeler inspected the girls' toilet and sink. He walked around the rows of desks, looking at notebooks and pointing out mistakes. Then he went up to the front of the room.

"Boys and girls," he began, rubbing his clean white hands together briskly. "Never mind your work for a few minutes. I should like to talk to you about a trip we took to Ottawa this spring."

Ottawa. That was a red circle on the map where Canada had a split. Only it wasn't a split exactly; it was the Saint Lawrence River, but to Francie it looked like a split.

Mr. Wheeler pointed to the circle on the big Nelson's Chocolate Bar map on the wall.

"We saw the Governor-General drive by in his carriage," he continued.

His story was like a fairy tale. There were big buildings in Ottawa, and one even had a clock on the outside. Servants in tight pants opened doors and bowed. Mr. Wheeler bowed to show how it was done. He rubbed his hands together and smiled at them.

"Well, boys and girls, that is what you may expect to see if you visit Ottawa someday. Meanwhile, you have a fine school and a good teacher. Keep working hard."

At recess they walked until they were through the porch, then broke and ran. Recess always lasted longer when the Inspector came. Maybe the teacher would tell him about the gophers. But then maybe she was ashamed of the boys and wouldn't tell Mr. Wheeler anything. But she would have to tell the school board, because the broken lock had to be fixed.

Outlaw and Joe stood apart, sniggering. They knew something that the rest of them didn't, but there was no sense in wasting a good long recess trying to find out what it was. They began playing Prisoner's Base.

Half an hour later Mrs. Kyraniak rang the bell. While the children walked into the school, Mr. Wheeler stood at one side of the room, nodding and smiling at them.

"Good-by, boys and girls," he said. "Keep up the good work."

They rose as one.

"Good afternoon, Mr. Wheeler." This time the words were loud and sure.

Mr. Wheeler bowed to Mrs. Kyraniak. He went out, smiling and feeling good. Mrs. Kyraniak slumped into her chair, trying to pull herself together.

They heard the car start, then stop. There was a dead silence. Joe snickered, and Outlaw bent over his desk, holding a hand over his mouth, his eyes rolling. A car door slammed.

Quick steps rang in the hallway. Mr. Wheeler jerked open the door.

His face is purple, thought Francie.

The Inspector beckoned to Mrs. Kyraniak. Everyone watched as she went out into the porch and closed the door.

They looked at one another for a clue, then at Outlaw and Joe, who had burst into an insane giggling fit.

Mrs. Kyraniak came back into the room, her face grey.

"All the grade sevens and under, go out and play until I ring the bell for you to come in. The grade eights may go, but Joseph and Jesse are to stay here."

Mystified, they trooped out. Mr. Wheeler was digging around in the trunk of his sleek car. His back looked very straight.

Then they saw. The tires were flat. All four of them. Flat as pancakes.

For once Outlaw and Joe were really going to get it. Mr. Wheeler would fix them. And after that, he might do the best thing of all: he would expel Joe and Outlaw for good.

CHAPTER FOURTEEN

The buggy wheel turned round and round. Francie sat beside her father on the hard wooden seat and squinted at the spokes flying by. Prince's shaggy feet clopped saucers in the fine blow-dirt creeping over the road. They were going to Field with the twelve-dozen egg crate and two cans of cream. It was Francie's first trip to Field.

The pleasant scent of her dad's tobacco made her hungry. Along the road the fenceposts leaned every which way, half-buried in soil. Dust devils danced across the summer-fallowed fields. It was August, and there would be no crop again. Dad and the boys had cut all the hay they could find and had piled it in two big stacks near the barn. They were going to fill the loft too, but they had to go farther and farther to find the hay.

It was nice going to town. They would get some money for the eggs, and maybe everyone would get a treat. The papers would have come. And they would get a few groceries. Not much, just sugar and matches and coffee. And a can of Vogue tobacco. Francie fingered her mother's list. The writing was small and crooked. She liked to look at it. It had fat little a's and o's, round and plump, just like her mother.

Prince blew through his lips, and his spit landed on her face. Prince was stupid. The boys hated working with him. He would trip when there was nothing on the road at all, and sometimes he would step on Harry's foot and just stay there, not feeling anything, until Harry swatted him hard or jerked the bit so that it hurt Prince and he would shift his weight.

Francie felt in her jacket for the cream checks her mother had pinned there.

"Watch so you don't lose dat money," she had warned the girl. "Daddy has to get grease and oil, so he won't have time to get da groceries. You have to go to da store and buy da stuff and stay dere till he come for you. And you tie da money what da storekeeper give you in your handkerchief so you don' lose dat. Iss very important. Da teacher say you can skip one grade, so you should be smarter now."

If the boys hadn't gone to the Other Place to cut hay today she wouldn't have had a chance to go with her dad. Pretty soon she would go all by herself with Prince, when the men were all too busy.

"Here, you hold da lines." Her father handed over the thin strips of leather that he had tanned and cut himself. Her father opened a tobacco tin and took out the red package of cigarette papers with a rooster drawn on it. Steadying the creased paper he shook tobacco on it.

Prince knew that she was driving. He walked slower and slower, his head sinking lower and lower. Francie shook the lines.

"Giddy-up," she ordered.

To her surprise he lifted his head. Again she shook the lines, and the horse broke into a stiff-legged trot.

He thinks I'm Dad, she thought. He's scared of me because he thinks I'm Dad.

A grasshopper stung her cheek. Prince blew spit again.

Three blue-grey elevators hunched close by, looking as if their hands were deep in their empty pockets. That was where her father hauled the grain, if there was any. She felt sorry that he wouldn't have any grain this year. The elevators were waiting, but no one would come. It was like that almost every year.

Dad took the lines as the buggy clicked over the railway tracks. She was too young to drive on the highway. He edged Prince to the side of the road.

The first building in Field was square and yellow. Francie stared at the paint peeling on the sides, and the big faded sign that spelled Field Hall. A rickety wooden sidewalk ran crookedly down the main street. A dark brown building had a big front window. Francie could see fly-stickers hanging behind the painted letters on the glass. Morgan's Store, they said.

There was a space with beaten yellow grass and fireweeds standing in bunches, and then a lopsided building that had once been painted white.

"Thatsa de post offeece," her dad said.

He flicked the lines. They turned off the highway toward a sturdy, reddish-brown building beside the tracks. On a wooden platform stood a wagon with no sides. Cream cans waited on it.

A fat little man came out of the building with a pencil behind his ear. His hat had a green shade over his eyes but no top on it.

"Hello, John," he called.

There was nothing much to look at in Field. There weren't any people stirring or children playing. A few houses lay behind the main street, but no sounds came from them. Field was a very quiet town.

Then her dad climbed into the buggy again and drove back to the store. "You go een dere and get de grocery," he said as she stepped down.

74

Francie pushed open the silvery door. A bell tonk-tonked over her head. Mr. Morgan waited in the cool, dim interior behind a cluttered counter.

Francie looked about with interest. He had a nice place. All kinds of boxes and cans lined the walls on three sides of the store. The strong scent of coffee perfumed the air, while other smells came at her from all sides. Francie loved boxes, and there were hundreds of them in the store, all shapes, all colors.

"You look after dis." Her father eased the egg crate to the slivery, dry floor. After he went out the door, Francie suddenly felt smaller.

She watched Mr. Morgan take the eggs out of the crate. He was old. There was no hair at all on his head. It looked like one of the smooth eggs he was handling. Thick glasses hung from his small ears. They kept slipping down on his nose and he kept pushing them back with one finger. His apron was square-cut with wide shoulder straps.

Francie thought it funny to see a man wearing an apron. Among the people she knew, only women wore them, except for Dad when he was scraping the hair off skins he was tanning. Then he wore a leather apron so that the lime would not eat his clothes.

And the women never wore white aprons, because white things got dirty too quick. Her mother's aprons were covered with little flowers and were dark green or brown or red.

Maybe all Englishmen wore aprons. But the man who took the cream hadn't wore one. He had that funny hat with no top and black sleeves from his elbows to his wrists. Maybe just the storekeepers wore the aprons.

Francie wondered if there were any mothers or girls in Field. The cream man and the storekeeper were not like her dad or the neighbors. They lived in, out of the sunlight, like gophers in their holes. Once in a while they came out and said, "Hello, hello," like the gophers who came out of their holes and squeaked at people.

"Do you know what your mother wants?" the storekeeper asked her. His eyes looked as if they were about to pop out from behind his glasses. From the side his eyes looked the same as anyone else's, but from the front they looked like a frog's eyes.

Francie offered the crumpled paper and unpinned the cream checks. Mr. Morgan shuffled about, gathering things. He kept writing something in a thick little book with lines. At the top of the page Francie could see that he had written "John Polansky". But she didn't tell him that he had spelled their name wrong. She would tell Dad afterward.

A bell jingled over the door, and a woman came in with a little girl. Francie stared. The woman had curled hair and a new blue dress. Her shoes were white and made hard sounds as she walked. They were like Mrs. Kyraniak's shoes.

The girl didn't look like Rosy or any girl Francie knew. She didn't look at Francie at all, but played with a balloon on a string. She wore a white dress with ruffles around the short sleeves, and when she reached up for the balloon, Francie saw that her bloomers were white and ruffly too. Her hair hung in long brown sausage curls down her back.

Francie twisted a bleached pigtail and watched the girl. She was wearing shoes — hard ones like her mother's. Francie never wore shoes in the summer. Suddenly, she felt sorry for the girl with her feet in those hard shoes.

Mr. Morgan looked up at the woman.

"What can I do for you, Ruth?"

"A package of Sweet Caps, please." Money rang on the counter.

Mr. Morgan put a package down in front of the woman. He picked up the money and punched buttons on a machine. A drawer flew open, and a tiny bell dinged somewhere.

She must be buying them for her husband, Francie thought. Her dad didn't smoke bought cigarettes. He rolled his own out of Vogue tobacco.

"Here you are, little girl." Mr. Morgan counted money into Francie's hand. She spread her handkerchief on the counter and laid the money in it. Then she began tying the corners.

The woman and the little girl watched her. Mr. Morgan watched her too. Francie's fingers grew clumsy. She began to feel warm.

The bell over the door announced her father's return. The woman and the girl went out, but the girl and Francie looked at each other until the door closed.

"Geev me nine of dos bags of popcorn for de keeds," her father told Mr. Morgan.

They were going to get a treat after all! The storekeeper put the slim bags of popcorn into a brown bag. Francie's mouth watered. She knew that the popcorn lay pink and sweet in those thin bags and that a prize lay hidden at the bottom.

Dad counted out a nickel and four pennies.

"How much you pay for de eggs?"

"Five cents a dozen, John." Mr. Morgan scratched his smooth head. "It's the best I can do. I sell them for seven cents."

John Polanski did not answer. He knew that it was hard to be a storekeeper too, just as hard as it was to be a farmer. He said to Francie, "You hava de money?"

It was a question. "Yes," she answered, showing him the handkerchief.

Mr. Morgan tore the page from his little book and gave it to her dad. Francie knew that at home her mother would study the page and count the money carefully.

"You know, John, there was hail south of here last night. Big as baseballs. Knocked the windows out of some houses and killed a few chickens."

"Ya?" Her father rolled a cigarette and licked the paper. "It doesn't matter eef eet hails on my land or not. Dere's not'ing dere!"

Both men laughed at the thought of hail. It couldn't hurt crops that had dried up. Let it come.

"Get your mail yet?"

Her father nodded.

"There's talk of war in the Old Country. The price of grain will go up if there's a war."

"Ya. Dere's always a war someplace in de Old Country. Dey got not'ing else to do, dem politishians. It's de beeg shots dat mak' de war."

That was a long speech for her dad. Francie believed every word of it.

"Did you hear that the King is coming to Canada?"

"Ya, I hear dat."

"It said on the radio that he's going to pass through Regina. You going up to see him and the Queen?"

"No, hell no. I don't haf time for dat. I see dem in de papers. Dat's enough." He paused and added, "De King don't get my hay cut."

The two men chuckled over the idea, and her father bent for the egg crate.

"Vel, ve start for home."

As the buggy crossed the tracks, a long, sad wail echoed through Field. Looking back, Francie could see black smoke churning into the dull blue sky. The train was coming in.

"Tramps veel be getting off dat train," her father growled. He hated the men with stubbly faces who walked out to the farms looking for work. He hated them as much as his wife feared them. Francie remembered the strange, wild look in their eyes when they were told that there was no work for them.

Dad clucked to Prince and the horse trotted briskly homeward.

CHAPTER FIFTEEN

Francie and Danny lay idly in the shade beside the house. "We have to go and pick cow pancakes," Bennie said, backing Prince toward the buggy. "In the calf pasture."

The three younger children climbed onto the back of the buggy, the best place to ride with legs dangling free. It was just a little way to the calf pasture, but rides didn't come very often.

Francie jumped off the buggy and ran to lift the wire loop that held the gate to the post. The calves saw them and thought that it was feeding time. They started coming toward the gate.

"Get!" Francie darted at them. They stared, then spooked in all directions. She flipped the loop back over the gate behind the buggy.

They dragged gunny sacks behind them over the short grass, picking up the dried calf dung. Some of the pancakes weren't dry when they were turned over.

"Just leave them to dry out," Francie told Danny, who was staring at all the ants running out from underneath a pancake he had overturned.

They filled their bags and lifted them onto the buggy. When all the bags were full, they drove back to the yard. Eddie carried one bag into the kitchen and emptied it into the woodbox.

"You didn' bring me no wet ones? Dey don' burn so good." Mrs. Polanski kneaded dough in the speckled pan.

"What should we do with the rest?"

"Put dem in da coal shed at one end. And go and pick some more. Daddy didn't buy much coal or wood this summer. Just for winter. So you have to pick lots."

Eddie carried the bag to the buggy. Their mother straightened with an effort, pulling the dough off her fingers.

"*Oi, Boza, Boza,*" she prayed, asking God to take pity on them, the times were so hard on a big family. It was going to be such a hard winter.

Back to the pasture they went. It wasn't much fun, gathering cow pancakes, but it had to be done. The manure that the calves made burned well. Horse manure didn't give as much heat. The one bad thing about *himnagayih* was that they made so much ashes in the stove. Tomorrow morning the ash tray would be overflowing. But it was better than nothing.

It was on the third trip to the pasture that Bennie whispered into Francie's ear.

"Let's smoke."

Francie thrilled. Only Dad smoked. He carried his tobacco can everywhere. His tobacco smelled so nice that she'd like to try it, just once, to know what it was like.

"What about them?" She nodded her head toward Stanley and Danny, who were tying a thread around the neck of a grasshopper.

"I'll tell them to get us a drink of water on the next trip. You go in the Other Room by the back door and get some paper, any paper. And some matches, but not too many or they'll know. I'll collect some tree leaves from behind the shed. They're dry and should burn good."

New energy ran through their tired bodies. The thought of fun made the work easier. While Bennie unloaded the dung on the trip back, Francie slipped through the back door.

No one was supposed to use the back door. Ever. Only Dad or Mum. And no one ever did, unless he was doing something wrong. Francie's bare brown feet made no sound on the worn linoleum. She stole to the partition where her parents slept. A double page of newspaper lay on the homemade desk beside the bed. It was the colored comic section from the *Free Press*. She grabbed a few matches and slipped out of the door again. As she pulled the back door to softly, she could hear her mother humming in the kitchen.

Bennie had the pancakes unloaded. He had filled his pockets with the crisp leaves which lay on the ground behind the shed, old before their time.

In no time they were back in the pasture. For a while they gathered the dung until Danny and Stanley wandered off with the grasshopper. Danny held one end of the thread, and the grasshopper flew madly ahead of him, wings rustling.

"Let's go behind the granary." Bennie looked back at the house. Nothing moved in the hot afternoon.

They left Prince switching his tail, dreaming. Bennie rolled the colored paper around the leaves. It made a very big cigarette.

"I have to squash it a bit." Bennie scrunched up the clumsy parcel.

"Whatcha guys doin'?" Danny had wandered back and stood watching them with interest.

"Danny, don't you tell!" Francie was angry. It was too late to get rid of him now.

Bennie struck a match and held it to the paper. A breath of wind flared the flame. The crooked cigarette started to smoke. Bennie tried to puff on it, but it burned too fast. So fast that the flames scorched his hands. He dropped the cigarette, and the wind caught it and blew the flaming mass over to the side of the granary, out where it could be seen. The grass caught.

"Holy smoke! Put it out!"

They ran to the wicked paper that was fast disappearing, stamping at the spreading flames.

"Hoi!" The bellow came from the yard.

Horrified, they saw Dad standing there, on his way to the house from the shop. He was staring at the little flames licking the grass in an increasing circle.

They broke and ran. Madly, madly, with their father's yells ringing in their ears and a terrible dry taste in their mouths. Behind the garden, through the oat field, through the pasture, north. Francie went blind, insensible to anything but the need for flight.

They fell on the ground, exhausted, in the north pasture behind some buckbrush. For a while they gasped for air.

Francie's round eyes sought Bennie's. They were to blame. Both of them. Never, ever were they supposed to play with fire. Now they had done it.

"What are we going to do?"

What could they do? They couldn't go home again ever. Dad would kill them, he'd be so mad. He was always talking about the danger of fire when it was dry.

Bennie poked his head up over the buckbrush.

"Lie still," he whispered. "Danny's comin'."

Sure enough, they could hear him coming, following their trail, whimpering because he couldn't see them. He was probably lost already. Francie lay with her ear close to the ground. Maybe he would give up and go back. They couldn't wait for Danny. He was too slow.

But he didn't go back. He came thrashing through the buckbrush, talking to himself, and saw them lying there. Dirty streaks ran down his cheeks.

"Francie," he said. "Dad's awful mad."

They sat up. Danny squatted beside them, turning his scratched foot over on the side, looking for thistles in his soles.

They sat there, weak. Once in a while Bennie peeked over the buckbrush to see if Dad was coming. Francie chewed on a rosebush berry.

But he didn't come. Then they knew that he was waiting for them to come back. If they had gone home right away, the licking would have been over by now. They could be in the house now, hurting and crying, but it could have been over. The longer they made him wait now, the more angry he would be.

"Bennie, what can we do?"

Bennie looked at the horizon around them. To the north lay the prairie, dotted with willow-ringed sloughs. Far to the west lived Grandma and Grandpa, who wouldn't feel at all sorry for them. To the east lay Field, with its English people who wouldn't understand. The only way to go was home, to the shelterbelt, but that was the one way they could not turn yet.

"Let's go to Uncle Paul's. He's not far from here."

They wouldn't have to tell Uncle Paul. They could say that they had just come to visit. Uncle Paul would be kind and give them a drink of water. Aunt Agnes made good cinnamon buns.

They dragged themselves toward their uncle's farm. Already, home seemed far away, a place of no return. Francie closed her mind to tomorrow.

Danny followed a little way behind. He was tired and a bit homesick. He was worried too.

"Danny, what did Dad do?"

Danny scratched his bottom. "He . . . he hit at the fire. With a sack. He was real mad."

That was why he hadn't chased them. He'd stopped the fire from spreading.

More than once Francie looked behind them as they neared Uncle Paul's, expecting to see their father's tall, haggard figure gaining swiftly on them. Dad looked more tired this year. He got mad easier too.

In the yard, chickens scratched in the fine dirt around the stone step. Bennie knocked on the door.

No one answered, even when Bennie pounded as hard as he could. The old dog who lay in the shade lifted his head and regarded them calmly.

"Nobody home," Bennie said and pushed open the door.

A good smell was coming from a pot on the stove.

Uncle Paul and his family had all just gone somewhere. They would be back soon.

Bennie peered into the pot on the squatty black stove.

"Looks like chicken soup."

All at once they were very hungry. Francie couldn't even remember what they had eaten for dinner, it was so long ago. They eyed the pot.

"If we take out just one piece for everybody, they won't know." Bennie answered the unspoken question that hung in the air.

He reached into the pot and grabbed a drumstick by the knobby end.

"I want this. What d'you want, Francie?"

81

"A wing."

Bennie used the drumstick to poke around. He fished out a steaming hot wing.

"Wanna grizzerd," Danny piped, watching Francie toss the hot wing from hand to hand.

Bennie poked around again until he found the gizzard.

"Holy smoke," he said, "does it ever smell good."

They sat on the front step and ate, watching the happy chickens frisk dirt over their backs.

No one came. They wandered back to the kitchen, sucking at the chicken bones.

"What should we do with these?" Francie held up her fleshless chicken wing.

"Here." Bennie dropped his drumstick behind the low kitchen cupboard.

"What's this?" Bennie lifted the heavy wooden cover off a small crock on the cupboard. "Brown sugar!" he exclaimed. "A full crock of it."

He picked up several hard lumps and gave them to Francie and Danny. Never had sugar tasted this good. They licked their fingers clean.

"Wonder what they've got in their Other Room." Bennie stood in the doorway, trying to see in there. The blinds were pulled down, and it was dark and cool. Francie could make out the high, plump pillows on a bed. And lace curtains. Uncle Paul had only one child. He could have nicer things in his house than Dad did. One child didn't wear out many things and didn't eat much.

They were through the door before they knew it. For a while they just stood there, looking. The smell of moth balls lingered on the air. Something rustled in the walls.

In one corner stood a varnished cupboard with glass doors. Various things could be seen inside of it — cups and saucers with flowers on them, silver spoons, little statues. Bennie saw the hair clippers first.

"Gee, I wonder how they really work," he said. He pulled gently on the door knob and the glass swung out.

They all looked at the clippers. Dad had a pair at home, but he never let anyone touch them. He cut all the boys' hair.

Bennie closed his hand partway on the handles as he had seen Dad do, and the clippers gave a click. The little teeth on the end moved sideways when Bennie clicked the clippers again.

"Do you think they work?" Bennie asked Francie.

She shrugged. She wanted to know though. She always watched when Dad gave haircuts at home. Sometimes the clipper pulled, and the boys cried a little.

"Let's see, Danny. I want to try them." Danny held his head still. The clippers clicked sideways over his head.

A neat white strip appeared halfway across Danny's head. Bennie tried to push the rest of Danny's hair over the bald strip, but it resisted. His hair stuck straight up all over his head, and the path that Bennie had cut looked like the path a binder made in a wheat field.

Bennie threw the clippers back into the cupboard. They scuttled out to the stone step again. Bennie didn't talk now. He kept looking at the road on Danny's head.

Francie felt sorry for Bennie. He would get it twice now. Once for the fire and once for cutting Danny's hair like that. He would get it worse than she would, because he was older.

The chickens scattered as Uncle Paul's old truck chugged into the yard. Uncle Paul and Aunt Agnes and cousin Bill were surprised to see them sitting there.

"Hello, hello," they called. "What are you doing here?"

No one answered. Even Danny said nothing and picked at his toes.

"What happened to Danny's hair?" Uncle Paul asked. They stared at Danny.

"We don't know." Bennie, as the oldest, had to say something.

"You don't know? That's funny, you don't know." Uncle Paul looked past them into the house. "How come you're here, anyway?"

"We just thought that we'd come over."

"Um-hmm." Their uncle didn't believe that. Then with an arm extended to the door, he asked them in.

"Hodeet du hatee."

They followed their relations into the kitchen. Aunt Agnes lifted the lid on the stove and pushed a stick into the fire. She took a quick glance inside the pot.

"We just came to see how you were," Bennie said quickly, trying to look away from the stove and the crock. "We're going home now."

"Just a minute, just a minute," Uncle Paul interrupted. "Let's talk a little. What's your dad working at today?"

They always asked a lot of questions. They didn't visit often, but they liked to know what people were doing. Bennie and Francie began to move toward the door.

Bennie tried to answer in Ukrainian.

"Tato . . . ," he began. All he could think of was the word for father.

"In shop," Francie said with firmness. *"Tato roboti* in shop."

Their relations laughed.

"E mama?"

Bennie didn't try to answer. He left it to Francie.

"Horobit hleba." Horobit was the wrong word to use. She had tried to say

that her mother was baking bread, but the word for baking eluded her. *Horobit* meant cooking, not baking.

Their relations laughed louder and longer this time.

"We got to be going," Bennie blurted, and out he fled. Francie and Danny were close behind.

"Good-by, good-by," their uncle called, standing on the step watching them. "Say hello to your dad for me."

They turned their faces to the fate that awaited. The sun was getting low in the west.

"It must be suppertime by now," Bennie said.

They longed to be home, sitting on the bench behind the table, eating the fresh bread. They wondered if the others missed them.

"You go ahead, Danny." He scampered off, glad. He didn't know why they were hanging back.

It was Bennie who went home first. Francie stood miserably at the edge of the oat field, watching him grow smaller and smaller until he disappeared behind the shelterbelt.

She sat on the warm ground and studied her feet. Bennie would be getting it by now. He was lucky. He would be over it and would be eating supper, and she was still going to get it.

Long shadows began to slant over the oat field. Joe came out from behind the shelterbelt.

"Francie!" he called, "Come on home and eat your supper!"

It was just a trick to get her into the house. She knew Joe. She didn't trust him, ever.

Joe walked nearer, coaxing.

"Hurry up, Francie, or Mum will be mad. She said for you to come."

She stood there in the gathering twilight, the cheerful sounds of a hundred crickets rising all around her. Something big and hard gathered in her throat. She wanted to go home. They would be lighting the lamp soon.

Joe could see her face now.

"If you go home now before Mum gets mad, you'll get an orange."

That did it. Oranges were only for special times. Francie tasted the sweet juice of one in her mouth. She was tired, so tired, and her mouth was dry. Her ankles ached from running through the stubble of the oat field.

Joe walked alongside her, talking about the orange. She knew that he'd been sent out there to talk her into coming home. He was fooling her as always, but she didn't care anymore.

The fear leaped up at her as she stepped into the doorway. But Joe was crowding in behind her. She couldn't get away any longer.

Mum was alone in the kitchen, piling the black bread pans on the cupboard. Her face was grave. She saw Francie standing there. She muttered something in Ukrainian and reached for the fly swatter. Grabbing Francie's wrist, she spanked the girl thoroughly across the legs and seat.

Francie danced as the swatter bit. Dad made the ends out of leather, and she was not pretending the pain.

"Now eat." A bowl of hot soup was placed before her. "Hurry up and go to bed before Daddy come back from da shop. You get to bed an' he will forget by morning."

Francie tasted the soup with all of her being. It steamed up into her face, making her nose run and her eyes cry. She cried all the way to the bottom of the bowl. Her legs still smarting, she stumbled gratefully up the stairs. It was so good to be home, to have the worst part over with. She would never try smoking again.

CHAPTER SIXTEEN

The dust storms came every day. In the morning the sun rose, distorted, and stayed, looking sick all day. A perpetual twilight fell over the prairie.

Dad's face burned to a darker tan. Often he sat in the kitchen in the afternoons, the big tin cup of tea growing cold as he looked away inside himself. It had been a long time since they'd had a party.

Francie grew tired of dusting. She would dampen a rag, then wipe the dust off the sills. The first wipe smeared the dust. By the time she was finished, there would be a fine grey film clouding the varnished wood again.

The drinking water pail had to be covered with a tea towel all day. Even so, dust crept into it and lay in a faint ring around the bottom of the container. The yard was stripped of all the fine topsoil that had felt good to the children's bare feet. It wasn't easy to walk across summer fallows. Russian thistles bounded across the open spaces, scattering their cruel, dry prickles before they came to rest, piled up in the fence corners. The page-wire fence that enclosed the calf pasture had a solid wall of Russian thistles on the west side.

"I don' know how we could get along wit' out dem cows," Mrs. Polanski sighed one dirty, windy day. *"Oi, Boza, Boza."* She asked God how much more hard times He would send, what else He would take from them. She turned to her one daughter.

"Frynca, it is time dat you learn how to milk. You have to help. Even if you can milk only one cow, it will make it more easy."

Francie perked up her ears. She wanted to milk. It would be nice to have a cow of her own.

"She could have Jersey. Or Muskety. They both freshened late. That way she won't spoil the good cows." Eddie pulled at the crisp corner of a loaf of bread on the side away from Mum. Corners tasted the best of all. Sometimes the bread looked as if mice had chewed on it.

With the left-over dough Mum was frying pancakes. The thick slabs sizzled in the frying pan. Here and there air bubbles rose in the dough. Francie and Bennie and the little ones stood ready with their plates.

Mum lifted out four pancakes, one for each. The children climbed up on the bench behind the table and tore their pancakes into bite-sized pieces. Over their plates they poured the golden syrup.

How good they were! Like *perogies* or *varinichi*. Everything Mum made tasted so good.

The baby dropped his bottle on the floor. He began to whimper.

"Take him to da Oder Room when you are finished eating, Frynca. You and Danny rock him to sleep."

The cradle was heavy. Danny helped Francie to drag it to the Other Room. At the sight of the two children, the baby became a little happier. Francie tucked the tattered blanket in around him.

The baby lay there, his eyes half-open. Francie straddled one end of the cradle; Danny, the other. Together they leaned one way, then the other.

"Wock-a-bye-baby," Danny sang, watching the baby's upside-down face. The baby would fall asleep fast today; he was tired. Rocking the cradle was fun if he didn't take too long to fall asleep.

"Slow down," Francie whispered. They rocked more gently, then slowed to a stop. Danny climbed off first. Then Francie slid off, and they were free.

"Go and get the cows," their mother told them when they returned to the kitchen. "And don' chase dem, or dey won't give much milk. Poor cattle is suffering too."

They called the dog and headed for the north pasture. Along the way they twisted off two willow switches. Willows were tough trees. Their branches really stung when they hit the cows with them.

"Stay on the cow path. There won't be any cactus on it," Francie warned Danny. The path wound around hillocks and buckbrushes. Somewhere at the end of it would be the cows.

Beside the north dugout some of the cows stood knee-deep in the dirty water, chewing their cuds and switching their tails. They knew that the children couldn't get at them, so they stared and acted stupid when Francie shouted at them to get going.

"Get 'em, Blackie!" The dog ran back and forth along the shore, barking with frustration.

Danny threw a stone. It missed a cow's nose and landed with a plop in front of her. The splash annoyed her, and she began to climb out of the water, sinking at every step. When she moved, the rest of the herd decided to move too. Blackie nipped at their heels as they staggered out of the water. He could get at them easily then because they didn't have their balance right away and couldn't kick at him.

Francie would have liked to stay at the dugout and catch a frog, but she knew better than to waste time when bringing the cows home. It took a long time to milk eighteen cows. No one could milk cows properly at night.

The water in the home dugout glimmered violet. Killdeers swung overhead, sending out wild, free cries. The cows stopped and drank as if they had never seen water before. The children waited for a while. It was good for milk cows to drink lots of water. Each nose made rings in the still water.

"Get going!" Francie knew that the cows were stalling. They chased the animals into the corral and tied the gate with wire.

Francie was eager to try her first cow. All the boys, from Joe to Bennie, had their cows to milk. Cows liked having the same person milking them all the time. They gave more milk that way.

Now I won't have to do all the supper dishes every night, Francie thought. I can go and milk, and Stanley and Danny will start the dishes so that there won't be so many for me to do afterwards.

They took the milk pails off the fenceposts and headed for the corral. Joe lifted the chain kickers off the fence. Mossie was his cow. She was hard to milk, because she often became excited and kicked a lot. Joe put the kickers around her hind legs so that she couldn't lift a leg and put it into the pail.

"Not that side!" Mrs. Polanski bent her babushkaed head and pulled on the udder of the best cow, squirting a few streams to the ground. "Always you milk from da oder side."

Francie wondered why cows had to be milked from one side only. Calves bunted their mother from all directions, sometimes even from between the hind legs.

Jersey turned her head and regarded Francie with friendly cow eyes. She swung her stumpy little tail back and forth in quick, nervous twitches. She had been born out in a field on a cold spring day, and her tail had frozen. She had only half a tail.

Francie squatted and placed the pail under Jersey.

"Don' put it under too far," her mother warned. "You have to be ready to pull it out quick if she kicks."

Jersey was a kind cow. Everybody liked her because she liked everybody. Sometimes she ate small raw potatoes from their hands, not because she liked the food but because she wanted to please them.

Francie put her left cheek against Jersey's smooth red belly. She could hear one of the cow's stomachs making funny noises inside. She gathered the front teats in her hands.

She squeezed. The teats were small, and nothing came out. She squeezed again. Jersey stepped away, sideways.

"Grab up higher," her mother instructed.

Francie followed the cow and squatted for another try. Jersey looked over her shoulder at her.

She grabbed the teats higher up. This time a stream of milk shot out from each teat. She tried to aim for the pail, but the streams flew all over. Some milk landed on Francie, some on the cow's legs, some in the pail. Jersey didn't like the way Francie milked. She kept stepping away, sideways. Once she kicked with a quick back leg and dirt flew into the pail.

"Doesn't matter if it get dirty da first time or two," Mrs. Polanski called. "Her milk no good for us to drink for three, four days anyway. We will feed it to da calves. Iss wery rich, dat milk."

Francie's legs started to ache from squatting. Her hands and wrists began to tire. Milking wasn't so easy.

She looked around at her brothers. They were all milking away, filling their pails with foam. Eddie sang cowboy songs as he milked, especially the Wilf Carter ones. Joe sat on a piece of wood under a different cow, the milk spanging into a empty pail. When a pail was filled, it was placed outside the fence, where Danny guarded it from cats and chickens.

Francie kept mangling the teats. The front ones gave out. The back set hung lower. They were so full that drops of milk gathered at the tips and dripped into the dirt.

She hardly touched them and the milk came out. Francie felt happier. At least she would have something to show for her work.

Jersey stood very still. It was good to have the pressure taken off. She chewed her cud rhythmically. Flies hung in clouds over her. She swung her stubby tail and thunked Francie on the head.

Francie moved her head back. There wasn't anything that she could do with that tail. It was just long enough to reach her head, but too short to be tied around the cow's leg.

Jersey swung her head back and chased the flies off her back. The cow's saliva flew into Francie's face. Then Jersey did a funny thing. She turned her dark, liquid eyes on the girl, reached back and gave Francie a friendly lick on the upper arm. Her tongue rasped like a file.

"See, poor Jersey, she like to get rid of dat milk. It hurting her," said her mother, carrying a pail of foamy milk to the fence. She came over and looked into Francie's pail. "Dat's good enough. Tomorrow she will give more. She is holding some milk back for da calf."

But Jersey wouldn't ever get her calf back. Francie knew why the cow kept looking over the corral and mooing softly once in a while. The cow was mourning for her lost calf. The boys had taken it and put it into the calf pasture. There it would be fed on skim milk after the milk was separated, and it would frisk around with the other calves who had been taken away from their mothers. Soon the calves would forget that they ever had mothers, and the cows would forget that they ever had calves. By the time summer was over, they would not know each other at all. It was sad for them, but that was the way it had to be with cows and calves.

Bennie squirted the first few streams of milk into the open mouth of the mother cat who waited beside the cow. Bennie aimed carefully. Joe didn't feed the cats that way. He just squirted milk all over them, making them wet and sticky. Then the cats had to lick themselves all over to get the milk. But Joe didn't care; he just laughed.

Muskety was hard to milk. Her teats were long and thin, like young carrots. But she was a quiet cow and good to practice on. Francie knew that she wouldn't get any good cows to milk until later on, otherwise she would spoil them. Cows didn't like to be fooled around with.

All the milk was carried to the house. The separator stood bolted to the floor in one corner of the kitchen. The big boys poured the milk into the screen pail and then strained the milk into the separator bowl.

"Francie, take your milk and go feed Jersey's calf. It so little it need da good rich milk."

Francie looked into her pail as she walked to the calf pasture. The milk looked blue and very dirty. She wouldn't drink it if she were the calf.

The calves were spread all over the pasture. Mrs. Polanski had trained them to come for food whenever she called her invitation in Ukrainian.

It was a crazy way to call calves, but they would not come unless they heard that call. Francie always felt uneasy when she had to call them in. One time she had yelled the words over and over on a windy day, only to find out afterwards that an insurance salesman had been parked in the yard behind and had taken a lively interest in the proceedings.

They could have been taught to come for any words — even words like "Here, calf, here." But Francie's mother taught them Ukrainian.

She crawled through the wires that were a part of the gate and yelled the words at them, *"Hoichee, hoichee, ni-ni-ni-ni!"*

It meant, "Come, come, I have something for you!" The words made her feel foolish. And the calves acted in a foolish way. They lifted their heads and turned their ears toward her. As if they had to find her with their eyes before they could believe the sound. Then they started coming, slowly at first, then running because they all wanted to be first. Jersey's little calf came with them, not because it knew the call, but because the other calves were running. The other calves were bigger. They bumped the little calf about.

Francie felt sorry for Jersey's calf. It didn't know what the fuss was all about. It was still very lonely for its mother.

She kicked at the bigger calves.

"Get! Danny get a stick."

90

Danny wiggled through the page wire head first. He picked up a long stick and menaced the big calves.

Francie had seen how the young calves were taught to drink. She had even helped to teach them. She pushed Jersey's baby into the fence corner. It had a clean, little, turned-up nose.

She held the pail in one hand and shoved the calf's nose all the way to the bottom of the pail.

The calf stayed quiet for a minute, then took a breath. Up shot its head, nostrils full of milk. The calf began to lick itself on the lips. It liked the taste. It sniffed around for more milk.

Francie dipped her fingers into the milk and offered them to the calf. It snuffled at the fingers, then started to lick them.

Francie drew her hand away with care, leading the calf's nose toward the surface of the milk in the pail. When the calf sucked noisily at her fingers, she pulled her hand under the milk. The calf continued to suck at her fingers. It was getting milk now. Francie moved her fingers out of its mouth.

The calf sucked once, twice, but it couldn't find the fingers. It bunted upwards, hitting Francie's hand holding on to the handle of the pail.

It stood blinking, licking its mouth and calling for its mother. Francie wet her fingers again.

The calf sucked right away this time. Francie could feel the tiny ridge of its teeth in the lower jaw. She lured the calf's nose into the pail again.

This time it took a few gulps when she pulled her hand away. Then it knew that the milk was in the pail. Like something gone crazy, it shoved its head to the bottom, taking big gulps.

Francie prepared herself. She knew that the calf would spill the milk if she were not alert. When the calf came up for air, she jerked away the pail. Danny laughed at the ring of milk up to the calf's eyes. The calf's ribs showed yet; in a few days it would begin to round out from the milk and the grass.

Jersey's calf was like its mother, not stupid like some of the other calves. It learned to drink the first time. It drank all of the milk and then stood with a smile on its calf face.

Bennie and Nick came with the milk for the rest of the calves. Bennie had to teach Muskety's calf to drink, but it was stubborn. And big. He had to wrestle with it. Nick fed the rest of the calves through the page-wire fence. Once the calves learned to drink, no one had to climb inside the fence. The calves just put their heads through the spaces in the fence and drank. That way the calves didn't step all over the children's toes or steal from each other.

In the house Mrs. Polanski poured the warm cream into an empty syrup pail with a handle.

"You go and hang da cream in da well, Bennie. Tomorrow we should have enough cream to fill da can. Den maybe Harry will take it to town wit da oder can. I don' want it should get sour, because den da test is not so good and dose bogers don' send much for dat."

Her mother got about five dollars a week for three cans of cream. Eighteen cows twice a day. Milking was hard work, but then twenty dollars a month was a fortune. They got their groceries and clothes with that.

Francie felt proud that she was helping. She was doing the same thing as the boys were.

CHAPTER SEVENTEEN

"I want to make da pantry before school starts and den dere's nobody to help," Mrs. Polanski said at breakfast one sun-filled day.

"Awright. Harry and Joe can get de things. De oders can mix." Dad sipped his coffee loudly from the tin cup. "It vill be good to have more room in de house."

Francie and the younger ones watched the proceedings with interest. Stanley had to watch the baby in the shade, so he couldn't help. The home dugout was getting low, so Bennie had to drive the cows to the south well to pump water for them. That left the rest of them to help.

Dad and Harry nailed the two-by-fours together and then attached the framework of the pantry to the north end of the kitchen.

The boys nailed slats sideways across the two-by-fours. The slats were close together, but the younger children could peep through the spaces.

"Francie, our pantry gonna have holes?" Danny asked.

"I don't know." Francie had never seen this way of building before.

Mrs. Polanski carried out the big, grey washtub. She placed it on the ground in the sun. Into the tub Joe dumped mud and dry horse manure. Their mother added dugout water.

"Why do we need the manure?" Francie asked.

"Because," her mother answered, "Da horse makes good manure. He eat da grain an' da grass an' chew it all good. Den when you put the manure in with the *hleno*, the walls won't crack because the manure hold them together. Now get in the tub an' mix wit your feet."

Francie didn't like putting her feet into the cold slush. Neither did Danny. At first they stepped slowly: down, then up. The mud made sucking sounds when they pulled their feet up, and the water began to turn to a dirty yellow-brown.

"Keep on, keep on," urged their mother. "It take a lot of mixing."

The children stepped a little faster. As they worked, the mud and manure turned softer.

"Tramp good," their mother warned. "Don't just stay in one place."

Dad came over. "Get out," he said. "Eet looks like eet is ready." He prodded the mass with a long stick. The boys helped to drag the tub over to the pantry wall.

Then Dad and Harry and their mother grabbed big handfuls of the mixture and slapped them onto the wall. They looked like little children playing with mud, plopping it over the slatted side of the building.

"Ve haf to go inside and plaster from dere too," their dad told the boys.

The younger children were set to tramping a second tubful. There was no time to be lost. One tub would be emptying, the other being prepared. When Francie and Danny grew too weary, Bennie and Eddie rolled up their pant legs and tramped. Their feet were larger and stronger, and they did not tire as easily.

It took all day to plaster the pantry. When it was finished, they stood back and looked at it. The mud walls looked black and moist. The house looked much bigger.

"Ven it is dried real good, ve put de lime on eet," Mr. Polanski said. "Een Poplar Valley dey used to make de houses out of clay, like dis. Dos houses was real good, just as good as de sod house."

He gathered his tools and went into the kitchen to cut a door in the north wall so that they could enter the pantry that way.

Francie thought of the new room with excitement. The pantry would be cool in the summer, and on its shelves food could be kept from meal to meal. In the pantry her mother could store the big speckled mixing bowl and empty sealers and the big pots that weren't used so often. The family would have a lot more room in the kitchen.

But she didn't like how black it looked inside. The only light came through a small window facing north.

"When it is dry, I put da whitewash inside all over. Den it will look real clean," said her mother. "Only I know dem darned mices like to make holes in da walls. We will have to set traps all da time."

After the mixing was finished, Francie and Danny looked at their feet and legs with interest. Mud and horse manure and water really cleaned the feet.

CHAPTER EIGHTEEN

Whenever Francie thought of the new teacher and going back to school, she became excited. The new teacher was a woman. She came from a big city called Winnipeg and had a very good education. She was young and had just married a farmer at Green Valley.

Harry spoke up at the supper table one evening.

"I want to stay home and farm. I don't want to waste any more time going to school," he said.

Their father chewed for a while before he answered.

"Harry, you are not yet fourteen. De law say dat I haf to send you to de school until you are fifteen and in grade eight. Of course if you finish de grade before you are fifteen, you can quit de school den. But you have one more year to go. Den you can stay at home."

"Better to get a good education, Harry," their mother joined in. "Times iss changing. Daddy have only grade t'ree in da Old Country. Dat wass da big education over dere. But here in Canada you should finish da grade eight."

Francie couldn't understand why Harry wanted to quit. School was a lot better than staying at home and working all of the time. Besides, there were many books at school. There was even a set of brown encyclopedias that told all about the world.

Harry didn't say anything more about quitting school. He would be fifteen on Saint Valentine's Day, and after that he would be a man.

"Today yous have to pull up all da peas," Mrs. Polanski told the children at the table. "Dere are not so many, but we haf to save da seeds for da next year."

Bennie, Francie and Stanley went out to the garden with their mother. The wind tugged at their mother's heavy babushka and flapped her faded brown apron.

"See. Pull out all da plants by da roots. Den pile dem on two piles, one at each end of da patch. We leave dem here to dry for a few days. Dey dry quick when it is hot."

It was almost sinful to pull up the plants after caring for them all summer. Each child took a row. After their mother had returned to the house to begin dinner, they began to pretend.

"Aahrrrrr!" they roared, and they charged at the helpless plants, frothing at their mouths. They were monsters bent on destroying anything that stood in their paths. They wiped the peas right off the face of the earth.

The piles, as high as Danny, stood in the garden for several days.

"Take dose grey blankets out to da garden," their mother told them one dreamy August afternoon. "Spread dem out on da ground and put da peas into dem. Den you carry dose peas to da empty granary an' t'row da peas on da floor."

They spread the grey blankets as they had been told. Bennie and Francie tottered to the granary with the first two loads. The peas were not heavy, but clumsy.

It was while they were gathering up the plants next to the ground that they discovered the mice. The animals had built large, loose straw nests under the piles of plants. When the ground was exposed, the mice, awkward grey ones, bumbled off in different directions.

"Mice!" Francie screamed. They darted after the fleeing animals. Some they tramped on, but the littler ones they caught.

They were nice, like the baby ducks.

"These are field mice," Bennie explained.

"They come from Field?" Danny wanted to know.

"No, no. There's two kinds of mice. The ones that live in buildings are house mice. They're the mad, biting kind. They've got big ears and pointy noses. These mice are fat, and they've got wee ears and squinty eyes. They live out in the fields and gardens. And they don't ever bite like the house mice do. Even the big ones don't bite."

"We could keep them for pets," Francie said.

"No," Bennie said, shaking his head. "Mum would be real mad if we kept them. Especially you, Francie."

After the noon meal their mother went out to the granary with the peas. She carried a three-foot two-by-two.

"You hit da peas like dat." She smacked the pile of peas hard. "You hit dem all over. Da peas get knocked out and dey fall to da bottom." She pounded at the pile, hitting the plants with vigor. Sweet dust rose in the granary. She turned some of the plants over and struck again.

"Now you do it." She gave the stick to Bennie. "Be careful. Only one hit da peas at a time, or you will maybe hit somebody."

After their mother left, they declared war on the peas.

"Take that!" Bennie struck down a bump. "And that!" He whirled to meet the enemy advancing from the rear. "Oh, so you think you're smart! Try this!" And he dealt the enemy a terrific blow that flattened him.

"My turn! My turn!" Francie danced about. "Bennie, let me do it!"

They fought, by turns, an unbelievable war. They killed thousands of men. The war left the peas flattened and broken.

"Dat's good," their mother said when she saw the pile. "Now we haf to lift up the plants and see how many peas dere are underneath."

They dumped the debris into the grey blankets again. All over the floor lay the wrinkled peas, mixed with bits of dried shells and leaves.

"How are we going to get the rubbish out?"

"I do it. You watch." Mrs. Polanski tied her apron into a pouch. She filled it with the rubbish and peas.

"I go outside in da wind. Go and bring me da washtub, Frynca."

The wind came in gusts from the northwest. Mrs. Polanski stood with her side to the wind. Then she put her hands into her pouch and tossed handfuls of peas up into the air. The wind caught the rubbish while the peas drummed into the tub.

"I haf to do dis again. The second time da peas come out cleaner."

Francie watched her mother winnowing the peas. The woman stood, solid and serious, her clothes blowing to the south, her face intent under the white babushka. As when she had planted the same seed in the spring, she looked like one of the gleaners in the picture over the school blackboard. There had to be seed for the following year. Her mother would be sure of that.

CHAPTER NINETEEN

One hot September day when the children walked into the kitchen, they found their mother wiping her eyes with the edge of her apron.

"Da horses dey getting da sleeping sickness. Today da King die."

They had never seen a dead horse. They ran to the barn without stopping for lunch.

King, the strongest and smartest work horse, lay quietly on his side. Flies buzzed in circles around his nose.

The children approached him warily. They had kept out of his stall when he had been alive. King had never liked children.

His belly swelled in an enormous arc. Bennie put a foot on it. It gave a little.

"Feels like rubber," he said. "I'm going to climb up on him."

"Maybe you shouldn't," Francie said.

"Why not? He's dead now." Bennie stood up on the dead horse's belly. He did not make much of a dent on it.

He gave a little jump. Then another.

"Sure feels like rubber," he said. "C'mon, Francie."

Francie wanted to. She looked at her father and Harry, who were bending over King's mate, Polly, in her stall.

"She vill not last till de morning," their father spoke with resignation. "Ve be lucky dey don' all die."

Francie stepped up on the dead horse beside Bennie. The great belly gave a little when she walked. It was funny, walking on the side of the fiercest horse they had owned.

"Let's jump together," she said to Bennie. And they jumped. Not too high at first, then higher and higher. When both of them came down together, the dead horse passed wind. They laughed.

Francie looked quickly at her father. They might get it, laughing and being silly when the horses were sick.

But her father stood beside Polly, his thoughts on the rest of the herd. King and Polly had been his most faithful workers, tireless and strong. If they caught the disease, what would happen to the rest of the horses who were not as strong?

"You get de tractor an' pull de King out to de pasture. Bring de tractor back to de barn. Ve be needing it again."

He took no notice whatever of the children playing on King. He went out of the barn, his shaggy head bowed.

It didn't stop with King and Polly. Jessie got the sleeping sickness too, and Daisy and Jackie, then big-boned Queenie. Several of the young, unnamed horses died too. Every day the tractor pulled yet another horse into the north pasture.

The children saw a helplessness settle over their father's shoulders. Grasshoppers he could face and gophers and the dry summer, even the hailstorms. But this was something else. He loved his horses. Like him, they were fierce, big, strong; yet this invisible blight took his animals from him with triumphant stealth.

Even Prince caught it. For two days he stood in his stall, head drooping, dreaming of something that horses dream of, not even bothering to switch his tail at the flies. But instead of lying down and never getting up again, he stood. After a week he roused himself and began to nibble at the hay in front of him. He disappointed the children. They had been looking forward to jumping on him.

When Harry led him to the dugout for water, they saw at once that he was going to be clumsier than ever. He kept tripping over nothing; his hind quarters moved awkwardly. He would not be of much good the rest of his life. He would be used around the yard with the younger children.

The vet came one day and gave some of the horses shots. It didn't do much good.

"Mosquitoes," he said. "They carry the sickness. You can't do much. If the horse is strong and can fight it, he'll be okay. If not, nothing will help." He shook their father's hand.

Half of the horses died. At night, Francie could hear the coyotes in the north pasture calling. Answers from other coyotes came eerily from all around the shelterbelt.

They must be standing out there in the dark in a solid ring, she thought. They fed well on the horse meat. At least they would leave the sheep alone when they had all that meat to eat.

One afternoon Dad came pounding into the kitchen.

"Qveeck!" he shouted to their mother. "Take de keeds and run to de trees. Dere is a twister coming from de west!"

Urgent calls rang out. Francie grabbed Stanley by one hand and Danny by the other. The whole family scrambled to the northeast corner of the shelterbelt.

"Lay down and hold on to de trees," their father instructed. "Don' you get up, no matter what happens."

Mrs. Polanski muttered prayers in Polish, her face strained as she held the baby close. They stretched out close to the ground.

A black, evil funnel loomed in from the west. Everything went quiet. Not a bird chirped. Even the dog was silent. It became very dark, even though it was only three in the afternoon.

"Francie, can I hang on with my feets too?" Danny asked.

"Sure." Francie bit into the bitter bark of the branch she was holding. "See, I'm holding on, tooth and claw."

Just behind the shelterbelt Dad and the boys had made a big haystack. The wind came in a gust and carried off the top of the stack.

A hen who had picked the stack to brood in was blown, cackling, head over heels out of the stack along with the hay.

"Bet that'll cure her," Bennie laughed. The hen tried to go back to the stack, but the wind, furious now, pinned her to the ground.

Above them the trees writhed and thrashed. Mum prayed louder. They didn't care if the twister took everything they had, as long as it left them alone.

A terrific gust of wind tore through the yard. They stared as a hayrack shuddered, slowly rose and then turned end over end like a giant Russian thistle across the yard, splintering as it went. With the roaring of the wind in their ears, they heard no other sound. The destruction of the hayrack was like a silent dream.

"Oi, Boza, Boza," their mother cried, full of fear for her family.

The twister angled off toward the south, toward Szodas. Rain began to fall in great, cold splashes.

"Everybody run to de house," their father commanded. "Hurry up."

They had just made it into the house when the hail began. What a noise it made on the roof of the kitchen! They crowded to the windows to watch the marble-sized hailstones bounce off the ground.

"Don' stand too close to da window," their mother warned. "Da lightning can hit you dere." She was still praying. She lit a holy candle and placed it on the table, asking God to protect the cattle out in the storm.

"Hey, the chicken house is open," yelled Eddie. "The door's gonna get blown off."

Sure enough, the old wooden door banged back and forth as the hail pounded it. If a chicken came out now, it would get killed by the door.

"I'll go shut it," Joe offered. He stuck a milk pail over his head and made a dash for the chicken house. They all laughed to hear the hailstones boinging off the pail. It must have made an awful racket in his ears.

He slammed the chicken house door, turned the wooden latch and sprinted back across the yard, hailstones ricocheting from the pail. Harry opened the door, and Joe fell panting into the kitchen.

The children were out before the last drops ceased. They ran through the puddles, splashing one another, inhaling the new-washed air in great gulps. A glorious rainbow arced across the eastern sky. On a wet, grey fencepost a meadowlark sang its high, clear song.

The rain barrel was overflowing. Their parents stood on the steps and looked around at the running water, the mud. If only a rain like this had come in June, the fields would not be lying barren now.

CHAPTER TWENTY

Behind the house the butterfly lifted tantalizingly out of reach. The wind caught it and trembled its beautiful silken wings. A mad desire for possession seized Francie. Without thinking, she suddenly hurled the rock she was holding. The butterfly darted upward; the rock flew insanely into a window, scattering the glass in a brittle shower.

For a moment Francie stood unbelieving. That this could happen to her just as she was innocently reaching for the unattainable — it was monstrous. Before she knew what she was doing, she dived around the corner of the house, but she heard her father's roar from the Other Room.

Where to go? Though she ran to the ends of the earth, her father would find her and punish her. He would never understand that she hadn't meant to do it. A window cost money and meant an extra trip to town. No one bought windows ahead of time. The knowledge that he wouldn't understand brought the tears to her eyes in a flood of anguish. She ran into the tall weeds skirting the shelterbelt and lay down, her heart beating wildly, hopelessly. Even then, she knew that she would have to face the consequences.

During the interminable afternoon, she heard Joe call her several times. In his voice she sensed a triumph and she wept anew. If only she had gone in right away and gotten her licking it would have been all over by now. Was it always going to be this hard to do what was right?

At last she could bear it no longer. She crept to the front door, tear-stained and shaking, her soft flesh already feeling the stroke of the strap. Her mother looked up from her work at the table. She checked herself and kept on ironing. Francie slipped into the Other Room to get upstairs.

But her father was right behind her. He had been coming from the blacksmith shop for a drink of water. As he saw Francie move soundlessly over the linoleum, his features darkened under the soot from the forge.

"Frynca!" he shouted, "you break de window?" Startled, Francie darted under the table. It did her little good. An angry arm reached after her, firmly gripped her ankle, pulled her out.

The first stroke of the strap was interrupted by the table. In a flash Francie knew that her father was angry, very angry, because he'd missed. Terror gripped her.

The trouble was that she couldn't fool Dad. If she didn't cry loud enough, he would think that he wasn't punishing hard enough, and then he would half-kill her. If she yelled too much, it made him mad, and then he hit harder because he despised cowardice. For an instant Francie hoped that she could display just the right amount of remorse; at the first tremendous stroke all her resolution vanished, and she screamed with pain as the leather bit into her upper legs.

Mrs. Polanski ran in from the kitchen, trying to hold his arm. *"Toh dosheit, Tato, dosheit.* She still just a little girl."

His anger spent, John Polanski drank deeply from the dipper, wiped his wet moustache and went out into the sunlight.

Francie stumbled blindly up the stairs, the smarting in her legs and across her back unbearable. But the pain would pass, and the thing that would remain was her feeling that he had completely rejected her. She had seen a butterfly, a beautiful painted thing, and tried to capture it. That was all. The thought of her heedless innocence brought on the tears anew. She had not deliberately come up to the window and put a rock through it. It had happened almost without her knowing.

"All of you can go to Regina to see the King and Queen," Mrs. Topchuck announced one day in May. "All school children have free passes to go by train."

Regina. Only Mum and Dad and grownups went to Regina, to the Army and Navy Store to buy winter clothes once a year. Now they could all go to Regina, and for nothing. It would be their first train ride too.

Francie looked with care at the framed picture of the King and Queen that hung over the front blackboard. The King had a thin face, and his crown looked too big for his head. The Queen had round cheeks and a round front. She looked happier than the King.

The second picture over the front board showed the Royal Family. There the King looked more like one of the salesmen who sometimes came to the farm. His face looked the same, as if he never smiled. And thin. The Queen's cheeks were pushed up because she was smiling. The two princesses stood with their parents, looking very clean and neat. Francie wondered if they knew what fun it was to play Prisoner's Base.

The two princesses had their hair parted very straight. Francie wondered who parted it for them. Rosy parted her own hair, never in the middle or on the side, but somewhere in between. And the part was always crooked. And because she didn't care how she parted her hair, Rosy's face looked crooked. People wanted to straighten Rosy out. Her mother fussed with her collar and rebuttoned the backs of her dresses, but it didn't help: Rosy still looked crooked.

The night before the visit of the King and Queen everyone took a bath. They had to get up very early the next morning to get the chores done. It was hard to do chores when everyone was so excited. Then they all climbed into the back of the truck with their lunches and Dad took them to school. At school all the other kids climbed on and the truck headed for Field. Mrs. Topchuck sat in the cab with Dad.

Francie had trouble breathing. What if they got a flat tire and missed the train? Oh, then they would all stand helplessly and see the train go by in the distance, carrying hundreds of the other happy children who had made it. She tried to dismiss the thoughts of failure from her mind. Inside her a voice kept saying, "Oh, no, Francie, you're really going to see a live king. You're really going to ride on a train. You're really going to Regina, the capital of Saskatchewan. All in one day."

"What a long train!" Rosy marvelled.

The engine heaved and chugged into the station, with heads and heads of school children sticking out of windows, cheering and waving small flags as if they were welcoming the Westfield children. Car after car slid by, and Francie began to fear that there was no room for them, that they would just have to go to school while the rest of the children on the train went on to Regina and saw a real king and queen.

"All aboard!" the conductor shouted above the din. With a delicious lurch, the train started on its way as they perched, unbelieving, on the plush seats.

"Hold hands tightly, or you'll get lost," Mrs. Topchuck warned when they neared Regina. A while later, the line of Westfield children wove in and out through the throngs of people in the streets.

"We're going to see a puppet show first," shouted Mrs. Topchuck. "In this building. All of you sit together."

Funny, stiff little people jerked around and said things in high, squeaky voices.

"The people are really just wooden dolls," Mrs. Topchuck said, " and real people who are hidden do the talking."

Sure enough, out on the back wall Francie could see the shadows of the strings that pulled the puppets.

After that it seemed that all of the people in Regina acted like those puppets on strings. Some ran this way, others ran that; they jumped up on fences and one or two climbed trees. They waved all kinds of flags, little silk ones and big heavy cotton ones. All of the Westfield children stood in rows alongside the street and looked across to the other side at children looking back at them.

Then there arose this queer, low roar that started somewhere way down the street. The roar grew louder, and all the flags started waving faster and faster. Francie watched a colorful parade of Mounties go by. Then she lowered her flag and stared. A low open car was driving by. In the back seat sat a pretty lady dressed in fluffy blue feathers. She was smiling and nodding her head this way and that, stretching out her gloved hands as if she were asking for something. Francie caught one quick glimpse of the man who sat beside the pretty lady. He looked thin and small and not at all happy.

Francie wondered why some people were crying and blowing their noses. The fierce roaring died down. They all turned to look at Mrs. Topchuck. She was blinking hard.

"Well, children," she said, "I hope that you'll never forget this as long as you live. This is the first time that a British monarch has set foot in one of the dominions. Always remember May the twenty-fifth, 1939."

Francie wondered where the King had set his foot. He couldn't do it unless the car stopped. And when they lay sprawled out on the train on their way home, she wondered if the King and Queen always had to ride around in an open car, jerking their hands like puppets and turning their heads from side to side, smiling and smiling.

CHAPTER TWENTY-ONE

One day that fall her doll disappeared. Just like that. Francie was sure that she had left it in its usual place on her pillow, half under the feather tick, just before she trotted off to school. She went upstairs to get the doll after getting home, to take it with her when she and Danny went for the cows, but it was gone. There wasn't even a sign that the doll had lain under the tick.

She threw back the bedcovers and searched every corner of the bed. She looked under the pillows. Then she looked in the improbable places: on the windowsill, under the bed, in the corners.

Maybe one of the boys had hidden it, just for fun. She decided to ask her mother.

"No. I don't see no doll." Her mother stirred the *varinichi* floating around in the big aluminum pot. "You never mind dat now. You go and get da cows with Danny."

Francie hunted through the house over and over again, until her mother sent her outside to play. Then she thought of the various places where she had played with it: the low branch of the maple, the shade behind the granaries where her brothers played farms in the dirt, the kittens in the loft.

She knew that she was too big to want baby things, but without the doll, what did she have? Only the boy things were left — the wooden tractors that ran like silly things, the carved wooden guns for playing cowboy, the make-believe fences and machinery for the play farms. Without the doll they meant nothing. With the doll she could accept them for a part of each day.

She questioned Joe about the doll. He opened his eyes wide and said, "Doll? What doll?" He repeated it to each of the other boys, until Francie's ears drove her out, in spite of herself, to wander among the granaries and look in stupid places where no doll would ever be found.

After school she would go upstairs and stand by her bed, not looking at it at all, looking at the corners of the room instead or even under the bed. When she could bear it no longer she would look at the pillow where she had seen it last. There was always the sharp, bitter disappointment, the anguish. The doll was gone, no one knew where; she would never see it again. What was she going to tell Rosy? When she was sent to gather the eggs, she would resolutely turn her eyes away from the last nest; the doll was in there, waiting for her. At the last moment she darted to the nest to find only an egg or two: plain, grim reality.

Joe acted nicer to her than he had before she lost the doll. He would ask her to join in the boys' games and even give her a turn first.

"C'mon, Francie," he coaxed one Sunday afternoon. "Play farm with us. You can have the soft patch of ground in the shade. You can use my tractor."

Francie had no tractor of her own. When she needed one, Eddie usually lent her his.

She sat on the patch of ground and looked at the farms thriving around her. Eddie was pushing little sticks into the ground around his fields. Harry had the biggest farm. He was using an odd-looking chunk of metal and pretending to be digging a dugout. Bennie and Stanley planted pigweed trees behind their buildings; they were making shelterbelts. Nick was driving his truck, a block of wood with spools sawed in half for wheels, along the narrow dirt road that led to Harry's farm.

Joe had buildings made of match boxes and broken shingles. He drove his tractor over to a patch of grass and began to cut his grain. He held a handful of grass with one hand and sawed at it with his jackknife.

Francie had seen all these actions repeated many times over. She had entered joyfully into the pretend farming many times. Now the game did not interest her. She was tired of pushing things around in the dirt and building farms.

She wandered off to the garden where the late peas had been pulled up and piled. There would be mice hiding under those plants, big, kind, easy-to-tame mice that would make good pets.

"Danny, Stanley." She ran back to the boys. "Help me catch mice under the pea plants."

Joe's eyes caught fire. "Yeah. We could pretend they were horses."

They surrounded the pile of plants.

"Whatever you catch, it's yours," they agreed.

Harry put his arms around the pile and lifted it off the ground. Mice ran in all directions, but slow, bumbling mice, half-blind and baby-clumsy.

Francie put her bare foot across one mouse's back and cupped her hand over two wee babies.

"Danny, did you get any?"

Danny was proud of himself. He had wet himself in the excitement, but he had caught his first mouse, a big grey one.

"Let's keep them together," Francie said. "Go and get a wooden box. The one you're using for a barn. They'll chew their way out of a paper box."

Danny's mouse was clearly the biggest. Francie was sure that it was a mother about to have babies, but she didn't tell Danny. He wouldn't stop watching it if she did.

"Whatcha gonna do with 'em?"

"Just play." It would be better to look after live things like mice than to drive tractors all the time.

"Let's see if they will eat." They shelled a pod that still hung green on a vine.

The peas rolled in front of the mice. The big grey mouse sniffed at a seed, sat on its haunches and began to chew the pea.

"Jus' like a squirrel," breathed Danny. "Jus' like a squirrel eats. My mouse is smart, Francie," he boasted.

"He sure is." Francie could see that these mice would be easy to tame. They would eat whatever was given to them and get to act like pets.

"Don't you tell Mum about them," she warned Danny. "Else she might kill them. She hates mice."

Danny nodded. No one was going to hurt his mouse.

They kept them in an empty granary beside the shop. A piece of old screening kept the mice from jumping out of the box, and a stone kept the screen on. The mice had all that they needed to live. They were fed peas and old bread crusts and were given a jam pail lid of water. Francie spent all her spare time with them.

One morning they found that the big mouse had died.

"It was the nicest mouse," Danny mourned. "Why for she have to die, Francie?"

Francie thought for a minute. The remaining mice seemed to be sluggish, stiff.

"Maybe they got too cold," she said. "Maybe mice need to be warm at night."

She looked at the three remaining mice.

"Promise not to tell, Danny, and you can have the next biggest one."

Danny promised before he knew what he shouldn't tell.

"We'll get an old woolen sock," Francie said. "A warm one for the night. Mice can't keep themselves warm. We'll put them away down in the toe of the sock when we go to bed and keep the sock rolled up in a ball between us all night. That way we'll keep the mice warm and they won't die."

Danny danced. "What if we lay on 'em, Francie?"

"We won't. We'll sleep far apart."

It worked. For three nights they smuggled the sock to bed, slept with the mice and woke overjoyed in the morning, glad to find that the mice were alive. The two littlest mice became very lively.

"See, they're really getting tame." Francie showed Danny how one mouse sat up on her palm, chewing at a pea.

"Jus' like squirrels." Danny sat on his haunches like the mouse. He, too, liked playing with live things better than playing farm.

Francie became so fascinated with the mice that she began to take chances. She slipped out of the house one evening without clearing off the plates.

"Francie! Dishes!" her mother called. Francie hastily put a mouse back into the wooden box and ran for the house.

"What you doing, all the time away from da house?" her mother scolded. "You getting too big to fool around anymore. Dishes is dishes. You wash dem first, den go and play."

Francie said nothing. She scraped hard on the plates.

The mice became so tame that they sat up when the children approached the box. They spent every minute they dared with them. Danny called his mouse Tiger, and Francie named hers Hans and Fritz, although she wasn't sure which was which.

"Ayeehhh!" their mother screeched one evening at the supper table, startling Francie so much that she dropped her spoon. Mrs. Polanski was pointing at Danny's shirt. His mouse had climbed out of his pocket and was creeping up his shoulder.

"Outside! Get outside!" roared their father. Danny didn't know why they were all so excited. He didn't know that the mouse was loose. He stood up uncertainly; the mouse plunked into his soup.

Chairs flew back from the table. Danny grabbed his mouse and fled, his father's rage reaching after him. Everybody wanted knives and forks washed off, and their mother couldn't eat her supper.

"Dem darned mices," she kept saying. "Dey no good, dem mices. Dey carry da diseases. Dey not for playing."

Francie thought about the mice in bed every night with them. What would their mother say or do if she knew what was going on? They would have only one mouse apiece from now on.

Danny didn't get a very hard licking. Mum felt sorry for him. "Don' you play no more wit dem mices," she warned.

The two little mice felt spunky the next morning. They ran on perfect little mousefeet all over the tick, twinkling their immaculate noses.

"Francie, I'm scared if Mum finds them," Danny whispered.

"Let's leave them in the sock in bed today," Francie said. "Mum might

109

go looking in the granaries for them. She thinks we have something hidden somewhere."

It seemed to be the best plan. Mum would never, ever think of looking in their bed. Anyway, she didn't have time to go upstairs during the day.

They saw the bedclothes on the clothesline as they rounded the shelterbelt on the way home from school. Francie's eyes rounded with horror.

She wasn't afraid of a licking from Mum. She felt sorry for the poor mice.

"*Doorna*," her mother began as Francie came into the kitchen. *Doorna* meant stupid girl. It wasn't a very bad word unless Dad used it.

"Why you keeping dem dirty mices in your bed? You such a big girl, and you do such crazy t'ings. You teachin' Danny to do dose same t'ings too."

Francie hung her head, hoping that her mother's anger would spend itself before her father came to the house. How could they have known that their mother would be washing clothes today?

"Da girl who plays with mices and t'ings — mices and gophers — dat girl will never make da good wife. Grandma always say dat. And it true. Her bread never raised and her cakes always fell." Mum ran out of breath, she was so mad. "You wait and see. When you start to cook you be no good because you playing wit dem dirty things."

She didn't give Francie a licking, but she sent her after the cows without a lunch. Danny walked forlornly beside her, swatting the mosquitoes that pestered his closely cropped head.

"We jus' can't have nothing." He cut off a dandelion's head with a stick. "I wanna go to school."

"School's better," Francie agreed. "At least there you can read and play crokinole or with plasticine. And you have friends."

They walked down the soft trail emptied of hope.

"Danny," she asked him for the hundredth time. "Do you know what happened to my doll?"

CHAPTER TWENTY-TWO

Mrs. Topchuck had new ideas for the concert. The big play this year would be *Snow White and the Seven Dwarfs*. It wasn't just a play. It was a musical as well. That meant that all those taking part had to sing a lot of different songs, and that those who were not in the play had to sing behind the curtains to help out. It meant a lot of practice and a lot of costumes.

"Rosy," said Mrs. Topchuck, "you will have to be one of the dwarfs. We don't have enough small boys."

She explained that Rosy would have to take off the overalls and put her legs into a sweater, with the neck hole at her bottom, which would be pinned shut.

"And you'll have to wear a toque and a beard," continued Mrs. Topchuck. "You're going to be Sleepy."

Rosy sat aghast. Oh, it didn't pay to be short; you got all the worse parts.

"We need six more dwarfs," Mrs. Topchuck continued. She gave out the parts to the protesting boys. The bigger boys hooted at each choice. But Johnny Szoda had to be Dopey and that was the funniest of all. He smiled with pleasure while the rest of the boys roared and beat on their desks.

After she had talked about the musical, Mrs. Topchuck gave out other parts. Then she wound up the gramophone and put on a record.

Wild, sweet music tumbled off the spinning disc into the room. Francie felt an irresistible urge to get up and caper around.

Mrs. Topchuck stopped the record.

"That's the *Hopa Cola*, a Ukrainian dance. You could do it, Francie."

"I don't know how," blurted Francie, astonished.

"It isn't hard to learn. You will wear a nice costume to dance in. There will be ribbons down your back, hanging from a wreath of flowers around your head. Your parents will be very pleased, and it will be something for the people from Field to see, too."

The ribbons did it. Francie saw herself twirling around, ribbons flying. She wanted to do it.

Right from the beginning she hated the dwarfs. They sang songs like "Whistle While You Work" and "Heigh Ho, Heigh Ho." Sleepy had to act stupid like Dopey.

But learning the dance made up for the dwarfs. At first she tried to imitate the teacher's smooth, lilting one-two-three movement with stiff, awkward little jerks. All at once the polka rhythm charmed her feet. She gave into it and it carried her away; then she felt that she could dance forever.

The special steps were easy to master then; they were done in between the polka. Francie danced through recesses and noon hours. She danced beside the heater at home with her mother smiling encouragement; she danced in her dreams at night, bright ribbons flying. She yearned for the music during school hours when dull work had to be completed; the dance possessed her utterly. Rosy didn't care for that kind of dancing at all.

They sang the *Snow White* songs a hundred thousand times. Mrs. Topchuck even made them sing while they were decorating. If it hadn't been for the dance, Francie could never have stood it.

On the night of the concert, she waited behind the center part at the back of the stage. Since she was dancing alone, she could not come in from the side. It would make the dance look unbalanced. Her mother had made her a full-sleeved white blouse, and Francie had embroidered the cross-stitch patterns on the sleeves in red. The gathered skirt was homemade too. Mrs. Topchuck had pointed out that the proper costume had a very straight skirt; but Francie's mother meant the skirt for Sunday wear after the concert, and no young girl wore straight skirts. So the gathered skirt had to do.

"What she t'ink, we rich like her? We have more dan one kid, and dey all needs somet'ing. I not making two skirts. I making da gathered skirt like young girls wear nowadays."

But her mother had insisted on satin ribbons.

"I don' like dose paper ribbons. Dey not hanging nice. I buy you da good ones an' you wear dem in your hair afterwards."

Francie waited out the eight introductory beats, her body lilting to the rhythm. Feeling the joy of the dance, she polkaed out onto the stage, straight to the front, where she changed effortlessly into the knee-out kick. She knew the routine by heart; she had danced it so many times.

Stamp-kick! The music called and Francie's feet obeyed. Polka, polka, it sang, and she polkaed round and round, four times. Step-slide, it commanded, and she answered gladly. The closing beats climaxed in a giddy reel, and Francie spun around four times across the stage, ribbons flying.

The applause was loud — louder than it had been for anything else. It didn't stop. People were shouting and stamping their feet. And whistling! Francie flushed with pleasure. Mrs. Topchuck beamed at her.

"Go on back," she had to put her lips to Francie's ear so that the child could hear.

Back she went. The gramophone received a second transfusion of energy, and the music coaxed the rhythm through her feet right into her head.

This time Francie ended up puffing. The excitement drained her. When the bedsheets were being drawn, she sank on one leg, her skirt spread wide under her outspread arms. She looked like a spent red poppy making its final gesture of joy.

No matter how long she lived, she would never forget the dance and the pull of the music. Nor would she soon forget the people from Field, rising to their feet and standing in a solid line, clapping and clapping. They were English, but they liked the dance anyway.

CHAPTER TWENTY-THREE

"There is not much feed for de cattle dis year," John Polanski said one day. "I am taking a load of cattle to de stockyard."

When he came home, he had a big radio, their first. Right away the radio became part of the family, for it looked like some living thing standing in the corner. Its two knobby eyes stuck out over a long narrow mouth of the dial, and shiny brown material covered its front. Dad and Harry hooked up the battery and ran an aerial wire through a hole bored in the storm window. Then Dad turned on the knob.

They sat on the floor, enchanted. They heard a band playing a march. Francie thought that it was the most beautiful music in the whole world.

No one moved until the music stopped. They heard the voice of a man telling the news. Dad wanted to listen to that. They sat quietly, wondering how this brown box could connect them to the whole world. There was much talk of war. Dad listened to every word of it.

They did nothing else that night except listen to the different stations. The following day they hurried home from school and discovered that there were comics on the radio. They listened to the Lone Ranger come galloping up on Silver. Tarzan thumped his chest and gave his victory cry. They thumped their chests on the way to school and yelled "Arrmaaanganeeee!" at the startled horses. They listened to the evil laugh of The Shadow and to the sirens of Boston Blackie.

Sundays were the best. Then they could listen for a whole hour to Lux Radio Theatre. And Fibber McGee kept opening his closet and letting all the junk fall out; Henry Aldridge kept gulping, "Coming, Mother"; and Charlie McCarthy with Mortimer Snerd kept making the man who owned him look foolish. They liked the name Mortimer. Harry named the big hog after him.

In the evenings they now could do something else besides playing cards and reading and embroidering. They still could embroider, but it was more fun when the radio was on, making pictures come into their heads.

Cowboy music came on for fifteen minutes at a time. Wilf Carter yodelled in most of his songs. Prosvigs bought a radio too, and on the way to school Rosy yodelled; the boys couldn't stand it and kept throwing her off the sled. She and Francie yodelled behind the furnace during the noon hours and were heaped with abuse for their efforts. They themselves thought that they sang rather well, even though they had no guitar.

One evening when a fine, stinging wind blew from the east, a bobsleigh jingled into the yard. The Mounties had come to see if Dad had made any whiskey.

"Go in de Other Room and play," he commanded, striding to the bedroom and seizing a bottle that stood on the night stand. He set the bottle on the window sill and yanked down the blind. Then he pulled on his sheepskin and went outside.

The Mounties had a dog with them. They walked past the house with the dog trotting in front, their fur caps whitened with frost.

Their mother kneaded bread dough in the kitchen, praying again. Francie wondered if God would listen to prayers if her father were doing something wrong. She hoped that he had no whiskey out there. But she wanted to have the Mounties come into the house, because she wanted to see a policeman up close.

Joe slammed the kitchen door.

"Where dey is, Joe?"

"Looking through the haystacks."

They found the whiskey, one gallon of it, where the dog led them in the hay. Francie and the little ones were not allowed to go into the kitchen when the Mounties came in. They listened at the keyhole but could not make out what was said. But Francie knew that it was bad, because everyone spoke so quietly.

After the Mounties drove off into the teeth of a blizzard, Dad sat at the kitchen table, drinking his tea and looking away into himself. Their mother sniffed now and then, and they knew that she was crying.

"Joe," Francie whispered in the Other Room. "What's going to happen to Dad?"

"He has to go to court. There will be a big fine."

They had no money to pay a fine. They got very little money in the winter time, because the hens stopped laying when the hen house got too cold and the cows dried up then, so there were no cream checks.

"Can Dad sell a cow and pay the fine?"

"Cows are worth about ten dollars. And it takes a lot of gas to go to Regina. No, I don't think Dad has enough cows to sell."

"What will happen then, if he can't pay?"

"I don't know. Maybe he'll have to go to jail."

That night as she lay in bed, Francie wondered how long they would keep her dad in jail. Maybe it would be for life.

The next morning Uncle Mike rode in on his horse. He wanted some *horeewka*. Aunt Caroline had a bad cold and needed something to make her feel better.

"I got no more *horeewka*," their father said in a tired way. "I don't make it no more."

When Uncle Mike heard what had happened, he brought his fist down hard on the table. "Dat's communism!" he shouted. "Communism! Why can't a man make whiskey on his own land? It's worse than Russia!"

"I know," John replied, his shoulders slumped. "But what you or I can do? I sell de wheeskey to put shoes on de keeds' feet. I sell it to buy de coal for de stove."

Uncle Mike wished that he had been there when the Mounties had come.

"I'd show dem! *Shlak traffit!* I'd fix dem!"

"What you can do?" John asked again, "Dey haf to keep de law. Somebody report me. But nobody else want to feed my keeds."

Then he soothed Uncle Mike. "Never mind." He smiled a grim smile. "If worse come to de worse, I go to jail. Me, John Polanski, go to de jail. But dey say dey don't want me in de jail. Dey tell me I can pay de fine a little at a time. Even if it take a year. Dey don't care."

Uncle Mike shook his head in helpless anger.

"Joust a minute," their father said. "Dey didn't look in de house. I still have one bottle left." He got the bottle from the windowsill in the bedroom. The glass was frosted over.

"Aha!" Uncle Mike laughed, glad to see that their dad had fooled the police a little bit. "We haf a drink to da politsmans' dog!"

They drank a toast with one gulp. Uncle Mike coughed, stamped his right foot, wiped his mouth with his sleeve.

"Ivan, I don' care about da polits. You make good *horeewka!*"

"It's *not* so good," Mrs. Polanski sniffed. "Somebody make da trouble for us. Big trouble. I always say, I don' like da whiskey makin'. See, now he get caught."

"Den, when dey put me in de jail, de ol' woman she can get rid of de ol' man," their father teased. Uncle Mike thought that was funny, but their mother just sniffed. She wiped the corners of her eyes with her apron.

"C'mon, *zinka*," their father invited. "*Miyiti sibee horeewka*. Dreenk a good one before it is all gone." He poured her a glass.

She didn't want it very much, but she drank it. Then she sat near them and began peeling potatoes.

Uncle Mike pinched Francie's bottom. She jumped and slapped his hand with surprise. He laughed and tried to grab her skirt, but she twisted

116

away. He thumped his feet on the floor, as if he were going to chase her and Danny, and they ran shrieking into the Other Room. He was fun.

The bottle kept filling the *koleeshooks*. Uncle Mike and Dad began to sing.

But they couldn't remember the words, and the tunes went sliding off into nothing. They began telling each other stories, which Francie couldn't understand, and slapping their thighs. Mum smiled now and then. The bottle kept busy.

"Dance!" roared their father. He jumped up and staggered backward. Uncle Mike fell into his arms.

"*Hoi! Hoi!*" they sang, staggering around the room, trying to make music, trying to dance. But their feet wouldn't lift off the floor.

"*Wazayti! Tum pietz!*" Mrs. Polanski warned as they leaned over the hot stove. They stumbled into the center of the room.

Over they went, with a tremendous crash that shook the kitchen floor. Uncle Mike's head almost missed the slop pail, but not quite. He lay there giggling, the bright red blood pouring from a gash across one eyebrow.

Mrs. Polanski ran to them, mad at both of them and sick at the sight of blood. Uncle Mike tried to get up.

"No, no! Lay still! Your face iss bleeding!" She dabbed at him with a tea towel, trying to see how much damage had been done.

Dad lifted himself on one elbow. He saw the blood, and a great pity came over him.

"Mike!" he wept. "Mihilovitch!" The tears ran down his cheeks. "I sorry! I so sorry!"

"No, no, Ivan! Ivan!" Uncle Mike began to cry when he saw Dad's tears. "Don' cry, Ivan! Iss all right!"

They comforted each other: Dad crying for Uncle Mike, Uncle Mike crying for Dad. Mum was awful mad.

"Come, I tie up your silly head! An' den yous both go to bed! You crazy, drinking in da daytime!"

It was safe for her to scold now. Dad felt too good to say anything, and Uncle Mike was Mum's youngest brother, used to getting scolded by her.

After Mum put a bandage around their uncle's head, he crawled behind the stove and began to snore. Dad felt the walls all the way to the partition and fell heavily across the bed. They heard him singing slower and slower; then he too began to snore.

CHAPTER TWENTY-FOUR

"Rosy!" Francie threw an arm around her friend's neck. "Mum said that I could go home with you from school today and stay overnight!"

"Hey, that'll be good! My ma is over at Mrs. Wilk's, to help her have her baby. We'll have fun, but I have to do the cooking."

A warm chinook breathed softly over the snow as twilight hushed the prairies. Jackie Prosvig cracked the leather whip over the horses' heads. Leaning into their harnesses, the two greys broke into a swift trot. The sled bumped, leaned dangerously. It got dark so fast in the wintertime.

"I'll show you all my Shirley Temple scrapbooks," Rosy shouted in Francie's ear. "And all the movie stars on my bedroom walls. We'll eat supper right away so that it will leave us more time for fun afterwards."

They scurried into the kitchen with the lunch pails. Rosy tossed hers onto the cupboard.

"Holy gee, the fire's gone out." She clattered the stove lid. "Just when we want to hurry. Mrs. Wilk must sure be having a hard time with the baby."

"Mrs. Wilk has grey hair already. How come she's still having babies?"

"I dunno. Maybe she's in the change."

"What change?"

"Quit having her monthlies. But not quite. Let's go down cellar and get the spuds. I'll get the flashlight."

Francie carved a large potato with the big butcher knife. She hardly ever got to peel potatoes at home. Her mother did that when it was time to get the cows.

Rosy attacked the stove and shook the grates furiously.

"The fire will take a little while," she said, dusting off her hands. "I know. Let's have a fizz drink while we're waiting."

"What's a fizz drink?"

"You put some water in a cup. Add some vinegar. Like this. Then you stir in a teaspoon of baking soda."

The liquid frothed in the glass. Francie tasted it gingerly.

"It cleans your blood. Dad used to drink it every day. This and the juice from dill pickles."

Rosy sliced the chunk of salt pork and plopped it into the heavy black frying pan. It seemed as if cooking was fun for Rosy. And easy. Not hard work like it was at home.

Francie sawed at the homemade bread and hacked out an assortment o chunky slices.

"Who murdered the bread?" Jackie asked, spearing a slice. Francie fel her face grow warm.

"You guys eat some fat too," big Kaspar Prosvig growled at them. He had quit school and did almost all the heavy work in the barn. "Don't jus pick out all the good pieces with all the meat."

Francie knew that Kaspar helped himself to his mother's wine bottle when she was not around. His nose stayed red all through supper.

"Bread."

"Meat."

"Pass the pickles, stupid."

"Like hell I will."

They dashed around the table, gathering the dishes.

"Don't be in such a big hurry," Kaspar growled at them. "You guys go all night."

The orange kitten appeared in the doorway to the living room, tai twitching. Kaspar fired a teaspoon at him. Seeing the cat move furtively under the cupboard, Kaspar slid back his chair.

"That damn cat has no business being in the house. Are we gonna le the cows in too because there's a little snow outside?"

He jabbed a broom under the cupboard. The cat moaned with fury.

He stepped over to the corner and picked up the well-used rifle.

Rosy's eyes widened with horror over the dishpan. "What're you gonna do?" she cried. "Not *my* cat!"

Kaspar paid no attention. He knelt on the floor and tried to locate the cat under the cupboard.

"Come on outa there, you refugee from a flea farm!" The girls stood unbelieving. He thrust the rifle under the cupboard.

"Ma's gonna be mad at you!" Rosy shrieked. "You're not supposed to shoot in the house!" Suddenly she hurled the soppy dishcloth at his head At the same moment he pulled the trigger.

"See what you made me do?" He stood up angrily as the cat thumped its life away under the cupboard. "I'm gonna tell Ma that you pushed me."

"I don't care," Rosy stormed, wiping her nose. "Nobody shoots inside of a house."

Kaspar pulled out the twitching form. "Just a damn freeloader," he growled. "One mouth less to feed around here." He slammed the kitchen door.

Rosy grabbed a tea towel and wiped her eyes angrily. "That damn big bully, just because I kinda liked that cat, he had to shoot him. I can never have anything of my own," she sobbed. "They always kill it or break it."

Francie had never seen Rosy cry before. She did not know what to say. It was stupid, stupid. But it was what a boy without a father would do if he drank too much wine. There was no one to lick him.

"Maybe he isn't dead yet," she suggested. "Maybe . . . ."

"When anything bleeds from the nose like that, it's dead," Rosy sniffed. "I seen lots of gophers die that way."

Francie wondered what her mother would say when she found out. She would never let her go to Rosy's by herself again. Better not tell anyone.

In Rosy's bedroom Francie studied the photos on the walls. "You sure have a lot of pictures of movie stars."

"I got some real red nail polish from the fifteen-cent store," Rosy said. "Ma doesn't like it when I put it on. Want some?"

A sudden burst of shouting rang out in the kitchen below them. Feet pounded on the stairs. Rosy readied a shoe.

"I'll bean anybody who comes up here!" she shouted.

It was Jackie, chased by Kaspar. An exchange of curses followed. Then doors slammed and all was quiet again.

"Hey, Lux Radio Theatre is just coming on," Rosy exclaimed. "It's a love story this week. Let's go down and listen."

The play had barely started when the boys trooped in.

"You shouldn't be listening to the radio," Kaspar began. "Ma said. The battery is getting too low."

"Let's go up into the attic," Rosy said to Francie in a low tone. "The boys will never go after us there. At least we can look at snapshots and old stuff."

In Rosy's bedroom, the attic door stood behind the head of Rosy's bed. Together they dragged the bed aside and slipped one at a time through the narrow door. The stale air inside promised mystery and enchantment.

Once inside they could not stand up because the low ceiling slanted right down to the floor. They sat on their heels and examined the clutter of wooden apple boxes, Rosy holding the candle high over her head. A fishnet of grey cobweb spanned the tiny panes in the small window. Dust lay everywhere, but it was a thick, comfortable kind of dust that clung to everything. Francie tipped a box toward her.

"Letters. And snapshots. Lots of wedding pictures."

"Let's look at the brides. They look funny, those people."

Solemn-eyed brides stared back at them from beside serious, moustached young men. Most of the time the groom held his hand over the bride's shoulder, as if to say, "Sit there!" None of them was smiling. Marriage was not for fun.

"Look," Francie pointed. "Here is a picture of a mother and her girl. They both wear those long black skirts that our mom wore."

"With black ribbons around the bottom," Rosy said, leaning close. "Always white blouses and white shirts. What a hell of a time they must have had getting them clean."

"Dad hates his white shirt. He gets it dirty before he even gets it on."

A faint fairy chime came softly from the black mantel clock that Francie bumped with her elbow. The hour hand was missing. Then it stood mysteriously silent, as if it had lost its tongue.

"Ma has lots of old letters," Rosy said, shuffling through the pile. "But you can't read 'em. They're all in Polish."

They studied the faded writing, trying to decipher the strange words. Some of the pages were stained a light brown, as if tea had been accidentally poured on them. Francie fished out a comb from the same box. It was made of tortoise shell and was the kind some married women wore to keep their hair back from their faces.

In the candlelight Francie could see the little scum of dandruff on the comb. Who had worn it, then put it here to lie in a dusty, spidery attic? Whose hand had tucked it firmly behind a small pink ear? And did she think that she looked prettier with it?

Rosy slid along the floor to another box, holding up the candle. Faded crepe paper roses, their wire stems a tangled maze, covered the things underneath.

Look. Here's an old prayer book." Francie flipped through the soft pages. It too was written in Polish and had black and white illustrations. Inside the front cover a bride and a groom were being blessed by Jesus. The groom stood straight and tall, with a manly bearing; the bride bowed her head forever to Jesus, not daring to look at Him.

A soft rustle came from the shadows. Rosy lifted the candle. On the frame of a glass-covered picture of the Sacred Heart, a tiny grey mouse quivered its delicate whiskers.

"Damn mice," Rosy shuddered. "They're always up here. I hate 'em."

Francie slipped off a shoe, steadied it and flung it at the animal. Shoe and mouse disappeared.

"I wish I could throw as straight as the boys." She crawled in among the boxes, looking for the shoe.

"The dogs!" Rosy cried. "The dogs are barking! Ma must be coming home. Hurry up, Francie! She'll kill me if she finds out that I had a candle in here. She's so scared of fire."

"Rosy! I can't find it anywhere! My shoe is lost!"

"This candle is getting pretty short. Hurry!"

"It has to be in a box or on the floor!"

"Holy gee. C'mon, Francie, let's get out of here for now and undress and get our nightgowns on. She'll think we were in bed. Then afterwards we can pretend we're going to bed, but instead we'll look for the shoe."

A chorus of voices rose from the kitchen. The girls scraped their sides as they hurried out of the small door.

"She might come up and smell the candle," Rosy worried. "Let's go down. You ask for a drink of water. She won't get mad at you."

Mrs. Prosvig, dark circles under her eyes, was unwrapping a long brown scarf.

"All right, have your water," she grumbled. "I thought you would be asleep by now."

"What did Mrs. Wilk have?" Rosy asked carelessly.

"Just another girl. Mr. Wilk, he so disappointed. He have just the two boys, you know. But I say to him, 'Another girl, another cow in the barn. The girls is better at milking.' But he say, 'I don't care about no cows. I got two sections of land and I have only two boys to help me. I not so lucky as John Polanski'."

They reentered the attic by the light of the coal-oil lamp.

"We have to be real quiet," Rosy whispered. "Ma's bedroom is right below the attic."

The black shadows made the clutter of boxes look monstrous. Somewhere in there was her shoe. Francie wished now that she had never thrown it.

"There's no floor board against the wall," Rosy whispered. "Maybe the shoe fell in there."

Francie felt carefully. Her fingers touched thick dust, splintery wood. Something moved under her hand.

She jerked back, knocking the lamp chimney to the floor. It broke into two neat pieces.

"Leave it," Rosy cautioned. "It's too hot to pick up right away. I'll put the pieces on my dresser and tell Ma it was an accident. She'll yell for a while, but she never straps us. I'm not gonna tell on you. You're my very best friend."

Francie put her hand into the opening quickly and immediately drew it out again. She had touched something solid. She reached again and she had her shoe.

"You're going to tell your mother a lie," Francie whispered as they crawled out.

"If I don't, she'll never let you stay here again," Rosy said practically. "I just lie once in a while. To keep her from getting mad."

They huddled close together under the cool bedclothes. Francie felt the warm, comforting presence of her friend. Where would she ever find another friend like Rosy? She could fix anything.

CHAPTER TWENTY-FIVE

Mrs. Topchuck resigned because she was going to start a family. A new teacher came one evening to the Polanskis' to apply for the school. She came with Mr. Miller.

The children looked her over with care. She had thick ankles, thick wrists and thick, bushy hair. Her eyes protruded from her long face.

"She looks like a darned old moose," Bennie whispered to Francie beside the radio. They burst into giggles and dashed out the door to dissolve into helpless laughter behind the house.

"Bet she's forty years old," Bennie gasped. "She's got grey hair! What did they get an old grandmother for?"

After she could keep her face straight, Francie crept back to the kitchen. Mr. Miller sat on his chair, his elbow on his knee, chatting with her dad and the new teacher.

"And it's not a bi-bi-big s-school, either, Miss B-Beaufort," he said. "A lot of the b-boys have quit since they finished grade eight. The girls too. There's just the Polanskis and the Prosvigs and us."

"Dere vill be de Vilk girl too," Dad reminded them. "She vill be in de same grade as Francie. Her parents is sending her to dis school now."

Miss Beaufort blushed to the roots of her hair. Their dad was looking at the teacher with kind eyes. The teacher fluttered her eyelashes, her big hands.

"Oh, Mr. Polanski, I'll do my best for the children. You don't know how much this means to me."

Francie was disgusted. No wonder Bennie didn't want to go to school. If she fluttered like that in the classroom, they would all burst out laughing.

"Is *that* gonna be our new teacher?" Bennie asked Dad after Mr. Miller and the woman drove away.

"Yah. She is not one of us. I t'ink she say she Norwegian. And she is not a Cat'lic. But I say to Mr. Miller that does not matter as long as she does a good job."

Bennie dragged himself reluctantly to school with them the following day.

"The Moose ain't gonna teach me anything," he muttered.

Francie watched Danny and Stanley lopping off dandelion heads ahead of them on the school road.

"She might not be too bad."

"Ugh. With a face like that she would be working in a canning factory."

A canning factory was the place Bennie would put anyone he didn't like. "Get lost in a canning factory" was his favorite expression.

They looked her over when she introduced herself. Rosy stared at the apparition, her mouth open.

She was just so big. All the other teachers they had known had been small. This one was like four little ones put together.

She talked slowly. She turned her great round eyes from side to side. At first Francie thought that maybe she was making faces, just to impress them; then she realized that the woman was really like that.

A bike scraped the steps. Claudette Wilk came in.

Francie had seen Claudette before, but only from a distance. The girl had been attending Green Valley School, but now that a community pasture lay between them and Green Valley, her parents wanted her to come to Westfield.

Claudette was very thin. And bowlegged. She wore shoes too, not nice girls' shoes but funny old women's shoes with ties and a heel. Her adam's apple bobbed on her thin neck when she talked.

"I'm sorry I'm late," she smiled at the teacher. Miss Beaufort didn't smile back.

"What can I do for you?" She stared at the new girl.

Rosy poked Francie under the desk. The teacher hadn't even heard Claudette.

Claudette swallowed, her adam's apple bobbing.

"I'm sorry I'm late," she repeated louder. "I'm Claudette Wilk."

Miss Beaufort stopped staring at her. "Sit down," she said.

She continued to talk to them. These were the things she expected of them. These were the things they should not do. Prosvigs began to move restlessly in their seats.

"And this is my name." She wrote it on the board in big letters. Miss Beaufort.

Bennie and Peter Prosvig doubled up in their desk holding their hands over their mouths.

Rosy looked questioningly at Francie. Francie dared not look into her friend's wide green eyes. It was the name. Francie knew what had sprung instantaneously into their minds when they heard her say, "Beaufort".

Whenever Bennie and Peter got going, they couldn't stop laughing. That was how the next thing happened. Bennie passed wind, loud.

Miss Beaufort snapped to at the board. "Who is making funny noises?" She glared at them all with her wild, white eyes.

Francie's stomach ached with the effort to keep a straight face. It wasn't nice laughing at her like that, just because she couldn't hear so well; but it was funny just the same.

Miss Beaufort began making a list of things required for the school term. She didn't notice that they were laughing themselves sick. Claudette kept her head turned straight ahead. Francie knew that she would not be as much fun as Rosy. Claudette wouldn't ever do anything wrong.

At recess the boys snickered, "Deaf as a post!" And they began calling her the name right away: the Moose. Bennie made it sound Ukrainian by calling her Moositco.

Claudette stood in the shade and watched them playing. She had tied a babushka over her neat curls. Rosy clopped past her to where Francie lay behind the scrubby caraganas.

"Get away, Rosy! Get away!" Francie yelled. It was not good to hide in the same place as Rosy; Rosy always got caught because she didn't care if they saw her or not. But Francie cared. On some days no one caught her. She loved the game.

Rosy made straight for Francie and the caraganas, her chunky knees lifting over the fox tails. She plunked down on her knees beside her friend.

Francie felt herself go white with rage. Here they were in plain sight of everybody, giving away a good hiding place behind the caraganas. And the one who was It could catch both of them just by peeking around the corner.

Before she knew what she was doing, Francie doubled up her fist and bopped Rosy right on the nose.

For an eternity they looked into each other's eyes. Rosy sank back on her haunches, rubbing her nose slowly, her eyes questioning, Francie angry to the point of tears.

Then she realized what she had done. She had struck her best friend in the face. For a game.

At the same moment they fell into each other's arms, babbling and apologizing.

"I'm sorry, pal. Did I do something wrong?"

"No . . . oh, *no*! I don't know why I did that!"

Rosy wasn't even mad at her. She never got mad at Francie. Here she was apologizing, sure that she had done something unforgivable. Not for a moment did Rosy think that it was Francie who had done the wrong.

What could be done with a friend like Rosy?

"One-two-three on Francie and Rosy!" came the triumphant cry.

After that recess Francie could not keep her mind on the work. She sat as close as she could to Rosy, her eyes filling whenever she thought of the shameful thing she had done, just for a game. Rosy grinned at her, the memory of the blow already gone.

Claudette had a serviette in her lunch pail. She wouldn't sit on the ground beside Francie and Rosy. She brought herself a block of kindling and sat on that to keep her skirt clean.

"What have you got?" Rosy asked Claudette as they opened their lunch pails.

"Lettuce and baloney." Claudette smiled a big, beautiful smile.

"Lucky," Francie sighed. They had peanut butter every day. It was okay, but they hated the marmalade. They couldn't buy jam because of the war.

Rosy lifted a soggy cocoa and cream sandwich. Cocoa and cream was the Prosvigs' favorite sandwich, even though the cream soaked right through the bread and into the corners of their lunch pails.

They walked part of the way home with Claudette. She was fourteen, like Francie, but she seemed to be a little old woman, with her old woman shoes and fringed babushka. She had very long, very clean nails.

"My mother and father are worried that my brother Frank will be called into the army," she said, pushing her bike around a rut in the road. "He's going to be eighteen next January."

"I know." Rosy and Francie laughed because both of them had spoken at the same time. They both had brothers who would be eighteen next year. It was all that they talked about at home: the war and conscription.

Bennie saw that it was of no use to argue with his father about quitting school. Both parents wanted him to get his grade nine.

"I wouldn't care," he told Francie on the way to school, "if Jim Miller hadn't quit, but I hate being the only one in grade nine. It's time I quit too."

He hated the Moose. He wouldn't answer when she spoke to him. He couldn't stand it when she fixed her great, troubled eyes on him and waited for an answer that he was not prepared to give. He even hated her slow plodding around the classroom. He began to busy himself with his jack-knife.

"Bennie, you're going to get yourself into trouble," Francie warned him when she saw him carving at his desk top.

"I don't care."

Francie didn't like what he was doing. She liked the teacher. Miss

127

Beaufort had already taught her how to organize, to outline, to plan compositions. Francie liked the ordering of things. She saw now how everything that had to be learned could be divided into little fences or pockets and learned much easier that way. She knew that Miss Beaufort was a good teacher.

"Bennie, did you carve your name on your desk?" The big, sad eyes waited for a reply.

"Did you, Bennie?"

Francie huddled miserably in her desk. Bennie was being mean.

"Well, Bennie?"

She kept Bennie in. He wouldn't talk at all. She kept him in all day, but he still wouldn't talk.

On the way home he laughed about his success. "I ain't finished yet," he threatened.

Francie worried about Miss Beaufort, not about Bennie. She hoped that the teacher wouldn't think that all Ukrainians were like him. She hoped that the teacher would not think that all Catholics were like that.

Two days later Miss Beaufort let Bennie have his recess. He still hadn't talked.

Bennie opened up his jackknife and went to work on the side of the school barn. He carved his whole name six inches high on a level with his head.

"She'll be happy to see that." Bennie grinned, pleased with his work.

The whole thing started over again, with Miss Beaufort asking Bennie if he had carved his name on the barn, and Bennie not saying a single word.

Then Miss Beaufort began asking the others.

"Rosy, did you see Bennie doing it?"

Rosy was trapped. She really liked Bennie too, and that made it worse.

"I seen him by the barn," she stammered.

"Francie," Miss Beaufort sighed. "I have to ask you. Did you see Bennie carving his name on the barn?"

There was no way out. Francie nodded.

Then Miss Beaufort lectured them all. But she meant it for Bennie. She talked about obeying the rules and being responsible. She hinted about expelling students who were a bad example. She talked for the whole period.

"See what you did," Francie hissed at Bennie when they were dismissed for lunch. "You're asking for it."

Bennie grinned, tossing his knife into the air. "Who cares?" He was getting what he wanted.

That day he carved his name in two places in the barn, on the mangers. He began carving on some of the fence posts.

"She won't find these for a while," he snickered.

They walked to school Friday, the September day scented with wheat musk. Shrews darted across the road in front of them. Snails had left shining trails across the path. The children inhaled the sweet morning air with rapture.

Bennie was especially happy. Francie hoped that he was over the crazy stuff; she wanted Miss Beaufort to like them.

But Miss Beaufort wasn't happy at all. She came in late, and when they scuttled to their desks, she didn't ask them to stand for the Lord's Prayer. She walked over to the window and stared out of it.

The silence grew. They looked at one another, wondering. Suddenly Miss Beaufort turned a haggard face toward them. Her voice broke.

"Go on — go home, all of you. I've had enough." She turned and walked into the girls' cloakroom.

For a few minutes they sat there, unbelieving. But she didn't come back out. She had meant it.

They collected their lunch pails and padded out in their bare feet. Rosy looked back, her feelings mixed.

"Told you I'd fix her," Bennie chortled. He trotted off down the road, anxious to tell his brothers that the teacher had cried.

Francie cringed inside. She was ashamed — ashamed of Bennie, of his happiness, of herself, of them all. Miss Beaufort was really soft and kind; she was being treated unfairly. How could boys be like that?

Rosy didn't like going home so early. She liked the teacher too. She also liked to get away from all the work at home. If there was no school, her mother would think up a lot of work.

They dallied as long as possible, but the inevitable had to be faced. Francie couldn't understand how Bennie dared to be so bad. He wasn't scared of Dad at all.

"When I'm old enough," Rosy said, "when I'm eighteen, I'll go to work and save my money for nice clothes. I won't live on a farm. I'll take care of a town house and never wear aprons or babushkas."

"I'll go to school until I can be a nurse," Francie replied spinning, her dream like a cobweb in the autumn air. "I'll work in a hospital and I'll always wear white."

When she walked into the kitchen, she found that Bennie had been sent stooking. Her mother looked up from the stove.

"You get some shoes on and go stook with Stanley. If you can't be good kids at school, den you haf to work in da fields."

Francie's eyes filled. "But it was only Bennie. Nobody else did anything wrong."

She hated stooking. It wouldn't be so bad if the sheaves were small. But the durum sheaves were taller than she was. They were so heavy that it took both her and Stanley to lift one off the ground.

Mr. Polanski drove to the school with the truck to see what could be done. It was serious, having trouble at school with the year just beginning.

Francie didn't like to think that she had a brother like Outlaw Turner, getting a bad name for making trouble for the teachers. Yet she couldn't stay mad at Bennie, because she knew that he wasn't really bad. He was just trying to make them take him out of school.

After dinner Dad told Bennie to get into the old truck. They drove back to the school.

"Bennie haf to go apologizéd," Mrs. Polanski told them as they did the dishes. "He haf to go tell it to her face. Daddy want to hear it himself. Den tomorrow yous will all go back to school again."

Francie knew that it wouldn't help much. Bennie would lay low for a while and then start doing stupid things again. He would wear Miss Beaufort out.

I wish I had a sister, Francie thought as she stood on tiptoe, piling the bowls in the cupboard. I wish I had at least one sister. It's awful having only brothers.

CHAPTER TWENTY-SIX

Harry would be eighteen in March. He would get his call to the army soon after that. The Polanskis hoped that the war would be over by then. Otherwise what would happen to all of the young men of the district? There were Joe and Eddie, the oldest Prosvig boys, the Millers, Outlaw, Cousin Bill. The war threatened all the big families, who needed their sons to work the land now that the fathers were growing older.

They were eating supper when they heard the news on the radio. The Canadian people had given the Liberal government the right to send Canadian boys overseas to help fight the war.

"Conscription!" Dad's face darkened. "Dat's all ve need now. I come here so I can live in peace, and now dey take my boys from me to go back into de war."

One day it came, a long envelope. After Dad read it, he got up and went out to the blacksmith shop without saying a word. Mum dabbed at the corners of her eyes with her apron all that afternoon.

The next day Dad went to Regina all by himself on the train. Harry drove to Field in the evening to pick him up.

"Dey give Harry until the harvest ees finished," their father said that night. "After that dey take heem."

"Dad, I want to enlist." Joe stood before his father, his eyes bright.

"What for?" Their father was dazed. "You gonna get killed sooner dat vay."

"I don't know. But if I wait till I get my call, they'll put me in the army. I want to go into the air force."

Dad shook his head. "No, no, Joe. Dat's de first place dey get killed, flying de plane."

"I don't want to fly. I don't want to be a pilot. I like the mechanics part of it. I want to join the ground crew."

They didn't own a suitcase. Joe tied up the brown paper box that held his extra pair of socks and a few books. He put on his faded blue jacket and plopped his orange cap sideways on his head.

"Well, so long, everybody. Francie, you write, eh?" He stood there, grinning at them all, the first to go. He was in a big hurry to get his uniform on, they could tell.

It didn't seem real when he went, in that old jacket and everyday orange cap on his head, because he was so young. And the next time they saw him he was wearing a smart blue uniform and cap.

Things were very quiet after Joe left. He went right at seeding too, so that made more work for Harry and Eddie. Even Nick and Bennie found that more work had come down the line to them; they had to clean the barn and pigsheds and look after the cattle.

Nick finished his grade eight and declared that he was through with school. Bennie and Stanley hated school more; they counted the days until they would be through with books too.

Francie had thought that she would never miss Joe. She'd thought that when he left home she would be ever so glad. But when he left, it seemed that all the fun had gone with him. He had always been the bad one, but without him nothing exciting happened any more.

"Shad up, Goddam you!" their father would shout if they were making a racket when the news came on. He kept a big map handy so he could follow the course of the war.

That fall there was a good crop. A big one. And on November the eleventh, Harry got his call again.

This time they would not give him extra time. Even though he was the oldest and they needed him, he had to go.

It was awful sad when Harry went. Mum stayed in the bedroom a long time after Dad drove Harry to the train.

Suddenly there was more room in the house. No more of Harry's felt boots or Joe's parkas; more room at the table for eating. When the boys came home on leave, they came as strangers — tall, straight young men, smelling of aftershave and shoe polish. They talked loud and stayed up late. Whenever they came home, they found a party going on somewhere and ended up with big hangovers the next day. Mum and Dad didn't say anything.

A shadow fell over the Polanski household. There were so many boys, five ahead of Francie. What would happen to them if the war lasted for four or five years? With a boy turning eighteen every year?

John Polanski's hair began to grey. He sat beside the kitchen table, drinking tea and discussing the war with Mr. Chorney.

"When I come to dis country, I come because dere was no war here. A man could farm and make a living. Now dey take my boys from me and send dem back to de Old Country and maybe kill dere own relations. It's de politishions an' de gooberment does dis. Ve don't want no war. Looks like

132

ve raise de keeds de hard vay just so dat dey can use dem for dere wars."

Mr. Chorney sucked his pipe.

"John, I don't t'ink you can keep on farming de old way wit dem horses. You need too many horses an' too many men to thresh. Your kids is too small for dat heavy work." He nodded to Francie who sat scribbling a letter to Joe. "You should get combine like I did. I got nobody but de old woman, and I get my crops in before you do."

"Dat combine waste too much of de grain. I walk through your field after you finish combining. I find grain and grain lying on de ground where you lose it. De combine waste too much grain."

"You waste de grain wit de horses too, what you t'ink? First you have to feed dem all. Den you need horses for de binder, horses for de hayracks, horses for de stook loader. You move de grain so many times you lose more dan I do."

"Yah . . . maybe." John's face worked. "But what you can do if you have sixty horses? I don't want to buy a machine when ve have de horses. Ve work wit de horses as long as ve can."

At school the days passed uneventfully. With Joe and Outlaw Turner gone, all the old exciting wickedness disappeared. Rosy was fifteen and in her last year. Claudette was Francie's age, a year younger, but Francie could see that in a year she might be the oldest student at the small country school and perhaps the only girl as well.

There were only ten of them at school now. During the breaks they ran happily after the soccer ball, making up the rules as they went along. The Miller brothers insisted that they play on the same team.

"Then I'm going to be on the other side," Francie declared. The young Millers were German, and her brothers were going to fight Germans. The Millers became the enemy.

They played the game fiercely with five to a side. Claudette wasn't much good. If she ran too hard, she got a pain in her side. She couldn't carry the ball across the field. A Miller could steal it from her with no trouble. Except when Claudette became excited and kicked with her pointed old lady's shoe. Usually she missed the ball but stabbed a Miller in the ankle or knee, and they would all have to yell "Time!" until the one kicked had a chance to get back on his feet again.

Claudette didn't care much for any of the running games that the rest of them loved. She never wore overalls or slacks.

"My mother says that girls should dress like girls," she said one windy day when she refused to play because the wind whipped up her skirt. And she always wore a black babushka over her curls so that her hair would not get messy. She looked like a little old grandmother running around on the playing field.

In their ragged jeans and bare feet Francie and Rosy enjoyed the game. They played to win and kept a day-to-day score on the blackboard. The Millers' team won once in a while. They played a defensive game; Francie's team always took the offensive.

The Polanskis were swift runners, but their bare feet had to move nimbly to escape the heavy, solid kick of the Millers' workboots. So they adapted to the game — they moved deftly because they were small and light; they passed the ball back and forth between them with no jealousy. The Millers waited for them, stolid and impassive. When the goalkeeper lurched across the goal to anticipate a feinted shot, Francie's victory was sweet as she drove the ball in with the side of her foot.

The war at school was all a game, but to them it was every bit as serious as the war that was talked about on every newscast.

"What you t'ink you want to be?" Mrs. Polanski asked, studying Francie's report card.

"I don't know. I never thought." It came to Francie in a vague way that she was not being told what to do. She was being asked. It gave her a heady feeling. At the same time it aroused an anxiety new to her. Playing games at school was one thing; finishing school and facing life was another. Maybe she should really think about nursing.

With the boys home on Christmas leave, the young people held party after party — at the Polanskis', at the Prosvigs', at the Wilks'. It seemed they were afraid that each party would be the last one ever, and they wanted to get as much fun as they could.

On Christmas Eve the Polanskis sat around the table in the usual way. Dad asked the blessing while the rest of them crossed themselves seriously, trying not to think of next Christmas. Their father waited until the table was cleared and then sang the old songs, looking into the candle flame. Harry and Joe sat beside their father quietly. The boys did not know the words of the songs, but the tunes were engraved on their minds. Every so often they would all have a drink.

"Somebody's here!" Bennie rubbed on a window pane, trying to see out. "I see two teams."

The Wilks and Chorneys filled the house with chatter. Frank Wilk pulled out a deck of cards.

"Who's with me for a game of poker?" he invited.

In the Other Room Francie watched behind the boys' chairs as they played. She could not understand how they could be so involved with the game. It was not like Durack. This game was fierce, real, and every move was important. The young men played together, but each one played apart from the others.

"C'mon, Eddie, Nick. We'll make men out of you." Frank pushed his chair over to make room for the boys who wanted to be in the game.

"We don't have any money," Eddie said.

"Use matches," Joe replied. "You're just learning the game."

The young men shouted at times over the singing of the grownups in the kitchen. Francie embroidered a flower for her new embroidery kit and tried to read *Little Women*. The grownups had each other; Stanley and Danny and Timmie played around the heater. The older boys had entered a man's world on whose fringes Eddie and Nick hung. She was alone. She fitted nowhere into the family structure, for she had outgrown her dependence on the younger boys and the older ones had begun to cast off the ties of home.

It was after nine when Eddie thought of it.

"Hey, you guys. It's a real quiet night. Why don't we hitch up a team and go once to midnight Mass?"

Midnight Mass was thirteen miles away at Green Valley. They had never gone to it before. The roads were impassable except by bobsleigh. It would be fun.

"We could stop at the Prosvigs and see if they want to go along. I'll bet you anything they'll go."

Their parents were pleased with their decision.

"Frynca, two feather ticks," her mother warned. "You will not get cold going dere, but da Mass take more dan an hour and when you come to go home, den you will gets cold. Dress warm. You don't have to be fancy to go to da church for da night mass."

They made preparations quickly. If Prosvigs came along, the evening would be perfect.

"Eef eet start to storm before you get home, stop somewhere for de night. Don' try to drive een de storm."

Francie sat under the ticks and looked up into a star-filled sky. There was not a breath of wind. Stars hung in great clusters, large and bright.

At first all of the boys rode on the sleigh. Then they began to pull each other off and tried to keep one another from getting back on the sleigh. Eddie walked and trotted the team by turn, teasing them.

At the front of the sleigh, Harry struck a match. The glow illuminated his face as he bent to drag on a cigarette, lighting one for Joe too. Francie was to remember the young, hopeful faces when the dark hours came later. They looked clean-cut, strong, alive. We might never again be all together like this, she thought. Maybe this is one of the last good times.

Rosy's face lit up when she saw Francie.

"Sure, old pal, I'll go along. Gee, it's a nice night for a sleigh ride. The Wilks left Claudette here. Let's ask her to come too."

Claudette had reservations about going that far on a winter night. But the presence of uniforms excited her; besides, how could she stay at the

Prosvigs' by herself? Along with Claudette, seven Prosvigs climbed aboard the sleigh.

The cool night freshened their faces. All at the same time the girls began to sing. An euphoria entered them as they inhaled the clean air and sang song after song. The boys in uniform crowded together at the front of the sleigh, smoking and talking, now and then choking over a quietly told joke. Behind the sleigh and clinging to its sides, the younger boys fought mock duels.

Just as Claudette began yodelling "Beautiful Girl on the Prairie", Jackie Prosvig dropped a chunk of hard snow in her upturned face. Spluttering, she scrambled out from under the tick, trying to get him back. But she couldn't tell who anybody was. There were so many of them, all in parkas, jumping about, yelling. She threw the snow awkwardly; it struck one of the horses. The team lurched forward; Claudette fell on top of the feather tick.

"Hey, girls, let's make a promise," Rosy suggested after they had resettled themselves. "Let's promise that no matter what happens or where we are, ten years from now we will get together and talk about this night."

At that moment, with the happiness of youth around them, they did not dream about possible shadows. It never dawned on them that they would grow old.

Scattered lights told them that they were approaching Green Valley. They quieted down.

"I hate Green Valley," Rosy said, in one of her rare sober moods. "The people here think they're too damned good for anybody else."

"I don't like Green Valley, but I like some of the farm girls around here," Francie said.

"It's a nice town, a real nice place," Claudette protested. "If you get to know the people, they're just as nice as they are anywhere else."

Francie and Rosy said no more. They knew what Claudette meant by "nice". It meant that you always dressed up and wore shoes all summer long. It meant having your hair curled and kept neat. Most of all, it meant that you talked to certain people because they were "ours". You could talk to other people too, but you did not get too friendly with them. You did the things that the old people liked, you spoke their language almost all of the time and you acted like one of them.

Claudette could do it. She wanted to be proper. Francie and Rosy couldn't stand it. The town inhibited them.

Brushing the snow off their clothes, they walked to the church. It's like a Christmas card, Francie thought as she looked at the violet and rose and blue colors falling on the snow through the windows. The people were singing "Silent Night" in Polish. For a moment they stood on the steps, listening.

I'm happy, she thought, I'm happy. It's Christmas, and Rosy is with me and a good feeling is in me. The three girls separated in the church and found niches for themselves in the jam-packed pews.

When the Mass began, it seemed to Francie that all the world was focused on the tiny doll-baby that lay in a small manger of hay in front of the altar. A statue of the Virgin brooded over the Baby; a donkey and a lamb looked into its face. The organ thundered overhead as the choir sang the Latin responses. In every row wizened, little faces gleamed, wrapped in dark babushkas. Old men leaned on the benches; army browns and air force blues were scattered throughout the congregation. Children of all sizes sprawled in sleep on the seats.

By the time Mass was over, sleepiness had overcome them. Ahead of them stretched the thirteen-mile trek homeward.

"Mother says that I have to quit school this year," Rosy confided as they snuggled under the ticks again. "I'm fifteen, and she says she needs me at home. I don't want to go to school anyway, but I don't want to just stay at home. I want the wild blue yonder."

A nagging regret clutched at Francie. What fun would there be going to school without Rosy? She and Rosy were like sisters. Deep inside, Francie knew that Rosy was a better person than herself. Rosy was so free of deceit, so loyal a friend.

"I'm not going to Westfield either next year," Claudette declared. "My mother wants me to take high school in the convent."

"We aren't going to see much of each other," Rosy mourned. "I wish we could all stay together in our own place."

"But we can write," Francie suggested. "All the crazy things."

"What are you gonna do, old pal?"

"I don't know yet. I can take eleven at Westfield, but after that if I want to go on, I'll have to board somewhere and go to a town school."

"Maybe your folks will send you to the same convent that I'll be in," said Claudette.

"Maybe." Francie wished a thousand times that it would be Rosy, not Claudette, who would be going on.

"Me, I'd sure like to get a job away from home," Rosy sighed. "Buy me some nice clothes and have a boy friend to take me places."

"I don't want a boy friend ever," Francie stated. "All I want to do is go to school. I like it. I couldn't stand having a boy friend. A boy is nothing special to me."

Eddie shouted at the horses as they floundered off the trail. The bobsleigh tilted but righted itself again. Big, feathery flakes began to drift out of the stars.

There is something about a snowfall at night, Francie thought. It makes the night holy.

"They need a waitress in Field's café," Rosy said. "Bet I could get a job slinging hash. Them travelling salesmen go through once or twice a month. Bet I could get good tips from those guys. And I'd be on my own."

"We'd better make time in case a wind starts up," Eddie said, giving the lines a hearty shake. They neared Prosvigs' farm.

"You girls try to come over during the holidays," Francie said. A morose look came over Rosy's face. Francie knew that Rosy would have twice as much cooking to do now. Her mother wouldn't let her go away even for one afternoon.

The horses came back to life after Claudette and Rosy left the sleigh. They trotted nimbly down the trail, yearning for the warmth of the barn and the manger of hay that waited for them.

Left to her own thoughts, Francie tried to anticipate the future. If the war continued, the boys would be called up, one by one. She would be in grade eleven next year. Then what?

Rosy could be happy on a farm, working for a bachelor. But Francie didn't ever want to settle down on a farm. It wasn't enough. And it was just a place of drudgery for a girl. She didn't know what she wanted. She would just have to wait for things to happen.

They drove under the bare crooked branches of the gnarled old maple on the edge of the shelterbelt. Francie wondered how the tree could stand there, living in one spot all of its life, watching and waiting, only to die at the end. She didn't want to be like that. She wanted to move around.

CHAPTER TWENTY-SEVEN

Miss Beaufort was leaving in June. Francie had become attached to her and felt sad when the teacher told the children that she would not be back in the fall. Not only would Miss Beaufort be gone, but Claudette and Rosy as well. Francie would be the only girl in the school with six boys, three of them her brothers.

"Would you please write something in my autograph book?" she asked the teacher after school was out for the day. Miss Beaufort allowed one of her rare smiles and accepted the battered little book. She wrote in a small, neat hand.

"What did she write?" Rosy and Claudette crowded close to read.

Be good, sweet maid, and let who will, be clever;
Do lovely things, not dream them all day long;
And so make Life, and the vast forever
One grand, sweet song.

"What does it mean?" Rosy puzzled over the writing. "I thought she'd write something funny. That's what autograph books are for."

It was a message. She had to make up her mind soon. Miss Beaufort had never spoken of Francie's future, but she knew.

Francie hated good-bys. On the last day of school, she walked blindly out of the door without looking at Miss Beaufort. I don't care, she thought. I don't care what she looked like. She was my best teacher.

If life was to be like this, a series of findings and losings, she wondered if it was so grand after all. When would she find another Miss Beaufort?

The long hot summer lay ahead. There would be days and weeks spent in the big garden; there would be the canning and preserving that came with the harvest. This fall Francie would have to drive a team. She hated the prospect.

The summer was endless. Harry was stationed along the British Columbia coast because of a feared Japanese invasion. Joe trained at Dafoe.

The harvest was early. And heavy. John Polanski mended the canvases and repaired broken harnesses. Every day would count this fall.

Although she was almost fifteen, Francie remained small for her age. Like Danny, she was frail. Both of them found that it took almost more than their strength to lift the five-gallon pails with chop or to carry the tall durum sheaves.

"Frynca and Stanley. You go and stook de oats today," their father said to them on a sunny August morning.

They did not mind stooking oats. Oat sheaves were small and compact. Besides, the bearded heads clung together once they were propped up.

"Gee. Look at how thick the sheaves are." Stanley looked at the field with dismay. The oats were still green in the low spots of the field, and there were many thistles tied into the sheaves.

They put on old boots to keep their ankles from getting scratched by the stubble. Francie lifted a sheaf, spiked it hard on the ground and held it there until Stanley did the same with another. Once the first four sheaves were in position, the others could be added quickly to the stook.

"Dat's no good!" roared their father, stopping the binder as he drove by. "You haf to stook in de rows, so dat ve can pick up de stooks vit de stook loader afterwards! You crazy, makin' de crooked rows!"

They re-stooked the few rows they had done. By then they were hungry and thirsty. The thistles burned into their hands.

Whenever their father clattered by with the binder, they re-doubled their efforts, slowing down when he was safely past. Francie squinted her eyes and looked at the sheaves that lay on the stubble. There were thousands, just thousands, of them. It would take forever to stook the whole field. And Dad owned a lot of fields.

During the noon meal their father voiced his unhappiness with their stooking.

"Too damn slow," he growled. What does he want, thought Francie. We can hardly lift some of those sheaves.

"Too damn slow. After dinner Frynca can drive de binder and I go stook."

Cold fear swept away her appetite. Drive the binder! She had never done it in her life. She wished that he had just left her stooking.

The horses stood switching their tails when her father told her to take the driver's seat.

"Hold on to de lines good," he warned her. "You haf to make sure dat de horses don' walk too far away from de grain and not too close in, because den dey will tramp it."

Francie squirmed, trying to find a comfortable spot on the hard iron seat that cut cruelly into her rear.

"Use de whip." Her father pointed to the long bamboo pole stuck in its receptacle. "You haf to hold de lines een one hand and de whip een de oder one when de horses get lazy."

Francie wondered how she could drive and ply the whip at the same time, but her father did not wait for her to ask.

"You haf to kick dat t'ing with your foot every time you drive past de row of sheaves. You can't let de sheaves fall all over de field. So watch out how close you drive to de grain and how fast de horses are going and where de sheaves fall."

Francie wished that she were at school, studying in a cool place, away from this horror of iron and sweat and horses and grain. Especially away from the wrath of her father.

"Geddy-up!" her father shouted to the horses.

They started off at once. Francie became distracted immediately. One of the horses in the middle stopped to eat a mouthful. She pulled the whip from its socket and struck the animal on the rump. It jerked forward, and she fought to hold her seat. As she jammed the whip back into its socket, she heard a roar from her father. What was she doing wrong? Driving right into the oats. Stupid horses. What made them do that anyway? She pulled hard on the right line, and the binder almost jackknifed away from the grain.

In the distance she heard her father shout again. She steered the horses back towards the oats. But she over-steered. Sweating profusely, she yelled "Geddy-up!" at the horses to make it look good. They had, by now, caught on to the fact that a novice was driving them. All of them were nibbling at the oat heads and dragging their feet. She grabbed the whip again.

Another bellow from her father. Horrified, she looked up to the side and saw that a large pile of sheaves had dumped themselves in the middle of nowhere. Oh, God, she thought, get me out of this mess; I can't do it.

The binder lurched over uneven ground, and she clutched the lines tighter to maintain a hold. Unwittingly, she pulled the horses into the oats again. She over-steered them out. Another pile of sheaves fell between the rows.

At last the team straightened out. But she was approaching a corner. Her dad had not said anything about corners. But he expected her to know, she knew that.

She heard a bellow behind her. Turning her head to see what the matter was, she saw her dad running behind the binder, yelling and pointing at the sheaves on the platform. Then she saw. There were no sheaves this time. There was only a vast pile of untied oats. The binder had run out of twine, and she hadn't watched.

She called out a loud "Whoa!" and braced herself.

"You get the hell off dere!" her father raged when he had found his

141

breath. "Can't you even drive a team of horses? So much education, an' you good for nothing on de farm. Get out, an' go stook!"

After riding the binder, stooking was heaven. Stanley had put up three stooks; all three had collapsed. They started the row afresh.

They had been exhausted by noon; by five o'clock they could barely move. But there was escape. One of them had to fetch the cows, another to gather the eggs. They rubbed cold cream on their scratched legs and gobbled fresh bread and butter.

Their dad would be mad at them. He wanted their stooking to keep up with the binders. They could never work that fast. He was beginning to see that he needed more help to get the harvest in.

"You are not going to school until de harvest ees over," growled her father at the supper table. "At least you can look after de cows an' water dem every day. You can start tomorrow. Bennie can drive de binder. You no good for dat."

She knew that she wasn't any good for driving the binder, but she wished he could see why. Nobody could learn to drive well the first time around the field. He expected them to know by watching. But watching wasn't the same as doing.

Francie held her peace. If she said something, it would only make him more angry, and he was already disappointed in her. That was the worst of all: he was disappointed in her.

Watering the cows was easy. There were about sixty head. In the morning she saddled the black horse and chased all the cattle to a well three miles south of the farm. There she climbed off the horse and pumped water into the big iron trough until the cattle could drink no more.

The first few days were hardest. The horse had to get used to her, and the dog too. The cows had to know that she was the boss, and with the first trip Francie learned the value of carrying a willow switch. The pumping made her arm and back muscles sore the first few days, but it was easy compared to stooking. After the horse took a good drink, she drove the cattle home again. They were very lazy coming home.

Once the cows were back in the pasture, she rounded up the horses that were not working and chased them to the same well. The home dugout was getting low and was saved for the working horses. Driving the horses to water was not the same as driving cows. Horses didn't wait for her when she had to open the gate. They began to run away as soon as she dismounted. She then climbed quickly onto her horse and tried to head them back toward the gate. But the black horse preferred to run behind the other horses rather than head them off. At times Francie cried from the frustration of it all.

The horses drank quickly and the speedier ones dashed off in different directions while some were still drinking. But the black horse felt like running by then, because she knew that it was time to head for home. France thrilled to the black horse bounding over the bleached prairie grass and kicked her heels at the horse's sides, with her blond pigtails streaming out behind her.

Watering the stock took up most of the day. After harvest was over, Bennie took the job over and Francie was free to go to school.

After the harvest Eddie spoke to his parents at the supper table.

"Dad, Mum, I'm going to enlist in the air force."

Francie saw fierce love and terror constrict her mother's face.

"You are not eighteen yet."

"Not yet, but I will be in December. If I wait till then, they'll call me into the army. I don't want to be in the army. I'm not as strong as Harry."

Their father began to chew his bread again.

"What you want to do in the air force?"

"Be a gun-armorer. I like guns. I'd be in the ground crew, Mum, so you wouldn't have to worry."

"I worry about all my childrens, no matter where dey is. Only you so young." Her voice broke.

"Well, it's better if I enlist now while I still have a choice. Once they put me in the army it's too late."

When Harry had gone, and Joe, it hadn't been so bad. They were tough and smart. Eddie was different. Always quiet and shy, how would he take it when they sent him miles away from home and even overseas?

Francie watched her mother pack socks and books in a brown paper box. She had sent each one of them away with clean socks and books, but the box looked awfully big with Eddie's things in it. Francie had never seen her mother cry so hard before. It wasn't loud crying; she didn't make a sound while the tears ran down her face.

Francie crept out of the house and sat under the big maple in the garden. A few chickens scratched in the dirt beside the fence. They could not get into the garden. But the whole world had invaded the Polanskis' lives, and no fence however high could keep it out.

When it was time for Eddie to go to the station, he grinned at her and yanked a pigtail.

"So long, idiot," he teased. "Keep up the letter writing." Then he swung himself up into the cab of the truck and was gone.

The new teacher was a girl in her teens. She had enormous brown eyes that looked frightened the first day. There were only seven of them. She instructed them in the morning ritual.

"Salute the flag." She tapped her pencil on her desk. She saluted, facing them, and they all saluted, facing the flag on the wall behind her. They kept their hands at their foreheads until she tapped a second time.

143

Then they found out. She sang off-key. It wasn't enough that she had them sing "God Save the King" every night and "O Canada" every morning, but because there was a war on, they had to sing extra songs, like "God Bless America". "Carry On" was her worst song.

"Not 'blast', Danny, 'bless'!" she corrected him as he sang lustily. She was pretty. And very young. And Polish.

"She is one of us," Mrs. Chorney said. "She will be a good teacher."

Miss Sobicki was all right with the younger kids, but she was unable to help Francie with chemistry since she had not taken it herself. Something about chemistry fascinated Francie. She made up her mind to take it, even though not a single chemical or test tube was available.

Francie wasted no time in getting started. She had missed over a month of school. But within a short time she ran into a snag. No one could help her. The work involved balancing chemical equations.

Day after day she went over all of the work leading up to the balancing of equations. She worried about it when she went to sleep at night and walked to school puzzling over it in the mornings. She was sure that there was some missing link that she had failed to grasp. The trouble lay in finding that link.

If countless other students could understand chemistry and its equations, she could too. The trouble was that she could not see in her mind what happened when equations were balanced.

The encyclopedias were too far outdated to be of any help. She read ahead in the course in the hope that a revelation would suddenly flood her mind.

She spent three weeks at it and felt thoroughly miserable about it. She could not go on until she understood how to balance equations.

Nothing can elude the mind forever, she reasoned. Sooner or later it will have to make sense. The answer is almost mine.

One day when she sat brooding over the impasse, she saw it. It came to her in a flash, and she saw that it was simple, so simple that she could hardly believe it. And all the time she had thought that balancing equations was immensely difficult and complicated.

She tested her new-found knowledge with several formulae. It worked. She surged ahead in chemistry, armed with new power.

There are always answers, she exalted. If I work hard enough and long enough, I can get any answer. People maybe give up too easily.

I can so do things. By myself. Maybe I'm no good on the farm, but I can do other work. I can do just about anything I want.

There was to be another day at school which burned itself into her memory. She was studying British poetry when she paused to look around at the few heads bent over school work. She was the oldest of them and the only girl. The rest of the students consisted of her brothers and young Millers.

And then she thought it. I am fifteen.

The moment she thought it she saw herself. Just as if she were a person apart, she looked at herself.

A thin, rangy girl with long bleached pigtails and bitten fingernails, wearing bib overalls and sitting in school with bare feet.

She glanced at her feet. They were not clean from the two-mile walk. A sudden shame swept over her. It was wrong, all wrong. Girls of fifteen did not go to school barefooted and carefree in patched overalls.

It had not occurred to her before that she was maybe different from most girls. She thought of all the girls she knew, and they filed through her mind like accusing ghosts. She was too old to dress like that any longer.

It was a long day. Francie did not accomplish much in her school work. When she walked home that evening, she looked about her and thought that everything looked different.

There leaned the grey-green willows that she had passed every day of her school life. They were so familiar that she passed them unseeing every morning and evening, yet it seemed to her now that she had lost something indefinable by not savoring their soft colors and ferny fragrance with every passing.

The old wooden bridge gleamed in the afternoon sun, its wood a silvery blue. She had heard the thunk-thunk of her steps over it for years. Yet as she looked at it now, she saw how clearly the graining in the wood showed in delicate veins of darker blue, how soft the splinters were.

A meadowlark caroled from a telephone pole. Birds grew up and flew and did all the right things, she thought. People are not like that. They have to learn and learn. "Go out in da garden an' get me some winter onions," her mother instructed when she reached home at last. "Why you take so long? Da boys is home long time already."

Francie didn't know which onions were the winter kind. She had heard her mother talking about them but had paid scant attention. Now she was caught.

In the garden she looked at both patches. There wasn't any difference really. She pulled an onion from each patch. They looked the same. She decided to waste no time. She would return to the house and simply ask her mother which patch she was to choose from.

She was not prepared for her mother's anger.

"You don't know where dem winter onions are, an' you pull da weeds around dem all year!" her mother began. "How can you be so old and get so much education and know not'ing?"

Francie was surprised at her mother's reaction. What difference did it make which onions she picked? They all looked the same anyway.

145

Her mother grabbed her by the shoulders and shook her.

Something unresisting about the girl angered her still further. She did not realize that Francie felt thoroughly ashamed. Supper would have to be ready soon; the onions were needed at once.

A pair of scissors lay on the table beside some material. Francie was too big to spank, but her mother felt that a shaking was not enough. She vented her anger in another, more terrible way; she seized the scissors and with them chewed off Francie's long braids close to her neck.

"Go get dem onions! Dey're by da trees!"

Francie ran out, tears blinding her eyes, her head feeling light and foolish. "By the trees," she moaned to herself, putting a hand to her hair. She felt two frizzled stumps where her braids had been.

She ran back to the house with the onions. Her mother was still angry.

"Go an' get dem cows. You walk so slow from school, maybe you should walk some more. Da boys is all busy. You no good for not'ing else."

The old dog responded slowly to Francie's broken voice. She trotted down the cow trail to the north pasture. What had made her mother so angry today? All that she had done was to walk home from school more slowly than usual. It was no sin not to be able to tell onions apart.

She could have told me in the first place, she mourned, feeling her mutilated hair. She could have said they were by the trees. She didn't have to cut my hair off.

She rounded up the placid cows, the tears running in a steady flow. What would the rest of the family say when they saw her? And what about at school tomorrow? What could she tell them if they asked? Her thick braids had been a part of her life ever since she could remember.

She loosened the shorn hair. It came to just below her ears. She knew that she looked ugly, uglier than ever, because when a girl's hair is cut straight from ear to ear she can't look nice. And Francie's hair was straight.

She took as long as she could, hooking the gate behind the cows when she got them home. She wouldn't go in and eat supper with the rest of them; she would milk first and then eat alone. It would be easier to face them one at a time.

Just as she was lifting a milk pail from a fence post, her mother called sharply from the window. "Come and eat first! Dem cows needs a rest before we milk dem!"

She had to go in. She headed for the washstand without looking at anyone. She had hardly entered when she heard Danny's "Huh?"

She kept her back to them, washing her face a long time and then her

146

hands because she could not stop crying. But at last she had to go to the table.

She looked at no one. They were all eating in silence. Danny passed the potatoes to her without a word; no one spoke. No one said a single word about her hair.

She forced a potato down, then a piece of bacon, although her throat hurt.

That evening she did not sing while she milked. She cried all the way through her four cows. Never again would she be able to grow hair that long and thick. She could not hate her mother; she wanted to understand how her mother could do a thing like that when she herself had meant no harm. She mourned for the hair of her childhood; she mourned more for the loss of trust in her mother.

At school the next day she kept her eyes down. No one said anything there either, but she knew that the Millers were looking at her. Francie put her head into her hands and tried to concentrate on her work. She wore her brown oxfords and an old cotton dress.

It was Miss Sobicki who started the tears again. Francie was the last one to go out of the door that afternoon, and the teacher smiled at her from behind her desk.

"Your hair looks nice short, Francie," she said. "It makes you look much more grown-up."

Francie rushed out and let the tears storm. If her mother had asked her if she wanted her hair cut, it would have been different.

Their parents had gone to Regina with cattle. Francie fried eggs for supper and heated potatoes. Danny looked at her small head critically as he drank his milk.

"Francie, where did your hair go?"

"I don't know. Mum threw it away."

He looked at her with wide, innocent eyes. It was no use to be mad at Danny.

"Pass the eggs, Danny," Nick ordered, and Danny forgot Francie's hair.

She did not look forward to her parents' return. Nothing in the world could bring back her hair.

The big truck rumbled into the yard after Francie had put the dishes away. The younger children waited eagerly for the parcels to be opened. Mrs. Polanski handed a slim box to Francie.

"Dat's for you."

Francie opened it obediently. A dress lay folded on white tissue paper. Why had her mother given her the box to open? The dress was an old woman's color, brown. Brown crepe.

Then she saw the size on the tag. Size twelve. Surely this dress couldn't be for her! She looked aghast at the large sweetheart neckline, the sprinkling of rhinestones.

She could hardly see. She knew why her mother had bought the dress, but it only made things worse. She hated brown. She hated the rhinestones. Most of all, she hated the big neck, through which her collar bones would stick out like bones on a thin chicken.

"It's expensif dress," her mother said. "You can wear dat to church and only things like dat. Dat's crepe. You can't wash dat when it get dirty."

Francie took the dress upstairs and hung it on a wire hanger. She lay on the bed and looked at its ugliness. On her thin frame the crepe would draw attention to her bony figure. Brown was only for grandmothers.

She hoped that they would never get to church. Winter would soon come on, and by spring she might just grow right out of that dress.

As she crept into bed she felt old. She thought of her youth, days when hair and dresses and acting grown-up hadn't cast shadows over her world.

"Dear God, help Rosy to make it. And me too. Let things work out some way. Help us to be persons."

It was no fun to grow up. Things hurt more when a person grew older.

CHAPTER TWENTY-EIGHT

That winter they listened to every newscast. No one dared to whisper when Dad had the radio on. Talk of conscription circulated in the district. Johnny Szoda had tried to enlist but was turned down. He became sulky and bad-tempered, for he had dreamed of the day when he could wear a uniform and have the girls running after him.

With spring the war grew worse. The Allies needed more help from the Canadian forces.

Harry came home on leave in March. He told them that he was going overseas that month.

There was a party held for him. It started out quietly. Everyone became drunk, and all of them ended up crying — Harry too. Francie did not take part. She did not care for the drinking or wild dancing. Harry went overseas on the *Aquitania*.

"We haf to write to Harry on dose air-mail letters," Mrs. Polanski said. "An' don' ask him when you write where he is, because the censors cut dat out."

Eddie came home on Good Friday with sobering news. He could spend Easter Sunday with them, but he was leaving for overseas on Easter Monday.

"So quick she goes. First Harry in March and now Eddie in April. *Boza, Boza*, what dis world coming to?" Mrs. Polanski prayed.

Eddie left with gentle good-bys that hurt. He had scarcely gone over on the *Empress of Scotland* when Joe came home on his last leave in May. Within three months the three boys were thousands of miles from home.

Then the letter writing began. It was Francie's job to write three letters per week without fail. The boys answered twice a month. Except Eddie. He became homesick very soon and wrote long weekly letters. His handwriting was beautiful.

"Emil Prosvig is stationed here too," he wrote. "It really makes a difference when you have a buddy."

Outlaw Turner and Joe had turned up in the same outfit. Joe sent home a snapshot of them together, leaning against a plane, their arms around each other's necks, grinning like the two fiends that they had always been.

Mr. Morgan, the storekeeper, borrowed the three photos the Polanski boys had taken of themselves before they went overseas. He displayed them in his store window on Remembrance Day, along with photos of all the other local boys who were in the services. The Polanskis were the only family with three boys in the war.

Francie took the cream to town one Saturday afternoon. Prince ambled toward the station where the agent unloaded the two cans.

"Getting a bit cool, eh?" he nodded to Francie, as she stood by.

She paused to look at the photos of the boys in Morgan's window. None of the other boys looked as nice as her brothers, she thought.

Two boys were lounging at the counter. When she approached Mr. Morgan they moved away, watching her. They flustered her a little. She was glad that she was almost completely hidden in her parka, because she felt shy of their eyes.

Mr. Morgan was more stooped, more wrinkled. He peered hard at things on the shelves and at the money in his hand. There was more money to buy groceries with now. Crops were better; cream sold for higher prices.

That fall Mr. Polanski had finally given in and bought a combine. The crop had been harvested much earlier than usual.

The three boys overseas had a mother's allowance sent home. Eddie sent home twice as much as the other two. He was the most careful with his money.

"I not spend dat," Mrs. Polanski told Mrs. Chorney, who teased about the great riches the Polanski family was now receiving. "I buy bonds wit da money. I saf it for da boys when dey get out."

"You haf to t'ink," Mrs. Polanski said to Francie one day. "You haf to make up your mind what you gonna do wit yourself. You want to quit school an' help me at home or you want to take da grade twelve an' den be somet'ing?"

Francie looked about the farm kitchen. Never would she stay here; never did she want to be a farmer's drudge. She could stay at home and help because there were still six boys to raise. On the other hand, she had a good education already; should she not do something with it?

The Chorneys visited one Sunday afternoon. Mrs. Chorney came into the house, her plump cheeks afire with health from the stinging north wind. She peeled off her coat and laughed at Francie.

"*Nooh*, Frynca, what you going to be when you leave school?"

Francie hated answering her. She made such awful mistakes with Ukrainian.

"Ya nezniyou," she replied, her eyes downcast.

"Ni teacher?" queried her bright-eyed tormentor. "Or you gonna help Mama like a good girl?"

Mrs. Polanski heard the last statement.

"I not stand in her way," she said proudly. "She has a good head for school. If she wants to go on den, we send her. What you can do wit a girl?"

"Oh, da girl can stay home an' cook an' get marry," Mrs. Chorney answered. "What do the book help you? Hey?" she prodded Francie.

"I'm not going to get married," Francie burst out.

"Oh, *yoi!*" Mrs. Chorney laughed. "You wait another year, maybe two. You find some nice Ukrainian boy and you will ask da Mama can you get married. I know, I know," and she enjoyed her own wit.

"We not getting da letter from da Eddie. Not for two weeks now, we not getting." Mrs. Polanski worried. "He write every week before dat."

"Oh, he write, he write, but maybe he is having too good a time with da girls over dere."

It was the wrong thing to say about Eddie. But Mrs. Chorney had no children. She didn't understand.

"I am afraid somet'ing is not good," Mrs. Polanski continued, as if Mrs. Chorney had not spoken. "It not like Eddie. He never miss a week. Ludwiga say dat Frank not writing either. Maybe somet'ing happen to dem both together. *Boza, Boza.*"

They never knew exactly where the boys were, but they knew that Eddie was somewhere on the continent. Joe had written home that he had been asked to train for an air gunner instead of staying in the ground crew.

"You write heem dat he stay on de ground," John Polanski instructed Francie with a harsh voice. "He go up in de plane, he die. Dey kill so many dem air gunners, now dey promise de young keeds more money and say, be air gunner. Dey talk like dat to de foolish keeds an' de keeds t'ink dey beeg, dey air gunners. You write heem not to change hees job. Or he's a dead man. Tell heem I say so."

Christmas Eve was very quiet. Dad sang the old songs with Mr. Chorney and Mr. Wilk. Francie could see the tears glisten on their cheeks.

Men didn't wipe away tears like women did. They were not ashamed to be seen crying. Mr. Chorney had no sons, but he cried too. Maybe it was for the sons he would never have; maybe it was for the sons of his neighbors. Eddie had been his favorite.

On Christmas Day Francie saddled the black horse and rode to Prosvigs to visit with Rosy.

Everyone was talking and yelling at once in the house. With no father to keep order, everyone did as he pleased. Francie found Rosy unhappy, even though it was Christmas.

"I wanna leave home," she confided to Francie upstairs in her bedroom. "Mother just wants me to stay home all the time and work. Never go out, even on Saturday night. Once I get out of here I'll never come back."

"But you can't just go and leave like that," Francie said, watching Rosy outline her mouth with a bright cupid's bow.

"I could so," Rosy answered with defiance. "I'm sick of staying here and cooking and washing for dem damned boys. I'm sixteen and want to have some fun.

"Look at them. They got their trucks and their liquor and their guns. There's so many boys around here. They can get together any place and have fun."

Sporadic laughter drifted up from the floor below.

"And me?" Rosy continued in a bitter tone. "Eight o'clock, and they're all yellin' for me to start the fire to cook breakfast. And I don't even get the dishes finished when they're yellin' about dinner. Then I get maybe an hour and they start yellin' about supper. I'm not gonna stay here the rest of my life."

"But, Rosy, where will you go?"

"First guy that asks me, I'm gettin' out."

"Rosy, what if he's an old man?"

"I don't care." The cupid's bow drooped at the corners. "I ain't stayin' in this badger hole forever."

Francie turned the black horse homeward, feeling sorry for Rosy. Her friend was in a real fix. She had quit school, and now she would have to work at home until she happened to meet a man and got married. Or she could leave home and get a job as a waitress or a hotel worker. Or even as a cook for a bachelor. The older women whispered about such jobs. Only bad girls took that kind of work.

"Any letters from da boys?" Mrs. Polanski asked when Nick came home from town.

"Yup. Two." They scanned the handwriting on the thin airmail envelopes. The letters were from Harry and Joe.

Four weeks and Eddie had not written. Francie hunted up his last letter, the one that he had written on his birthday.

"Are you still having pillow fights in the dark?" the letter read. "And do you still play war, or are you too old for that? Gosh, I never thought I'd ever be in a real war when I used to play that game."

That week Mrs. Prosvig received word that Emil had been killed in action.

"*Oi, Boza, Boza,*" Mrs. Polanski wept when she heard the news. "First she lose her husband, den her oldest son. And he was so good wit dem kids."

The unspoken question hung unanswered over the household. Buddies chummed together. Emil and Eddie had been close ever since their earliest school days. They were almost afraid to go to town, to look in their mailbox.

Why Eddie, Francie asked herself as she scrubbed the kitchen floor. Why not Joe or Harry, both strong and tough? Why the one who was kindest of all? She knew that she was not thinking in the right way about her oldest brothers. But why did it have to be Eddie? And Emil?

The following day the younger Wilk rode to the Polanskis on horseback. After he had warmed his hands by the stove he asked for news about Eddie. He shook his big head sadly when he learned that nothing but silence had come through.

"Gun-armorers don't work in such dangerous places," he said. "But you don't have to go to the front to get hurt. The Germans are sending over those buzz bombs."

He flushed scarlet when he saw the start his words gave to Mrs. Polanski.

"Maybe you could come and visit my folks tonight," he said. "We got a telegram this morning about Frank." He swallowed hard. "They say he is missing and presumed dead."

"Dead!" John Polanski's face turned grey.

"There's always a chance that he will still turn up," the boy continued. "But it's hard on Mother and Dad. They will sure need somebody in the evening. That's why I can't stay long."

After he had gone, Mrs. Polanski sat heavily in her chair beside the stove, wiping her eyes.

"Such a nice boy, dat Wilk boy. He like my own son. And such a good farmer. *Oi, Boza.*"

The letter came the next day. The writing on the envelope looked spidery. Francie trembled as her mother tore the envelope open.

She looked, then gasped. "I t'ink it from him. I can't read dat. Here." She thrust the paper at Francie, her face working.

Francie snatched the thin blue paper. It's not a telegram, she kept thinking. It's not a telegram. Eddie must be all right.

She blinked hard to clear the mist from her eyes. The writing slanted crazily across the page, the words hardly readable. But Eddie's name was scrawled at the bottom.

"Dear everybody," she read, puzzling over the elongated letters. "I can't write much yet. We were bombed and I ended up in the hospital with a broken collarbone. I was working on planes when a buzz bomb exploded. Emil was standing in the doorway. There was nothing left of him." Francie found it hard to go on. "Wish the damn war was over so we could all go home. I can't stop crying."

Danny looked at the handwriting.

"Why didn't he write in straight lines?"

"Because he was hurt, what you t'ink," retorted Mrs. Polanski. "He haf to get somebody else to address it too."

Francie thought of Rosy. Would she change her mind now about leaving home? Emil had been good to Rosy. Maybe now she would go sooner.

They studied Eddie's letter under the lamplight. He had been such a neat writer. They could see where he had forgotten to cross his t's and where his hand had shaken when he had tried to loop the l's. But the letter was from Eddie — he was alive and safe.

CHAPTER TWENTY-NINE

The war was over. At first they could not believe it. They went wild with happiness.

Then the fears and doubting began. What if the ships carrying the boys home were sunk by some mistake? What if a storm came up and swamped the big ships filled with thousands of men? Not until the boys swung off the train at Field would they believe that the long nightmare was truly over.

In late January a long list of returnees coming to Canada aboard the *Aquitania* was read over the radio. They were sitting around the radio, embroidering and reading, when all of a sudden they heard the announcer speak Joe's name.

"Joe! Joe's coming home!" the younger ones shouted.

"Leesten!" their father commanded. "What else dey say?"

The ship was due in Halifax on February the second.

In February heavy storms raged off the Canadian coast. They listened to every report on the radio. The *Aquitania* had run into heavy seas; she did not reach port on the second or the third. She finally docked on the fifth.

They were jubilant. In a week or so Joe would be home. Really home.

He came to Field and was fetched home by sleigh. He came into the house looking taller, thinner and much older. His mother embraced him briefly.

Francie looked hard at Joe. He wasn't like the old Joe at all. He hardly ever smiled. He talked quietly about the war, his cigarette burning away between his fingers, not noticing. His mind was still overseas.

And so a quiet stranger entered the house. He donned old work clothes and gave a hand at the chores, but he was far away in thought.

"Joe yelled last night," Danny rubbed his eyes when he came to the breakfast table. "Real loud. He woke us all up."

"What did he yell about?"

"He kept sayin' 'Kill 'em, kill 'em!' and then he just yelled like he was fightin'."

Joe slept till noon that day. He looked hollow-eyed at the dinner table. No one asked him any questions.

When Eddie came home in April, the whole family climbed on board the truck and drove to Field in a body to welcome him off the train.

Again they met a stranger. Eddie's face carried the marks of suffering. He was very quiet on the trip to the farm. Once he was home he passed around a few souvenirs — a wooden shoe, foreign coins, a necklace for Francie. But he didn't talk about the war.

"Boy, it's good to be home."

"Yeah. Doesn't the place look a lot smaller?" Joe grinned his old grin. "Before I left I thought we lived in a pretty big house. Now I don't see how we all ever fit into this place."

Eddie took his turn with the chores. He hunted rabbits a lot. He would go walking with the dog and his gun and be gone, sometimes for all day. When he came home at night, his face looked clean and ruddy.

In the evenings Joe talked about his war experiences. He described the air fights especially. He talked about the night bombings, the air raid shelters, the people overseas. Eddie said very little. He listened but didn't say much. He seemed very glad to be home.

"Een de spring," their dad told them, "you can each have a quarter section of land to start farming."

Harry returned to Canada in June, just at the time when Francie was writing her grade eleven exams. She passed all of her subjects, her highest mark being in chemistry.

"How you can get such a good mark when you don't even have da kemikals in school?" her mother wondered.

"It's easy," Francie shrugged. "If I go for a nurse, I'll need chemistry."

When Harry came home in July, the old house bulged at the seams. The boys put up beds in an empty granary and sat up telling war stories half the night. Once in a while Joe woke them all with his nightmares. He would be shaky the next day, but no one said anything about it.

Francie had a room to herself at last. She would lie in solitary splendor across her bed, looking at the stars sprinkled across the summer sky, listening to Eddie plunking on the banjo. Just before she fell asleep, she heard the tinklings of the sheep bells and the ragged howls of the coyotes who encircled the shelterbelt.

"I'm getting married before harvest," Harry told his parents. "We'll live with June's folks until we build a house of our own."

Joe gave his girl an engagement ring, the date being set in November.

At mealtimes they had to eat in shifts. The older boys took up so much room now. There was no place to put away the shoes, the clothes, the souvenirs. It was hard to keep things neat. Francie longed for new books, for regular hours of study, for girls to talk to.

"I'm going to be on my own. A bachelor," Eddie announced. "I'm not going to bother anyone else. I want some peace and quiet."

He knocked together a shack on his quarter of land and moved his possessions into it.

"You should find yourself a nice girl and get marry," worried his mother. "Den you haf a cook and a housekeeper too. It better dat way."

"Nope. Don't want any old lady buggin' me. I've had enough of people for a while. I'm staying a bachelor so I can come and go as I please."

One Sunday afternoon Mrs. Polanski and Nick drove the thirty miles to the convent where Francie would board while taking her grade twelve.

Francie looked eagerly at the skyline of the small town. A giant steeple dominated the elevators and trees.

"Dere be lots of girls here from da farms taking dere education like you. But it cost lots of money, you must know. Mrs. Wilk tell me dey charge twenty dollars a month for da room and board."

It was a lot of money to spend on a girl's education. But if a girl wasn't much good on a farm, there wasn't anything else that could be done. Just let me have a chance, Francie said to herself. I'll learn and learn, and the money won't ever be wasted.

The Mother Superior was all smiles. She readily accepted Francie as a student.

"We don't allow the girls off the grounds," she told Francie's mother. "We have regular hours for school, for study and for recreation. I'm sure that Frances will do well here."

Francie sat between her mother and Nick on the way home, her hopes high. Mrs. Polanski sighed.

"Dat's going to be so expensif. Twenty dollars a month; dat's lots of money. *Oi, Boza.* Somehow we haf to pay it. You haf to do good in dat school or Daddy will be so mad if you waste da money."

Francie counted the days until the start of the school term. The two weddings coming up did not excite her very much. Like her, the boys were leaving home, but not forever. It was time.

On the Sunday evening before school was to begin, Francie put her few possessions into a small cardboard suitcase. She had to have pajamas, a toothbrush, a hairbrush, underwear, a lot of things. Danny stood by on one bare foot, watching her pack.

"When are you coming home again?"

"I can come home only once a month. The rest of the time I have to study."

"You're not going to live here anymore?"

Francie looked into his dark blue eyes. Danny would always remain her favorite, along with Eddie. Eddie and Danny. She felt sorry for Danny now.

"I'll write all about it. It isn't so far. And you have to go back to school too, so it won't seem too long before I come home to visit."

After she entered the clean-smelling convent and the truck drove away, she felt small and altogether alone. She was only thirty miles from home, but as she followed the sister to her curtained alcove, she thought that she might as well have gone overseas.

"This will be your bed," smiled the young sister. "You are lucky. You have a window. You will be responsible for keeping it open or closed depending on what the rest of the girls want."

Francie looked at the double rows of beds, one along each wall of the dormitory. A washstand, a chair and a plain white pitcher adorned each cubicle.

"At night, when you are preparing the bed or ready for sleep, your curtain must be drawn separating you from your neighbor. Lights go out at 9:30. Everyone rises at 6:30 for Mass, which is followed by breakfast. Then you must come back here and make your bed. There will never be time to waste."

It sounds like the army, Francie thought. But she didn't mind. She wished it were tomorrow already and that she had her new books.

Girls began coming into the dormitory with suitcases and arms full of parcels. Most of them brought so much. Francie hid her homemade pajamas under her pillow and put her toothbrush into her glass. She hung the hated brown crepe dress along with a skirt and a blouse in a small closet beside the door.

Many of the girls knew each other. They called back and forth, unpacking mounds of clothing. Francie took as long as she could to put her writing paper and envelopes into her drawer. Nick and Mum would be home by now. She thought about the dark silhouette of the shelterbelt against the night skies.

A familiar face with a wide smile came toward her.

"Francie! How nice! They gave me a bed next to yours!"

It was Claudette. Here was a link with home.

They chattered away happily while Claudette put her things away. She could not get all of her dresses into her locker.

"No one is ever allowed to wear slacks here," she said. "I made sure that I brought enough clothes. You can wash them only on weekends, you know."

Francie did not know. She was glad that she knew someone who could tell her how things were done in the convent.

She would need more than two outfits. But how would she be able to tell her mother that? Twenty dollars a month for room and board was enough to spend on a girl from a big family.

"Lights go out soon," Claudette warned. She paid no attention to the arrivals around them. Francie watched them covertly. "Let's do our hair. You can't do it after dark."

They went to the bathroom to fill glasses of water. Claudette inspected a pimple on her chin with great care.

"Gee, I wish the water wasn't so hard here," she sighed. "My hair will look like something awful before long. And my skin! I'm going to go home every weekend to wash my hair in rain water and do my clothes."

"But they won't let you go. They told me that I could go home only once a month."

"Oh, once they get to know you, they'll let you go," Claudette smiled. "If you're a good little girl and obey the rules."

They sat on their beds and dipped combs into the water. Francie's hair was shoulder-length. She twisted a curler around a hank of hair and fastened it.

"You're done already?" Claudette frowned. "It takes me a long time to do my hair right."

A tall, dark, curly-haired girl came into the dormitory. She talked loudly and constantly.

"Hi, everyone. I'm Jennie Jones. From Regina. Back again for my third year. My folks can't handle me at home so they send me here." She jerked back the curtain that separated her cell from her neighbor's.

"Keep away from her," Claudette whispered. "She's really tough. She's a Protestant too."

Francie regarded the tall girl with interest. Would a Protestant have to get up at 6:30 in the morning and go to Mass too? She looked like an easy-going girl. Somehow she didn't look bad. Or tough like Outlaw Turner had been. Francie's heart contracted. Outlaw had been killed the day that the war ended.

They discussed their families as they prepared for sleep.

"Frank is dead. We're sure of that now," Claudette said as they waited in the line-up at the bathroom door. "They finally sent word that since there was no trace of him, he was officially dead. I think that someday he'll show up."

"Maybe he got amnesia," Francie whispered back. They were not supposed to talk when they got ready for bed.

"How come we have two sheets?" Francie whispered to Claudette as she pulled back the covers.

"One you sleep on. The other you sleep under, so that you don't get the blanket dirty. You have to make your bed right too, or they'll make you strip it and do it over again in the morning."

They lay separated in their cells, divided by the thin white curtains. A nun walked down each row of beds, checking to see if all was in order.

"Good night, girls," she called, and they answered sleepily. She turned out the light. Francie could see the window outlined against the autumn sky. She heard the nun's feet walk up and down, up and down between the rows of beds. A faint clicking of her wooden rosary could be heard. All of the nuns wore rubber-soled shoes so they walked quietly.

Francie wondered what the school would be like. Home was far away. Home would be full of the sound of the hissing gas lamp and faces crowding around the table. Danny would be reading some old comic, stretched out on the floor behind the stove. Mum would be making the yeast for baking bread in the morning.

She wondered if they would miss her. She thought of all the work her mother would have to do, and a pang of guilt went through her. Then she said to herself, the younger boys can help a lot. And then a small mouse thought nibbled at the corner of her mind: soon they will not even miss me at home.

Francie was the first one from the district to take grade twelve. Claudette was in eleven. They would be the first two to finish high school. The future was as black as the soft night air that wandered in through the black rectangle of the window.

CHAPTER THIRTY

Francie enjoyed life at the convent. She had been the only student in her grade for so long that hearing a teacher address a class of mixed sexes was a novelty. She wrote copious notes and memorized them each night during the study hour after supper.

She made friends quickly. The convent girls came from all parts of Saskatchewan where there was no easy access to high schools. She learned to take their joshing. She began to eat. There was never enough food on the table for her. When she went home for her first visit, her family reacted.

"You grow two inches," her father said. "Dey must feed you good dere."

"Not so good," Francie answered. "I'm always hungry."

"Ask for more den. We paying good money for you," her mother said.

"It's no use asking. They cook only so much."

"Da English peoples is always like dat," Mrs. Polanski stated. "Dey cook just enough for one meal. Dey so stingy wit da food. Dat's why dere is none of dem fat."

But if the family was surprised by the change in Francie, it was nothing compared to how she was appalled by them. Never before had she spent a month away from home. She couldn't believe that the wall around the washstand could be so splashed; that the towels were changed so seldom; that the wash basin always contained curdy grey water. It was like coming back to a different house.

She scrubbed the washstand and the wall behind it. She hung out clean towels until her mother protested. She scrubbed the splintery board floor. She made all the beds every morning.

Her mother took a stand. "Why for you do all dat? We is not dirty peoples. We was da same before when you was at home. Maybe dat convent makin' you too good for here."

Francie looked at her mother kneading the dough in the speckled blue pan. How many pans of dough would she knead in that chipped old container until the last child had gone? Her mother would be able to measure her life by the pans of dough she kneaded and baked for their sustenance.

"It's the boys," she said to her mother. "They don't wash their hands clean when it's time to eat. They just wet them a little and then put all of the grease on the towel. Some of them don't even wash at all. Not even their faces in the morning."

A white rage rose in her mother.

"You t'ink dat all a farmer got to do is wash his hands? Dat farmer dat keeps his hands clean is not a good farmer. A good farmer has to be dirty!"

Francie began to dish out the potatoes as the boys began to file in.

"Not dat bowl! Use da blue one. I always put da potatoes in dat."

Francie dumped the potatoes from the white bowl into the blue one. Now there will be another dish to wash, she thought. What difference did it make which bowl she used anyway? They got eaten just the same.

After the dishes were done, Francie approached her mother.

"Mum, I should have a brassiere." Her face turned pink.

"What for you need da brazeer? I don' wear none. You just hinting you want what da oder girls is wearing. You don't need no clothes. You have enough to wear. Here we working so hard on da farm and you just t'inking what you want to wear."

Francie wished that she had not mentioned it. Couldn't her mother see that she wasn't being vain, that she really needed the undergarment? She had begun to fill out quickly, and it embarrassed her to put on one of her few tops, a blue sweater.

When she returned to the convent on Sunday evening, she felt miserable. She liked the work at school; she wanted to like home as well. But only a miracle would get her mother to see things in a new way.

Strangely enough, it was Mrs. Chorney who helped Francie with her personal problem. On her next visit home, the Chorneys visited. Francie was glad to see them. They were as comfortable as old furniture.

Mrs. Chorney began her usual teasing.

"*Yak tum schola?*"

"School *dobra*," Francie answered. All her life she had been saying *dobra* to Mrs. Chorney, not only because it was easy to say but because saying "good" was an appropriate answer for many questions. It was the best Ukrainian word to know. It always made people happy.

Mrs. Chorney watched Francie wiping off the kitchen table.

"*Frynca fina jewchina,*" she praised.

Mrs. Polanski thought that it was not good to have her children told that they were handsome.

162

"*Toh chas.*" She meant, so what, it's about time. Francie's pleasure weakened under the off-hand comment.

But Mrs. Chorney continued to praise the girl.

"*Toh jewchina. Malinka, ali jewchina!*"

Mrs. Polanski turned to look at Francie. She suddenly saw how much the girl had filled out, grown, changed. Her face grew pensive.

Mrs. Chorney thought that school for girls was a waste of time. She pointed out that Francie would be better off learning how to cook and keep house, because she would be getting married anyway.

"No, no." Francie shook her head emphatically. "No marry, me."

Mrs. Chorney laughed. "Why sure you marry. Wait, wait, you change your mind. When you meet de nice Ukrainian farm boy, you t'row away all dose silly books. Wait and you'll see!"

Never, Francie seethed with indignation. I'd sooner be an old maid or a nun.

"You spend lots of da money to send a girl to school like dat," observed Mrs. Chorney. "And you get not'ing back for dat money."

Mrs. Polanski showed her stubborn side. "We send her as long as she do good. If she no good in da school den we not sending her."

"But you need da girl at home. You should be helping da moder," Mrs. Chorney said to Francie.

"Ya, it is lots of hard work," sighed Mrs. Polanski. "But God He helping me, and da kids is growing up. She is interesting in dat school only. I don't want to see my daughter have such a hard life as I have."

When Francie came home on her next visit, there was a parcel for her from Eaton's. In it she found a stiff, new brassiere.

It was a little large, but it would shrink. At least she could wear the sweater now without feeling so sloppy. Her mother did not speak about it.

Rosy wrote to Francie often. She was very unhappy at home.

"Francie, old pal, I'm just about dying. I hate it so much," she wrote. "A guy from Green Valley came around last Saturday night and asked me to go to a show with him. I said go to hell. I never liked them Green Valley guys, they're after only one thing. But Mother's mad at me now. She wanted me to go with him because his dad's a big farmer.

"Emil was the only one who was ever good to me. And you, Francie, you're my best and only friend. Don't ever give up on me, eh? I can't stand it much more; I'm just about eighteen and then I'll be free. I want to live my own life."

Claudette and Francie spent much of their free time together. The fact that Francie was taking her grade twelve and Claudette her eleven presented problems. They moved in different crowds.

One afternoon when school was let out, Linda, Francie's closest friend in her grade, pelted Francie with snowballs. Claudette walked sedately behind. She didn't want to get her hair wet. She disapproved of the other girls rolling in the snow. The air was warm and fresh; it was perfect snowball weather.

"Really, Francie." Claudette brushed snow off her sleeve and frowned. Something about Claudette chafed Francie. She was so old already.

That evening after the lights were turned out in the dorm, Francie heard Claudette banging about in her basin.

"What are you doing?" Francie whispered, pulling aside the curtain that separated their beds. No one was supposed to be out of bed once the lights were turned out.

"Brushing my teeth," Claudette replied. "I forgot."

As she lay in bed thinking about how fussy Claudette was, so particular that she wasn't much fun half the time, she heard her friend begin to gag and retch.

She made a lot of noise. All the girls in the dorm heard it.

"What the heck's the matter now?" Francie whispered, sitting up.

Claudette choked. "I-I thought that I had the toothpaste," she gagged. "But it was the Brylcreem."

The girls nearby burst into giggles. A nun came running into the dorm with her flashlight. Claudette dived back into the bed, her mouth full of greasy hair preparation. All of the other girls lay quietly, their sheets pulled up over their shoulders.

The nun was suspicious. She walked back and forth between the beds for a while, saying her beads. Claudette had to wait for half an hour.

Francie smothered her giggles in her pillow. It was so funny; it was good for Claudette because she was so particular about things.

Francie began to visit the chapel during her free time. She relaxed in the soft atmosphere, the sounds of the busy building muted in the distance. The vigil lights flickered softly in their colored glass jars; the white candles on the altar breathed a serenity into the room. She began to wrestle with the problem of her vocation in earnest.

No answers came. Questions ran around and around in her mind. Should she go in for a nun? She thought not. She was not good enough. If she did become a nun, what would her parents think about it after spending all that money on her grade twelve?

She was sure that she would never marry. There were better things to do than housework and cooking.

Most of the grade twelve girls said that they were going for teacher training because there was such a shortage of teachers. Perhaps she could become one too.

The nursing profession attracted her. As a nurse she could do much good. Every act she would undertake would be of help to someone. But it

164

took three years of training. Francie knew that her parents could not spend that much money on her.

"Give me a sign," she begged the invisible Presence in the tabernacle. Sometimes Linda knelt in the chapel too, lost in a reverie, unconscious of Francie's presence. Linda spent hours in the chapel on her knees.

"A letter for you, Frances," Sister Vera announced one day. The postmark was that of a small hamlet.

"Dear old pal," the letter began. "I hope all is fine with you. I just had to write you that I'm not at home any more. I left. I seen this ad in the paper and this old man wanted a housekeeper. So I told Mother I was going to answer. She screamed about it for two days. The man came and got me so I went. He's real nice to me, about fifty or so, and I don't have to work hard. Just wash his clothes and cook. That ain't bad after what I had to do at home. And he's paying me $60 a month.

"Write me a letter, eh, when you have the time. You're my only true friend. There's no young people around here.

"I hope you're not mad at me for taking this job. I want to be your friend. You know how it is at home."

Rosy would never have a home to come back to now; her mother would never forgive her. She would have to keep working for different people until she met someone nice and got married.

When Francie went home that weekend she found that Rosy's leaving home was the talk of the neighborhood.

"She will get into da trouble yet," Mrs. Polanski prophesied darkly. "Dem girls dat leave dere homes like dat, especially a moder that is widowéd, get into da trouble. She will be sorry. No nice boy will want to marry her now."

There was also talk of the oncoming marriage of Miss Sobicki.

"She ever make a good farmer's wife," Mrs. Polanski marvelled. "She can cook and sew nice. And she likes to drive da tractor and work on da field. Dat boy who get her be sure lucky man."

Both Harry and Joe had married. They lived on farms nearby. Eddie had gone batching as he had said he would. Girls were of no interest to him. With his gun he hunted for rabbits, wild ducks and prairie chickens which he cooked for himself. He rarely visited.

Claudette tightened her hold on Francie.

"You shouldn't mix around with all those other girls so much," she said one night as they washed up. "We have enough of our own. There's you and me and Jeanette Tworowske and Angie Kerowatsky. We don't need the other girls. A lot of the English girls are Protestant, you know."

Francie scrubbed the back of her neck hard.

"I can't help talking to them," she protested. "They're in my grade. Sometimes they help me with my work."

"Oh, I don't mean that. But after school you go back to the convent with a different girl every day. You never wait for me. And at recess you talk to everybody."

Claudette is too precious, Francie thought. How can I tell her? I want to be friends with everyone. It's no fun being with her all of the time. She wants me to think like her.

The problem solved itself. Claudette had permission to go home every weekend. She returned to the convent on Monday mornings, late for the first class.

One Monday morning she did not walk into the class, late as usual. Francie decided that Claudette wasn't well. Perhaps she had stayed at home. Francie felt free and happy. When she sat down to eat in the refectory, the table was buzzing.

"Hey, Francie, did you hear that Claudette went back home again?"

"You mean she was here this morning and then left?"

"Right. Her brother came for her in a truck, and she went back home after she came on the train. She was here for only an hour."

"Maybe she forgot her toothbrush," one of the girls suggested.

"Maybe she's sick again," Francie offered. "She gets sick often when she rides on trains."

"She didn't look sick to me," a junior piped up. "I saw her sitting on her bed in the dorm, and she looked mad, not sick."

When school was over that afternoon, Sister Vera stopped Francie in the hall.

"Sister Mary wants to see you right away in her office," she said.

Sister Mary! No one liked her. She dealt with the girls who were wild or who wrecked things. Francie could not think of anything she could have done, but she obeyed the summons.

Sister Mary was tall and thin. She gave Francie a sweet smile in the consultation room.

"How well you look, Francie. And I'm so pleased to hear that you are doing so well in your studies." Her smiled stayed pasted on.

Maybe they searched my washstand, Francie thought. Maybe they found those chocolate bars.

"And you're such a good friend of Claudette's, aren't you?"

Francie nodded.

"Dear, dear Claudette. She comes from such a nice family, you know. She's so clean, so neat, so painstaking."

Francie saw that the nun was eyeing her shoulder-length hair. She winced inside. Claudette had short, very curly hair. Maybe the sister wanted Francie to get a haircut and look neater.

"Such a nice family. So clean and neat," the sister went on. Then she smiled a bigger smile.

"Do you know something? I am going to tell you a secret that I want you to promise you will never, ever tell anyone else as long as you live."

"I promise."

The smile grew strained.

"It is so very strange. We all know how neat and clean Claudette is. And her family. But somehow, somewhere, Claudette picked up some lice in her hair. We know that she couldn't have gotten the lice at home because the family is so clean. She must have been in contact with someone else who had lice."

Francie looked at the nun's red face. She couldn't see why the sister had closed the door and made such a big thing out of Claudette's troubles. If Claudette had lice, that was why her brother had come to get her. The nun must have found out and told her to stay away for a while. But why did Sister Mary have to tell her all about it?

Sister Mary lowered her eyes.

"Francie, dear. Claudette picked those lice up *somewhere*. And since you're such a dear friend of hers and so close to her, I wondered if you'd mind if I checked your hair to see if *maybe* the lice haven't gotten into your hair too."

It was the first time in her life that Francie had seen a red mist before her eyes.

"Will you allow me to see your brush and comb, dear? Then I'll just comb out your hair. Sometimes people have lice and don't even know it. It will take only a few minutes."

They climbed the stairs to Francie's dorm. Francie didn't speak. Sister Mary continued to chatter.

"Of course, this has been *such* a shock to Claudette and her family. But you understand, don't you, dear. I'm asking this favor of you because you are her best friend."

They came to Francie's cot, and the girl handed her brush and comb to the nun. Sister Mary examined them closely while Francie stared stubbornly at Claudette's empty bed.

"All right, dear, we'll do the combing." Francie bent her head in obedience. The nun combed slowly and carefully. She went over every inch of Francie's head. A puzzled look appeared on her face.

"Well." She smiled. "It isn't you, Francie. Your scalp and hair are very clean. So are your brush and comb." She handed the brush and comb to Francie and hugged the girl by the shoulders. "You're a pet, Francie. Poor Claudette must have picked up the lice on the train. From leaning back on the seat, you know. That's the only way it could have happened."

After Sister Mary had gone downstairs, Francie laid her burning cheek on the windowsill. Claudette must have told the nuns that the Polanskis were a big family. And big families were not always clean. Well, they didn't wash every night like the Wilks, but they washed when they were dirty enough. Slowly her fury subsided. Ha, ha, Claudette, she said to herself. Ha, ha.

It was hard to keep the secret. She wanted to boast a little. The next time she went home she told her mother.

"What dey t'ink, we such pigs because we have lots of kids?" Mrs. Polanski was indignant. "Never mind. Dose small families dey is always more sickish. Dey get sick because dey are too clean."

Francie enjoyed her freedom while Claudette stayed at home for two weeks. After Claudette returned to the convent, she saw that Francie's friendship had cooled.

"I had to wash my hair in coal oil," she grimaced. "Twice. It was awful."

"Maybe you shouldn't have gone home on the train so often." Francie couldn't resist the shot.

Claudette tried to reassert her old hold upon Francie.

"It's good for us to make other friends," Francie said firmly as the two girls trudged to the school one day. "When we leave here we will have to get along with all kinds of people. English, German, Irish. Even Protestants. It's better that we start learning how to do it now."

In June the grade twelve girls were allowed to study in private rooms until midnight. Francie read her work aloud and tried not to think of the future.

One evening she came across a poem by George Eliot while she was looking through her anthology. Something caught fire within her as she read it.

> O may I join the choir invisible
> Of those immortal dead who live again
> In minds made better by their presence: live
> In pulses stirred to generosity,
> In deeds of daring rectitude, in scorn
> For miserable aims that end with self,
> In thoughts sublime that pierce the night like stars . . .
> So to live is heaven;
> To make undying music in the world . . . .

She had found her answer. Her life would be one of service to others. She was not quite sure yet what she would do, but she did know that she would never stay on the farm or get married. She dug fiercely into her lessons.

On the last day of school, after the exam was finished, the girls said their life-long farewells to each other.

"Has anyone seen Linda?" Francie asked her dorm in general, as she returned to it after a fourth fruitless search for her friend.

Claudette looked at Francie curiously. "Didn't she tell you? You're her best friend."

"Tell me what? Did she go home sooner?"

"No. Margaret went into her cell by mistake. Sister Mary was in there, measuring Linda's wrists."

Francie sat down suddenly on the bed.

"What!"

"Didn't she tell you?"

Francie looked wordlessly at her, her eyes filling.

"She's going in for a nun. I don't think she wants to see anybody."

The girls shouted with joy at one another as they threw clothes into their suitcases. Francie put her belongings into the cardboard suitcase without speaking.

Linda had chosen already. And kept it a secret from her, her best friend. It was as if a death had occurred. It was the death of a friendship.

Nick came to the door after the lunch hour. He greeted Francie quietly as he bent to carry her suitcase to the truck. Francie waved to the girls grouped in the doorway and turned her back on the convent for the last time. Sudden exhilaration came over her. Finished, finished at last. Never again would she have to worry about school.

"How's everything, Nick?" Francie had not been allowed to go home during the last month because of the exams.

Nick's hands twisted around the steering wheel.

"There's bad news, Francie. Awful bad."

Something has happened at home, she thought. Dad, or Mum . . . . Nick's face was working.

"Eddie. Eddie —"

"Oh, what? What about Eddie?"

Nick drew a long breath. He gripped the wheel.

"Eddie shot himself yesterday."

The truck rumbled over the graveled highway, and little specks of light shot across Francie's eyes. She could hear Nick breathing hard.

"What for? Why? Is he still alive?"

"Eddie's dead, Francie."

She began to cry with great intakes of breath.

"But why? How? Did he trip over something?"

Nick's voice was firmer. "Francie, Eddie shot himself. On purpose. He committed suicide."

"Suicide! Eddie!"

"He left a note. Just said that he didn't see any sense in living."

"But how, Nick, how could he shoot himself?"

She looked into his face. He waited a long time before he told her.

"He put the barrel into his mouth and pulled the trigger."

169

She felt saliva drool from the corner of her open mouth, wiped it with her hand and looked at it with horror.

The truck rumbled on, the box pounding and rattling.

"The funeral is tomorrow."

Funeral! Fresh tears came to her eyes. Then Eddie was really dead. The Eddie who had carved little spool tractors for them all, the Eddie who had gone away to war and had come back homesick. He had not even waited until she got home.

She put her face into her hands at the last thought. Why should he wait until she got home? What did she matter, or anyone else, when Eddie didn't want to live?

"We didn't phone you because you still had that exam to write this morning. They're keeping things pretty quiet. The police really went through everything and asked a lot of questions."

"Eddie wasn't like that, Nick. He would have thought of how Mum and Dad would feel."

"He was sick, Francie. Ever since he was hurt in the war. He wasn't himself. Sure, he lived alone, but something was bothering him. He never talked about the war. It must have got so bad that he couldn't live with it."

And just this morning, she thought, just this morning I was one of the happiest girls in the convent.

"The thing that bothers me," Nick said, and his voice turned hard, "is that the priest said that Eddie can't be buried in the cemetery. We had to dig his grave outside the cemetery."

Grave! While she had been writing exams and joking with the girls, they had been digging a grave for Eddie.

"Why can't he be buried with everybody else?" she sobbed. "What's wrong with him? He can't hurt anyone if he's dead."

"The priest said that they can't bury suicides in with the rest."

"Is that what they're calling him?"

"Well, sure. He shot himself."

"But he was sick! To bury him like a dog! Dad say anything?"

"Dad isn't talking much. Mum is taking it real hard."

"Who found him, Nick? Where did he do it?"

"Joe. He stopped in yesterday to give Eddie some mail. He found Eddie in his bedroom."

Something prevented Francie from asking any more questions. She did not want to know any more. She couldn't stand it.

The truck rumbled into the yard. Cars and trucks waited beside the house, and many people could be seen through the windows. Oh, Rosy, Francie whispered to herself as she stumbled across the yard. Rosy, I wish that you were here.

CHAPTER THIRTY-ONE

Francie's marks came from the department during that summer of tears. Her marks were very high.

"What you want to do now?" her mother asked.

"I want to go in for a teacher,"Francie answered. Since Eddie's death she wanted nothing to do with nursing.

"All right, we send you. You doing good. No use for you to stay on da farm. Maybe you have easier life dat way."

Her mother took a perverse pride in showing Francie's marks to the Chorneys and Mrs. Prosvig when they visited. The marks were proof that she had been right in insisting that her girl get an education.

The neighbors looked at Francie with new interest.

"Ya — my girl she no good. She go to work in dat café. Home is not good enough for her," Mrs. Prosvig said.

Francie flinched. Rosy would never have left home like that if she had been treated in a different way. But she said nothing to Rosy's mother, not even about Rosy's letters.

"Ya. We see if Frynca can be da teacher. I t'ink it not long dat she get married to a nice farm boy. Dere's lots of boys around here. What for you want to keep going to school all your life?"

Francie refused to answer.

Her mother interposed. "Once you get married, you married the rest of your life. She have lots of time to get married. I marry when I fourteen. Nowadays it different."

They talked about the Normal School in Moose Jaw.

"Oi, but it will cost and cost. We haf to buy you da good suitcase now. And you haf to get some clothes. But not too many. We haf to pay for da room and board too."

When the morning came for Dad to take her to Moose Jaw, Francie's throat hurt. Her mother brushed back a wisp of greying hair.

"Study hard and write home lots."

Danny scratched himself behind an ear. He felt awkward about saying good-by.

"I'm gonna have your bedroom now. Me an' Stanley."

With his words her childhood was stripped away. She would always be coming home as a visitor now, not as one who belonged.

Her mother's apron flapped in the wind as she waved. Francie looked at all the familiar old things: the dugout, the old grey barn, the blacksmith shop, the crooked house with its broken step. Then a blur of faces suddenly grown dear, a waving of hands, the swaying of the trees in the shelterbelt and the road.

The first mile was familiar. Down this road she had skipped happily for eleven years of school life. Then Dad turned the truck westward.

For the first time in her life, Francie knew what it was like to have male teachers. They dominated the staff at the Normal School. She regarded them with great interest, seeing a likeness in their thinning hair, pale faces and scruffy clothes.

Students by the hundreds milled around her. As long as one sat in a classroom, he could busy himself with work. But the breaks between classes were awful. Francie found it difficult to walk past a group of well-dressed, idle young people talking together and watching others go by. She felt that her cheap clothes screamed "farm" to them, and she wished that she could be invisible. She wondered how they could stand to waste time when getting ready to teach was so important. The ghost of Eddie followed her to every room.

They don't know anything, she thought with distaste when she saw handsome young men lounging in the doorways. They haven't been to a war; they haven't worked hard on farms.

She soon found that there were others who felt out of place. They wore the same clothes all of the time; they did not join the smiling groups that hung around in the doorways. They smiled shyly at her when she smiled at them. She began to make friends with those who sat nearest to her.

Some students never did return her smile or speak or talk about the work. They sat alone, reading during the breaks and speaking only when called upon by a professor. Suddenly a desk would be vacant, and the whisper went around that so-and-so had been asked to leave. Francie became haunted by the fear that she wouldn't make it either.

No friends from the convent had appeared. Whether they had changed their minds over the summer or found employment, she did not know.

Claudette was finishing her grade twelve and wrote sporadically. Her health was poor. In her loneliness Francie wrote long letters to Rosy. She was her one link to the past. In the evenings she poured out her feelings in a diary.

For the first time she learned the repression of limited space. She worked in her room after school, and after a light supper continued to work on assignments well into the night. She wondered about those bright crowds at the school who hung around the doorways and discussed their evenings of entertainment.

I must be awfully dumb, she thought. I could never go to shows and dances all the time and keep up with my school work.

Those students who had grown up in city or town schools spoke up well in class and often argued with the professors. Francie would listen, shocked, when a young man no older than herself defied the professor's ideas. It never occurred to her to argue. She accepted what she was told and kept her work up-to-date. Nevertheless, she began to dislike the motions of going to class and the homework night after night. She ached to be out on her own, doing something that really counted.

While attending the school, Francie had looked over the boys in each room and separated them into categories. So many were big mouths and conceited; so many were too quiet and maybe had dirty minds; so many seemed nice and acted much like her brothers. In her music class a thin, pimply faced boy with nervous hands sat nearby and often watched her. She didn't like him one bit. He had blond hair; she hated blond hair on boys. She thought too that he acted somewhat like a girl, with his light, nervous gestures and delicate hand movements. Never for one moment did she take him seriously.

One day she was standing in the hall, arms full of books, looking in through the window of the gym. Someone came up to her; she turned and looked into the shy eyes of the pimply faced boy.

He gave her a half-smile. Francie resisted the urge to bolt. She didn't want him near her.

"I'm Reggie," he said, trying hard to keep looking into her eyes. "I've noticed you in music class."

She nodded, wondering how she could end the conversation.

"Would you like to go to a show tonight?"

She stared at him.

"There's a good show with Alan Ladd. We could go to the early one at seven if you like."

Of all the boys in this school and in the world, it would have to be the ugliest one of all. Not only was he pimply faced, but also smaller than she was and decidedly nervous. Whatever would they talk about?

She didn't want to go. How could she refuse without acting green? She couldn't say "No, thanks", as if he were offering her a piece of candy. She looked around to see if there was anyone near.

"Okay."

"Where do you live?"

This is how you get all messed up with a boy, she thought. After you say okay then he has to find out where you live. And after that there will be no getting rid of him. She gave him the address.

"See you then," he half-grinned. "About twenty to seven." He walked away.

Why had she said yes? She hated the sight of him. And God, what if someone who knew them saw them together tonight?

She walked home, her cheeks afire. He picked me because I'm ugly, she thought. He's the ugliest boy in the room, and he couldn't get anyone else to go with him, so he picked me because I'm ugly and he knew that I'd say yes.

Whatever would she wear? She rummaged frantically through her sparse wardrobe. Everything in it she had already worn to school. But she didn't want to look too nice. Not for him. She wasn't ever going out with him again. He would see that she was ugly and never ask a second time.

She could scarcely eat her supper. She wished that it was tomorrow already so that she could forget the whole thing. Tomorrow I'll have to be nice to him in class yet. Maybe he'll start to talk to me in class. Then everyone will know that I went out with him.

She dabbed on a bit of lipstick, then blotted it all off. She combed her hair half a dozen times. The landlady called her from downstairs.

She came down the stairs unwillingly. Reggie stood stiffly at the door. He nodded at her as they went out into the early evening. She knew that he should walk on the outside, so she stuck close to the hedges.

Reggie talked about the school, the classes, the tough assignments.

"Do you like going to Normal School?" he asked her.

"Not much," she answered. Then, fearful lest he tell someone, she added, "I'd rather be teaching already."

"So would I. Wouldn't it be nice if we got schools close together? Then we could see one another often."

A wave of horror swept over Francie. So this was how one thing led to another!

They were on Main Street now; Francie glanced at their reflection in a shop window. She was nearer the window and saw herself first. Her hair stood out on the sides of her face; her feet looked big. She was ugly. But Reggie was just as bad. He hunched himself over, facing the wind, his eyes on the pavement, his hands in his pockets.

Francie looked around furtively. People hurried in different directions, but none wore familiar faces. When they got out of the theater it would be dark. It would be better then.

Reggie bought popcorn which they shared gingerly, careful that their hands didn't touch. Francie didn't want to owe him anything. It was enough that he had paid for the show. She wondered what he would do in the theater after the show had begun. Would he get fresh and try necking? She grew faint at the thought. She wanted no part of that pimply face.

Reggie liked the film, a war story. Francie enjoyed it too until it was half over. Then, just as Alan Ladd grabbed an actress on the screen and poured passionate kisses on her face, she remembered the walk home.

How could she have been so stupid and forgotten about that? In comparison with the walk home, everything else was as nothing. They would be all right on Main Street, where the lights were bright and there were crowds, but what would he do when they had to walk those last two blocks past a park?

What did he have on his mind? Did he maybe think that she was dumb, being from the farm, and that he could take her to a show and then pull her into the park? Parks were the worst place girls could walk through at night. They had no lights, and there were many hedges. Anything could happen to a girl who even dared to walk past one. Someone could be hiding behind a hedge, waiting for a girl to come along.

She never did remember how the show ended. Reggie buttoned up his light jacket and turned to her as they walked out of the glass doors.

"Like it?" Francie nodded her head. They walked with the wind now. She waited.

"How about having a sundae?" They paused in front of a café.

"All right." Anything to stall. Maybe with a sundae inside of him he would not get bad thoughts about her.

They looked at the couples sitting in the booths, their faces sick-looking under the fluorescent lights. Reggie put a nickel into a little box above their table, and the juke box began to play "Linda".

"What grades do you think you'll like the most?" Reggie squashed his ice cream against the side of his dish.

"The primary grades, I think. I don't know. I really like them all."

"I don't care for primary. I'd like to teach grades seven and eight."

He wasn't big enough for them. Francie eyed him as he dug around in his dessert. He looked like a grade six kid himself. And he messed around with his dessert like Danny did.

Much too soon they were back on the street, walking toward the park. Francie answered Reggie's questions with only half her mind. With the other half she was planning her defense when they got to the park.

How could you be so stupid? one part of her mind asked her. There was something unclean about a boy whose face was covered with pimples.

"What's your last name?" she asked when a silence lasted too long. She kept walking as fast as she could to get off Main Street and not to be seen by one of the other students.

"McLeod." So he was Scottish or Irish. She wondered if they were all pimply.

They turned off Main Street and Francie's heart began to pound. They

175

were nearing the park. So far he hadn't done anything. He hadn't even put his arm around her during the movie.

They began comparing families. He was the youngest in his family, and he had four sisters.

"You've got eight brothers?" he whistled. Francie felt proud of her family for the first time in her life. She thought of Eddie with a pang.

They were at the park. Francie was ready. If he pushed her at all, she would run right into the middle of the street and scream.

"Let's take a short cut through the park," Reggie suggested.

"It's kind of gravelly in there," Francie answered faintly. "My shoes . . . ."

They looked at her shoes. Open-toed, sling-backed.

"Maybe not," Reggie said. They walked on in a silence that seemed to grow and grow. Now he knows, she thought. Now he knows that I'm not that kind of a girl!

They turned in at the gate and walked up to the front door.

What if he wants to kiss me? Francie quailed. Don't I have to kiss him after he paid for the show and the treat?

They reached the door. She turned toward him and spoke with a rush.

"Thanks ever so much, Reggie, I really enjoyed the evening —"

"We'll see each other again," he interrupted, holding out his hand.

His hand. He wanted to shake hands. She thrust out her cold fingers, and they pumped each other's arms.

"Well, so long, Frances. See you tomorrow."

"So long." She was through the door and up the stairs. In her room she fell on the bed, laughing hysterically.

Never, never, never again would she go out with a boy she didn't like. It was stupid, wasting time talking about families and movies. And she was lucky. She had gotten home safe this time. But next time he wouldn't be so shy. He would have to be watched. Boys were like that. They acted really smooth until they got a girl to trust them. And then . . . .

Francie hung her coat in the closet and took out her writing pad. She entered the date and began writing.

"Dearest Rosy. Guess what? I've just had my first date. With the ugliest guy in the school . . . ."

Each day new want ads appeared on the main bulletin board in the Normal School. Throughout the province schools were being closed because of the teacher shortage. Students wanting to work left the training institute at the end of September to take teaching positions. They would teach for a year and then decide whether or not they wished to complete their training.

One grey October day Francie scanned the board as students buzzed and milled about her. She wanted to be out of it. She knew that if she was given a small country school she could manage it; she had gone to such a school for the better part of her life.

She read the letters carefully. She did not care for town and city schools. She felt that she would be out of her depth if she tried for one of those postings.

Tomorrow was her turn to make a speech before the class. Just a short one, describing her past life and future ambitions.

I've never made a speech in my life, she thought. I'm scared. More scared than I would be if I were to go out and take over a school right now.

Reggie stopped beside her, hitching up his books on one hip. "See anything interesting?" he half-grinned.

Francie tolerated him now. She still didn't like him, but she could talk with him a little.

"Yes, one," she said, but she didn't say which. After all, it could be taken already.

She practiced her speech that evening before the mirror. No matter how she said it or what she said, it sounded stupid.

"I'm Frances Polanski and I come from a farm near Field. I am seventeen and I hope to become a teacher. I like sports such as volleyball and riding horseback. I also like art and poetry . . . ."

It was stupid, stupid. Who would remember what she had said after she sat down? Who would even remember her last name? She didn't care what the others spoke about; who cared about what she said? It was all a silly waste of time.

When her turn came to go to the front, her legs could hardly carry her there. She turned and nearly reeled from the impact of eyes.

She didn't think there were so many of them. The room looked different from where she sat in the last desk.

"My name is Frances Polanski and I come from a farm near Field . . . ."

They were clapping politely and she was walking back to her seat, moving sideways between the rows. She could not remember what she had said.

She felt the perspiration break out all over her after she sat down. It was someone else's turn; she did not care who it was. She only knew that she had to get out of that building and begin doing something useful.

After classes she scanned the bulletin board again. A new letter announced that a teacher was required for a country school with an enrollment of fourteen, grades one to nine. A boarding place was available. The salary was $1100 a year.

Francie wrote down the address. That evening she mailed her application. Two days later she had an answer. She had been accepted.

CHAPTER THIRTY-TWO

French, French, French. That was all they talked. Francie dipped her spoon wearily as the conversation flowed around her. Her widowed landlady presided over the table, the oldest son, Henri, sitting on her right. Francie sat on her left and next to Lucille, who was older than Francie and no longer in school. Across the table sat two of Francie's students: Maurice, in grade eight, and Robert, in grade nine.

Robert was sixteen. Not for one moment would Francie have him know her age. Both Robert and Maurice were a foot taller than she; both shaved daily. They were neither boys nor men, and their size appalled her.

"You like more peas?" Lucille asked Francie shyly. Francie shook her head. She did not enjoy the meals in this house. She sat like a stranger through the meals while the mother talked gently to her family in her native tongue.

Her family answered in a respectful way, always in French. Sometimes Francie caught the old woman's small, shrewd eyes resting on her. She wondered what thoughts went on in that grey head.

Once in a while, in an effort to be polite, Henri would say something to Francie in English. His two brothers would blush furiously, especially if the remark concerned their school progress. But as soon as Francie answered, glad to be talking, the old lady began to speak. So the meals went.

After supper Francie spread out her papers and did her homework. There was so much to do and she knew so little. If only there weren't anyone in grade nine. She had to be sure that she was ready for Robert in case he asked a question; her greatest dread was that she would not know an answer for him. And then she might lose the respect of the other students.

And she couldn't lose their respect. The eight boys, from grades seven to nine, were all bigger than she was, except for roly-poly Eugene. They looked mean and ugly, with sparse moustaches and big hands and feet. They were not at all like the boys with whom she had gone to school.

During school hours they answered her in broken English, but the minute recess was declared all English was dropped. Francie heard nothing but French during the breaks at school, at her boarding place and in church during the sermon on Sunday. In the evenings Mme LaPointe listened to the French station on the radio. Francie's isolation was complete.

She knew that no disrespect was meant her. It was the custom to follow the traditions of the elders, and she could see that Mme LaPointe ruled with an iron hand in her household.

The school children were headstrong. Francie saw at once that she would have no trouble with the girls. For the most part the boys were replicas of Outlaw Turner. They liked to bait a young female school teacher; they boasted of the "fun" they had had with the previous one.

One noon hour Eugene laughed and laughed. He would not come out and say it, but he made it clear that the former teacher, a very young one, had met with some unfortunate treatment.

"You wouldn't believe me," he choked on his sandwich," but we really fixed dat one." He looked around for approval. "We — we tied her to dat chair you're sitting in, with wire."

"This chair?" Francie frowned. "I don't believe it."

"Honest to God, we did. And then we — then we — " He looked to the other boys for help, but they would not meet Francie's eyes and grinned foolishly with their mouths full of bread.

"And then we — then we — " he could not get himself to say it.

"Then you what?" Francie was curious now. She looked toward the girls, but they too were looking away.

Eugene could not let the joke die. "Hey, Miss Polanski, you won't be mad if I tell you?"

"Of course not," Francie answered impatiently. She was growing tired of waiting.

"Okay. Okay. You promised. Remember dat. After we tied her up with wire, we all wet on the ground behind her chair."

The other boys turned red, and Eugene choked over his food, remembering. Francie sat rigid. She looked at their silly faces and knew they were ashamed. She knew that Eugene was not telling a joke.

"That was awful."

"Oui, oui," Eugene gasped. "An' we could do it to you too, we could. You wanna make bet?"

"You try it, and I'll expel you." Francie felt cold fear and simmering rage at the same time.

"You know, I think she would." Eugene turned to Robert, hulked over his lunch pail. "Expel us, I mean." He looked at Francie and grinned, his cheeks full of bread.

She had a bad time for two weeks. Their names were so much alike:

179

Marcel and Margot, Lucien and Louise, Louis and Lucille. It did not help when she called out a name and then looked expectantly at the wrong student for the answer.

Although Eugene made his threat, the boys obeyed the school laws she had set down. They liked a joke on her, and she learned to tolerate them. They saw little sense in the schoolwork they were taking, but for most of them grade eight was soon to be completed, so they did what they could.

She rode horseback across the mile and a half of prairie to the school. One Saturday she asked Maurice to saddle the horse so that she could go to the school and do some extra work there over the weekend. It was a better prospect than sitting in the house and listening to French all day.

The sharp west wind blew the grass sideways as she rode between the willows toward the faded structure that would be hers to work in for the next few months. Francie felt proud of herself. She was only seventeen, but she already had a good job. She would really teach these children something.

Mme LaPointe was obviously perplexed because the teacher went to school on weekends. Francie found that getting out of the house made life bearable. On some days she read to get ahead of the students. At other times she twisted crepe paper streamers over the small windows. At the school she could be herself.

One afternoon after school was let out, Francie looked up from her desk just in time to see an object strike the door and fall to the floor of the porch right behind Margot, who flew into the classroom. Francie heard the angry French words of the would-be assailant.

"What's the matter?"

"Robert chased me. He got mad at me. He threw that horse manure at me."

Francie stepped out into the porch. Robert stood beside the barn, laughing with the others who were saddling their horses.

"Robert, come here," she said as sternly as she could, hoping that he would obey.

Robert came toward her. He planted himself a few feet away and asked, "Well?"

All of the other boys were wasting time harnessing and saddling the horses. Francie turned toward the school.

"Come in," she said. "I have something to say to you."

As he stepped into the porch, she pointed at the manure which still stuck to the door.

"Did you do that?"

He looked at her with level eyes.

"Yah."

"And you swore at Margot?"

180

"Yah." He cocked his head and waited.

"You are the oldest boy in the school. You should be acting a little better than that. Come in here and clean the door. And sweep it off the floor. And then you come into the school."

He grabbed the broom and swept the manure off the door. Then he held the door to the outside open with one hand and swept the manure carelessly outside. A whoop of laughter came from the children at the barn.

"It not my fault, mine," he said in a low, furious voice. "Margot she asked for it."

"I don't care if she did or not. You have no right to throw such things into the school. So clean it up."

In the classroom Maurice pushed the big stiff broom he used to clean the floor every afternoon. He was the school janitor. In the morning he rode to school early and lit the fire before the rest of them got there. He looked now at his brother throwing out the manure and back at the teacher at her desk.

Margot cleaned the boards. She did not dare go outside to clean the brushes because Robert was still working in the doorway. She pushed up a window and began clapping the brushes together.

Robert threw the old broom into the corner of the porch. He walked with big, heavy steps into the room. He stood in front of Francie, meeting her eyes.

"Me, I know how old you are. You are just one year older than I am."

Margot stopped clapping the brushes and turned to look at Robert's back. Maurice regarded Francie with his great moon eyes.

Francie wondered if Lucille had gone through her dresser.

"Never mind how old I am. You acted in a shameful way for a big boy like you. You're in high school."

He towered above her, his thumbs hooked in his belt. He could have smashed her face in with one fist.

"Here." Francie thrust a page of foolscap at him. "Write on there, one hundred times, 'I will not throw anything into the school again.' "

"One hundred times!" Robert staggered from the blow. "Just for throwing a little piece of horseshit at that - - - -!!"

"You say one word more and it'll be a thousand!" The cold fury in Francie's voice checked him. He threw himself heavily into a desk and pulled a pen from his pocket.

Francie was glad that the French taught their children to respect authority. Else what could she have done with this hulk of a man-child?

Robert wrote a few lines. His face worked.

"One hundred lines. That's a lot for a little thing like dat."

"One hundred lines." Francie checked at a notebook.

Maurice swept near her chair, and she got up to move so that he could finish up. He had not said a word, but he watched his brother and the teacher.

Robert's face turned a darker red. Margot had finished cleaning the brushes and was standing them up on the ledge of the blackboard. There was the cause of his humiliation.

He muttered something in French.

"Pardon, Robert?" Francie asked.

He repeated it, louder this time and with much feeling.

Francie looked toward Margot, who would not meet her eyes.

"What did Robert just say, Margot?"

Margot's face turned pink. "He called you a name."

"What kind of a name?"

"He called you an old turkey."

Robert shouted the words at Francie and Margot. Over and over again.

"Get your books," Francie said carefully when he tired. "Take them all, and get out of here. When you are ready to come back to school and apologize to us in front of the other students, then I may let you come back."

"Hey! Me, I don't care." He stood up and crumpled the foolscap on the floor. Maurice looked at Francie and swept it into the refuse. "I don't need to go to this shitty school. I'll never come back."

He dug his books out of his desk, pulled his cap down hard on his head and stomped out. Margot waited for a few moments, then followed him out. Her home lay in the opposite direction.

Maurice looked at Francie again.

"Robert, he has the awful temper. When he can't get his way. Me, I get mad too, but I don't talk like dat."

She stared at the work in front of her. Robert would reach home ahead of her. She would have to face him across the supper table and in front of his mother.

Maurice put away the push broom. "Well, good night," he said, even though he was going to see her again that evening. She was glad that he had witnessed the whole thing. Brother would testify against brother, she knew, and Maurice was the more stable of the two. The family would know all about the incident long before she got home. The whole district would be talking about it after church on Sunday.

She put off going home as long as possible. There were five of them to face. She wondered whose side they would take. Whatever happened, she couldn't accept a student who called her names. Robert was the idol of most of the other boys.

She came out of her room when Lucille called her to supper. It was quiet in the kitchen. Lucille shot a quick look of sympathy toward Francie, but the mother looked straight ahead. They bowed their heads and said grace. Francie stole a look at Robert. His color was high and his chin stubborn. Evidently, there had been a heated discussion.

Henri commented on the fine weather. "It will be good for haying, Miss Polanski. How would you like to drive the horses for me tomorrow while I load the rack?"

They all laughed a little because they knew that he was joking. In a family of three boys, no girl worked in the field. Francie knew that he was trying to make her feel better. She picked at her supper and wondered when things would come out in the open.

On Sunday after the Mass, the congregation walked to the post office for the week's mail. It came by truck on Saturday nights; most people picked up their mail on Sunday after church. A few women smiled at Francie and spoke to her; the incessant French drove loneliness into her like a sharp needle.

When Robert did not appear for school on Monday, all the children were sobered. They made little jokes about him. They looked at Francie in a different way. She pretended that nothing was changed, even though she felt depressed.

"There goes Robert!" one of them yelled the following day as a great rack full of hay lumbered past the schoolyard. "He's hauling hay! Ha, ha, Robert!"

Robert ignored them. He did not even look their way.

It was the custom to send the smaller children to the board to practice their spelling. The French children had real problems with English spelling.

Fat little Eugene tired of writing the words over and over again. One afternoon Francie saw him grinning from the board at the seated students.

"Eugene, you want to beat the old score," she warned. "Don't fool around up there or you'll have to practice in your desk."

Francie went from student to student, helping in whatever way she could. If only they knew their English, she thought. School would not be such a drudgery for them.

They liked her to come to their desks and to point out the better work. Sometimes they made jokes about their bad handwriting so that she could praise it.

In their own way they were like her family had been. They had their own way of life, but sooner or later they would have to make it on their own. Many of them would become farmers, but what about those who would have to leave the close-knit family structure and try to compete in a mixed society?

"Oo-w-w-w!!!" Eugene jumped straight up from the teacher's chair, holding on to the seat of his pants. The other students dissolved in laughter.

Francie watched, wondering what had happened. They were full of little jokes and tricks, these children.

"Me, I put a tack on your chair, see. But you stay in the back of the room so long I forget and sit on the tack myself."

He grinned. She knew that he had not forgotten; he had wanted to inject some energy into what was a dull session for him.

"Back to your seat. One hundred per cent now, Eugene."

The following morning Francie reached the school earlier than usual. Nothing had been said by any of the Lapointe family concerning Robert's expulsion. He had sat across from her during every meal, his face sullen and wind-burned. Only Maurice looked back and forth across the table at the two of them.

She was dusting her desk when a shadow fell across the doorway. Robert stood there, his books under one arm.

"Me, I come back to school if you let me."

"If you apologize in front of the others." Francie found her voice weak with surprise.

"Okay." He looked at his old desk. "Can I have my desk back?"

She nodded. He pushed his books into the desk, his eyes taking in all the changes that had taken place while he was away — the Hallowe'en stencils, the harvest decorations. He went out into the sunshine quietly.

After they had sung "O Canada" and said the Lord's Prayer, Francie spoke: "Robert has something he wants to say."

The big boy went to the front of the room and stood there awkwardly.

"Miss Polanski, Margot, I'm sorry I called you names. I promise I won't do things like dat any more."

Francie nodded as he took his seat. The children looked at Robert with new respect. It took courage for a man to say he was sorry to a woman. Not even a woman, just a girl.

Robert buried his face in his books and disregarded the rest of the students. Francie called the beginners to the board, a lightness rising inside of her. She caught Maurice's eye. He smiled and bent his head quickly so that no one could see.

Winter began early. During a Friday morning a white wind stormed out of the west, and soon it grew so dark in the school they could scarcely see to read. Francie told the children to put away their books.

"Mebbe we have to stay here overnight," Maurice suggested.

"Wouldn't dat be fun, Miss Polanski, wit the mice and rats running over us?" His big eyes shone with the thought of it.

"I'd like four of you boys to carry in a pile of coal from the barn. Robert, will you take charge? Carry in enough so that in case we have to stay here late tonight we will have dry coal handy."

The worst of the blizzard blew itself out by two o'clock. The temperature sank. Even with all the coal being fed into the stove, the school became colder.

"Put your coats and boots on," Francie directed. The fingernails on the small children had turned blue with cold.

"Let's do some P.T."

The boys cheered.

"But there's no room in here to do anything," Emile protested.

"Move all the desks right up to the stove," Francie said, grabbing the nearest one. "Then we'll put another ring around the first one. The smallest get to sit closest to the stove."

They swung and pushed the desks cheerfully. In a few minutes the desks cluttered the back part of the room, right up to the door.

"Now." Francie clapped her hands for attention. "Stand anywhere and do arm exercises." She gave them a moment as they scrambled for standing room. "One, two . . . ."

From the arm exercises they swung into running on the spot. This exercise warmed all of them in their heavy parkas and boots. The most fun was the great stamping noise they could make with their boots. The boys grinned at one another and tried to outdo each other with the noise.

Finally, Francie called for a halt. They were breathing heavily, enjoying the respite from work. No one liked social studies.

"Now for the hard stuff. Spread your legs apart on the count of one and clap your hands over your head at the same time." She showed them in slow motion. "At the count of two, bring your legs together and slap the sides of your thighs. Everybody try it once or twice."

They jumped about like ungainly scarecrows. The big boys felt like horsing around.

"One-two!" Francie yelled. "One-two!"

The angled stove pipe parted, and a shower of soot sprinkled the desks around the stove.

They crowed with delight.

"Robert — Maurice — do something quick, or we'll get gassed."

"Yeah, we'll get da gas!" Eugene laughed, enjoying the novelty. "Quick, boys, push dem together again."

They shoved the sagging pipes back into place.

"Look at our dirty desks!" Margot exclaimed.

Just then they heard the knocking on the door.

185

It was a persistent knocking, as if it had been going on for some time. But of course one could not have heard it in all the bedlam. It could be one of the older brothers come to drive some of the smaller children home.

"Come in!" Francie shouted.

The door opened a foot, then bumped the desk standing closest to it. There was a silence as they all watched and waited to see the visitor, who tried pushing the door in a little farther.

A man stuck his pink face around the door. He had red hair, neatly waved, and was wearing a heavy coat with a fur collar.

"May I come in?"

It was the awfullest moment in her life. Of all days, this was the one the superintendent had chosen to visit the school.

The children read her fear. The big boys moved the desks away from the door, and the smaller children climbed into their desks and wiped the soot off with their sleeves.

"Mr. Madsen, Miss Polanski." He shook her icy hand warmly. "How are you making out?" He looked at the children in the desks around the heater, trying to look busy.

"We — we were cold," she stammered. "I had them doing a little physical education."

"Umm. It *is* rather chilly." He looked at the thermometer on the wall. "Sixty-three. A bit too cold to study effectively."

Francie was shaking as if she had just come out of the water after a cold swim.

"Would you like to see my register?" He nodded and busied himself at her desk. "Just go right on with your work," he said pleasantly. "I have some reports to fill out, as you know. You don't mind if I use your desk?"

It was the only place where he could sit. Francie picked up her day book and placed it in front of him.

For the first time in her teaching life, she found time passing at an incredibly slow pace. She went from desk to desk, offering help. Some of the students looked up at her face in abject fear. They knew that they should be working, but at what? She repeated instructions.

The superintendent was not simply filling reports. He glanced around the school, at the windows, the stove, the thermometer. He was listening too to what went on between Francie and the students.

Finally it was recess. Francie dreaded what was to come. She knew that she had done no teaching whatever while he had been there; the school was a mess from the soot. She tied the last of the scarves and then pulled a desk away from the front of the stove to replenish the fire.

Mr. Madsen walked back and forth across the short space of floor, his hands in his pockets. He was cold too.

"Tell me, is it this cold every day?" He frowned all the time.

"No. Only on days when the temperature really drops. It's better on quiet days because it isn't so cold then."

"It must present problems. Those children working in their parkas . . . . Tell me, are you having any problems here?"

She wished that she could tell him of the awful loneliness that came from living in a French community, about the tears in bed at night. Something held her back. His business was to look after the school, not her. He might think her weak if she told him the truth.

She told him of Robert's expulsion.

He tried to look out of a frosted window. "Under the circumstances, you should have reported the incident to the secretary of the school board right away. I am to get a report from him in such cases. However, I'm glad that the problem settled itself."

Francie prepared herself for criticism.

"I realize that crowding the desks around the stove does not make for ideal teaching," he remarked, "but I would like to see you teach more. From the front of the room, not in going from person to person. The individual help should come after the lesson has been taught. You could save yourself a lot of back strain by stating the assignment to everyone at once, you know." He smiled to offset the criticism.

"I must leave right away because the roads are anything but good. Just keep on doing your best; I can see that the pupils are on your side. I'll see you in the spring."

He let himself out, a gentle, concerned man. Francie waited a few minutes before she rang the bell. It was all that she could do to keep the tears from spilling over. She had been in this school barely three months; it had seemed like eternity. That she could teach she was sure; that she could continue to live in an environment as barren as the winter world outdoors she could not be sure. Mr. Madsen had been her only contact with the English-speaking world. His encouragement overwhelmed her.

The children trooped in, stamping the snow off their boots, their cheeks blazing from the cold. Francie helped the smallest ones undress and untied scarves. She felt the stirrings of fondness toward them. She liked them for the way they had rallied behind her when the superintendent had been present.

CHAPTER THIRTY-THREE

The snow fell deep and soft, obliterating the prairie trails. Telephone poles shrank to half their height and fences disappeared.

The mail came from Durham twice a week by sleigh. It was twenty miles to the nearest railway station. When it was time for Henri to take Francie to the station for the Christmas holidays, his mother sent them outdoors with a huge pile of quilts. They travelled in a light, open sleigh. Francie enjoyed leaving the closed-in country behind; she could see the sweeps of smooth fields, the occasional poplar bluff, the mirages on the horizon.

She had ordered Christmas gifts for the whole family from Eaton's, delighted by the fact that she was in a position to buy gifts. She settled happily on the train, and the miles flew by. The crisp air, the fresh scent of the snow, the ruddy cheeks of the conductor excited her. For the first time in six months, she was going home.

Danny and Nick met her at Field. She was the only passenger. They gaped at her luggage.

"Whatcha got here, anyway?" Nick grinned as he heaved the box of gifts onto the sleigh.

The shelterbelt was a hoarfrost relief against the greying evening sky. The trail curved like a wing between the opening trees.

The old grey house leaned to the south; its windows were frosted over, but here and there Francie could see a hole rubbed into the frost so that someone inside could see out.

She climbed stiffly out of the sleigh. The door swung open with its old protest. Stanley and Timmie ran toward her.

"Hi, everybody," she sang. Her mother looked up from the kneading pan and began to pick the dough off her fingers.

"You get cold?"

"Nope." Francie unwound the scarf from her neck. "It's very nice out."

She looked for a place to hang her coat. There was the usual row of parkas on the big hooks beside the kitchen range. She could not hang her coat with the barn things. She went into the Other Room to hang her coat at the foot of the stairs.

Her father sat beside the heater, rolling a cigarette. He licked the paper and sealed the cigarette.

"Well, how she goes?" he asked, after he lit it.

"All right," Francie answered, feeling shy with him. Here, at home, she was just Francie. At her boarding place she had been Miss Polanski. She wished that they could see her here as others saw her at her job.

Stanley and Timmie became excited when they saw the box of gifts.

"That's for Christmas Eve." Francie dragged the box into the Other Room. "If you snoop in here I'll kill you."

Dad lit the gas lamp and hung it on the big hook where it swung to and fro, hissing with cheer. The boys brought in coal and wood. Francie removed her heavy clothes and then busied herself setting the table. At last she felt that she was really home. No one made a fuss. She felt a little disappointed. She thought that they would see how much she had changed, how responsible she was. But her dad smoked on and read the paper; her mother dished out the doughboys.

"Betcha you'll think this food isn't good enough for you now," Nick teased.

"I never ate doughboys and Jewish potatoes in all this time," Francie said fervently. "I used to think about them though."

"You not look so good now," her mother said. "Is hard work, dat teaching?"

"Not so hard. You have to get used to the food and different ways."

"How much dey paying you?" asked her dad.

"Eleven hundred a year," she boasted. "My check is a little over ninety dollars a month. I pay thirty for room and board."

"You doing not so bad."

After supper Stanley got the cards, and they began the old game of Durack. Francie found herself holding cards at the end of the third game.

"Teacher! Durack!" they hooted.

Christmas music started coming over the radio. Francie huddled on a chair beside the heater and looked about the Other Room.

She would still sleep on the pull-out bed in there. Tomorrow she would decorate the house. She had bought streamers and icicles and tree ornaments. She would lay the gifts under the tree so that they could squeeze and shake and maul them for a few hours.

She lay in the lumpy bed that night, happy to be home, most happy to be among her own people. At the same time a vague dissatisfaction nagged at her. The bed was truly uncomfortable. It was too short. The feather tick

189

was stifling; she had become used to blankets. And she did not like being without a private room.

The next day was Christmas Eve. The younger boys helped Francie tack streamers to the low ceilings. Their mother looked on without comment until she looked at the clock.

"Why for you spend money on dose t'ings," she scolded Francie. "You can't eat da decorations."

"They make the house look nice," Francie said, a little hurt. "We can take them down and put them up every year, so it's not a waste of money."

"Ya, if you wants to do all dat work," her mother said. "But I need someones to clean da wheat. You hurry dat up so dat I can cook da wheat for supper. It take a long time to cook, you know."

"I'll put up the rest," Francie said to Danny and Stanley. "Better start cleaning the wheat."

Toward evening Nick brought in the old sheaf. Happiness welled up in Francie. Then Stanley carried in the fragrant hay.

Quiet descended on them as they took their places at the table. In the Other Room Christmas carols could be heard on the radio.

Nick was the first of the family to get the bread. Eddie should have been sitting there. Francie's heart contracted painfully.

Their mother sniffed. "Leave some pieces of the bread for the dead," she said to their father. "Put dem in da small saucer by da candles."

It was believed that the souls of the dead relations came during the night to partake of the Holy Bread.

After supper Harry and Joe came visiting with their wives. The Chorneys were not far behind.

Mrs. Chorney looked at Francie with surprise. "You grow up," she said, trying her best at English. "You skinny, though. You should eat more." And she laughed, looking much like a rosy Eskimo, with her fat face and braids coiled around her head.

It was then that Francie discovered that Rosy was not going to be home for the holiday.

"Not home for Christmas? Why not?"

"Oh, her moder is mad dat she work for dat old man. People iss talking. And Rosy have a boy friend too, and her moder iss scared she get into da trouble yet. She want Rosy to come home or go work close here, like at Green Walley, but Rosy she won't do dat."

Without Rosy it would not be like Christmas. Francie had saved all her good news to spill out to her friend over the holiday. She had hoped too that Rosy would fill her in on some gossip.

On Christmas Day her parents went visiting. Francie stayed at home. There was nowhere to go. She pulled on her heavy melton ski pants and slid around on the dugout ice for a while, delighting the younger boys who scored goal after goal upon her. The clean, fresh air invigorated them. They trooped into the house, happy and ravenous for cold turkey.

And will it be like this next year? And the next? Francie thought about it as she sliced the turkey.

There is nothing here for me anymore. I might as well have stayed at the boarding place.

She decided to return to the school district on the day before Three Kings.

"You should stay yet for the holiday and go tomorrow night," her mother said.

"I want an extra day before starting school. You can't just walk into a school and start teaching." She hoped that she sounded important.

As she packed her suitcase, she thought of how restless the older boys had been after they had been away from home for a while. They had paced around and around the house, the yard, unable to sit down. She felt restless too. She didn't fit in anymore. Not even her dad understood that she had a responsible job, every bit as important as farming. But as long as she stayed home she would be just an ordinary girl.

CHAPTER THIRTY-FOUR

"There is going to be a Valentine dance at the parish hall on Friday," Lucille said to Francie as they did the dishes one evening. "You want to go? I think I will."

Francie hesitated. She loved to dance. But to go attached to one man — no. Lucille read her mind.

"Henri will take us. You can come home with us or whoever you like. The dances are fun. There's lots of young people there that you never meet otherwise. There's lots more boys than girls. So if you go, be ready to dance a lot!"

Francie agreed that it might be fun. As long as she didn't have to go as Henri's girl.

Mme LaPointe went visiting that Friday evening with Maurice. After supper everyone else began preparing for the dance.

Water had to be heated three times for their baths. No wonder they started getting ready before supper! Henri had found a bottle somewhere and became more talkative. Francie sensed that he was afraid of something; either he didn't dance well or it bothered him to go out all dressed up.

Francie stood before her mirror, brushing out the fine corn-silk hair that flew up and around her head in a static halo. She wondered what the dance would be like when she didn't know anyone. Maybe she would sit all night and no one would ask her to dance.

Finally, her hair lay close to her neck. I will look as out of place at the dance as I did at home, she had a sudden, swift thought. There are no fair French people. At least I haven't seen any yet. They're really dark, most of them.

And then she remembered. That story her mother used to tell about Dad and the Old Country. His mother had worn long yellow braids. She had been held in respect by the people of the village because of the unusual color of her hair. Maybe that was where Francie's blondness came from.

I will never marry a boy with yellow hair. She applied lipstick and then blotted most of it off. He will have to have dark hair like all the boys at home. Light-colored hair on a boy makes him look like a sissy. With a smile she remembered Reggie in Moose Jaw.

"Miss Polanski, may I come in?" Henri was at her door. Whatever did he want? He swayed in the doorway there, a pink box of dusting powder in his hand.

"Would you be kind enough to powder my face for me?" he asked, emitting a small alcoholic burp. "I cannot do it myself. Lucille is still in the tub."

Francie stared at him. He had been drinking, but he was not drunk. But what kind of a man wore face powder? His mild brown eyes entreated her.

"Turn your face more to the lamp," she said. She spread the powder over his shaved jaw, down his nose. He was perfectly serious, standing as if he were a little boy having his hair cut. He turned his face patiently.

Wait till she told them at home. They would never believe her. But then, maybe all Frenchmen powdered their faces when they went out. But with such sweet-smelling powder? Obviously, it was Lucille's.

He regarded himself in the mirror. "Now, just a little bit of lipstick," he said. "Not too much, just enough to give the lips some color."

"Hold your lips tight," Francie said. He made a crazy face and swayed toward her.

"You know, Miss Polanski, you are a nice girl. A real nice girl."

Francie pushed him toward the mirror. "Do you like that now?"

He was diverted instantly. "You made a good job," he praised, bringing the bottle to his lips again.

Lucille hurried into the bedroom, looking at her brother in anxiety. She saw the bottle flash and broke into a torrent of French. Francie understood that she was worrying about his ability to drive.

"Me, I drive like a damn," Henri slurred, stumbling out of the room. Francie handed the box of powder to Lucille.

Lucille rolled her eyes. "He thinks he need that," she said scornfully. "Powder won't get him a wife."

The dance hall was full, dusty and noisy. Crowds of young men hung at the back of the hall near the entrance.

As soon as Francie sat down beside Lucille, she felt the scrutiny of a dozen eyes. She looked toward the mob of young men. Some were pointing openly at her, telling one another who she was. She turned her face to the orchestra.

Henri came to claim her for the first dance, an old-time waltz played in a springing, lilting rhythm. Henri stumbled through it. She was angry with him for spoiling a good dance.

"See that tall man over by the window?" he breathed in her ear, his

193

breath strong with the scent of whiskey. "That is Charles Duval. He is most anxious to meet you. I will introduce him to you."

Francie looked over Henri's shoulder and studied the man. He was not cavorting around with the others. He stood apart, untouched, a bit distinguished.

"Miss Polanski, Mr. Charles Duval." Henri staggered between the two of them. Charles held out his hand, looking at her intently. Francie smiled at him. It would be good to get away from Henri. He was beginning to sweat profusely.

Charles swung her easily into a fox trot. He began the conversation immediately.

"You are from?" And she told him. He was the only son living on a farm nearby. Francie guessed him to be a little older, twenty-eight or thirty perhaps.

His manners were wonderful. After weeks of little communication at her boarding place, Francie began to thaw. They talked about farming, the community, the orchestra. He spoke of his travels. They sat out a polka to talk.

The next dance was a waltz. To her delight Charles waltzed beautifully. He held her a little closer at the end of the dance.

"Will you do me the honor of having supper with me?"

Why not? Francie asked herself. No harm can come of it. He has a nice face, and at least I can talk to him.

She felt proud that such a thoroughly nice young fellow had singled her out for the evening.

After the sandwiches and coffee were passed around, there was an interval of eating and talking. Then the coffee cups were collected, and there came the business of sweeping the floor with two push brooms. The crowd began to disperse. No one liked sitting on the benches, holding up their feet while the push brooms reached under for papers, half-eaten sandwiches and bottles. The dust rose, thick and cloggy.

"Let's go for a short drive," Charles suggested. Francie did not hesitate. There was something about him that inspired her trust. Knowing looks went around the hall as he helped her on with her coat. That Charles, they would say, he took out the school teacher from LaPointe's school.

Charles drove the car to the edge of town. The stubblefields lay pearly in the moonlight. Black tree branches arched over the car.

For a time they sat there — Charles with one arm draped over the steering wheel, Francie with her hands pushed deep into her pockets, her chin buried in her coat. It was peaceful after all the noise in the hall.

"Do you like teaching?"

"Yes. Very much. But I don't know enough yet." They laughed together at her candor.

"You do not need to teach forever, you know. A year or two, then settling down. Isn't that the way it happens?"

Francie wondered if he were one of the serious ones.

"Not me. I'm never getting married."

There was a short, sharp silence.

"But that is no life for a girl," he teased, lifting a soft curl and turning her hair around a finger. "Who wants to be an old maid?"

"Who wants to be an old housewife?" she asked, and they both laughed again.

"Housewives don't have to get old. They can travel and have just as much fun as single girls."

"I don't see them doing it though. They have too many little ones and too much work to think of fun."

He lit a cigarette. "How old are you anyway?"

"Just turned eighteen," she said, thinking of the birthday spent away from home.

He whistled. "That's pretty young to be teaching school."

The moon dodged behind a cloud.

"Why is it that you've never married?" Francie asked him suddenly. After all, he was older than she.

He held the cigarette in his fingers for a time, the smoke curling upwards. He dragged hard on the cigarette. An inscrutable look hooded his face.

"I'll tell you." He started the motor. "If you promise me that you'll go to the dance at St. Claude with me next Friday. I'll tell you then."

"I'd like to go."

"Good. I always keep my promises."

He slid the car to a stop beside the hall.

"There is one thing though, Charles." A shyness came over her. "I want to tell you right now. Before you take me to any dances. I will not ever get serious."

"You have someone then?"

"Oh, no. I don't want to hurt anybody."

He looked at her, sitting determined and serious.

"Of course," he laughed. "We'll go out for a good time. Agreed?"

She smiled with relief. He could have said "Okay, if that's how you want it, better find yourself another fellow." But Charles opened the door for her with good humor. The orchestra was already playing.

They danced together most of the night. Along one wall sat the older ladies of the parish. They whispered behind their hands as they saw Francie and Charles swing through dance after dance.

"May I take you home?"

She did not hesitate. "Yes."

She found Lucille to tell her that she had another ride home. Lucille's dark eyes widened.

"See, you 'ave found a nice fellow already. I will tell Henri."

They drove home in a companionable silence, the night a white and shining thing all about them. Charles helped her out of the car and walked her to the door.

"Till next Friday then. I will be here at nine."

He put his arms around her and kissed her full on the lips. He did it in such a sure, practiced way that she knew he must have been out with many girls. His kiss was light, deliberately so, and he looked into her face afterwards.

"Thank you for a wonderful evening," he said.

Francie tiptoed in, confused and happy for the first time she could remember. A charming young man had danced with her tonight and talked with her and even kissed her. She had something to look forward to now.

On Friday Lucille smiled when she saw Charles get out of his car.

"You 'ave the nice boy friend, no? He is a good man."

They drove down a winding road that followed a lake shore. Dances were held at the Fun Palace only during the summer season and once or twice in the winter.

"There may be a rough crowd there," Charles said. "All kinds of riff-raff show up at lake dances. I'll take good care of you though." He smiled out of the corner of his eye.

They parked on a bluff overlooking the lake. Charles dragged thoughtfully on his cigarette.

"I was engaged to be married this last fall," he said, his eyes searching the expanse of ice before them. "I should say we, not I. I had gone with Ann for several years. But when we told her folks about our plans for marriage, that was the end of that. They went crazy over the fact that I was Roman Catholic and that she was Protestant."

Charles lit another cigarette. "Ann is a very nice girl. I'm twenty-six; she's twenty-four. Both of us are old enough to make up our own minds. But her parents wouldn't see it that way. The fact that I owned my own farm didn't matter; they wanted no Duval for a son-in-law."

They watched the last of the color fade out of the sky.

"What did she do?"

"She did what they made her do. They broke us up by sending her down East to an aunt's. She's been gone since September. I may never see her again."

He looked at her serious profile, shrugged and smiled. "So you see, *ma petite*, there is a reason for my being single and unattached. Ann was the only girl in my life. You don't forget that fast."

"Why don't you go after her?"

Charles shook his head. "That would make matters worse. The family thinks that if she stays away long enough, she will meet someone else and forget Charles Duval."

"She might be hoping you will come."

"She could write. All it would take is one letter." He rubbed the steering wheel with his fine hands.

"Now you know. So let's hear all about you now. Any steady boy friends at home? Here? Surely you have someone. No girl as pretty as you, with spirit, could be without an attachment."

"You will have to believe me when I say that I have no attachments, none. I have eight brothers. In our community there were so many more boys than girls. There have always been boys around. I don't mean to be insulting, but when I see another man I think, so what?"

Charles threw back his head and laughed heartily.

"No, but really. I want to teach for a few years and then go into something else. I haven't the slightest wish to settle down and get married and grow old."

"I can think of nothing nicer than getting old, as you say, with the right person."

Francie looked at him with curiosity. "Weren't you all broken up when this happened?" she asked.

"Yes. But remember, that was almost six months ago. I can look at it more easily now, where before it hurt."

"What did she look like?"

It was the wrong question. He frowned.

"Ann was about your height. She had dark hair and dark eyes. She was all for fun."

She knew then that he had not forgotten the girl. The pain showed on his face.

They danced often that night, other men cutting in. Charles didn't like that too well. Some of the men smelled of perspiration and alcohol; others held her so close that she became embarrassed. Charles suggested that they leave at lunch time.

"Sorry about the dance," he said as they headed for the car. "I knew that it wasn't the nicest place to take a girl, but there is nothing going on anywhere else tonight."

When they parted, he kissed her with more intensity. Francie slipped into her room, troubled. With the slightest encouragement, Charles could fall in love with her. He was not at all unlikable; he was mature; he seemed to be honest. But he was on the rebound. And what would happened if Ann returned home, as she undoubtedly would?

They dated often. On Sundays they watched ball games, stuffing themselves with spicy hot dogs and fizzy drinks. Charles knew a great many people and introduced Francie to a bewildering number of them. They visited his mother, crippled with arthritis and living with an aunt. She liked Francie on the spot.

When the school year drew to its close, Francie sent in her resignation. It was discussed with some surprise at the boarding house.

"Me, I thought that you would stay on an' get married to that Duval in the next year," reproached Henri.

Never, never would I live in this community. Francie thought of all the lonely nights before she had met Charles. But to Henri she said. "Oh, no. I will stay single for a long time yet."

"You are making a mistake," he said. "I am a little older than you, so I can give you some advice. If you stay single too long, then you won't be able to get married. Take me for example."

She regarded him with sympathy. He was not a bad sort, but to her mind he seemed to be womanish. Perhaps that was because he was the oldest son and had to carry out the wishes of his mother.

In June Charles proposed. She was horrified.

"Charles, I told you — right at the start — nothing serious."

"That was before we knew each other. But you have begun to care for me?"

He lifted her downcast face and smoothed the cornsilk hair around her face.

She sensed the trap closing in upon her. How easy it would be to say yes and to never have to go working again. How nice it would be to become the mistress of a large farmhouse, the wife of a respected fellow like Charles.

"I can't do that to you," she said. "Charles, I do like you. You are the nicest man I have ever met, but I don't — don't love you. I never pretended I did."

"Who knows what love really is?" He lifted her chin. "So we marry. We live together, have children, have everything two people need to make them happy. Love will come later."

"What if Ann should come back?"

"She is back."

"Then — then you haven't seen her?"

"No. I know that she is at home. I don't care to go and see her. I have all I want right here with you, Francie."

He tried to pull her close.

She covered her face with her hands.

"Please, please, Charles — don't insist. Don't *beg me!* I thought that we could have a good time together and that it would help to pass the time away for both of us."

"Maybe you are not ready yet," he said softly. "But there will come a day. When you feel that you are ready, write me. Promise?"

He will never get that letter, she told herself. I don't want to get married. Marriage is forever. If only I can get away far enough, I'll be safe. He will see Ann again and forget all about me. I'll never go steady with a guy again.

If he weren't so nice, she could just tell him off. How could she do that to a man who had already been badly treated?

The following morning Francie made her farewells. Charles waited at the car while Francie took leave of the family.

Henri took her hand in his big warm one. "You did a good job, Miss Polanski. Too bad you don't stay a little longer."

The boys shook hands, red-faced, and escaped to the barn. Lucille she embraced with real affection. Then she turned to the matriarch.

Mme LaPointe regarded Francie with her cool, grey-glass eyes. Impossible, thought Francie. We are worlds apart. With her high pompadour and her air of dignity she could well be a French queen. They shook hands.

Charles talked all the way to the station. He spoke of redecorating the house. It was with pity and fear that she listened to his plans. If only he would take a final no for an answer. But he was adamant.

When the train chugged into the station, she braced herself for the good-by. A few people were about. One minute more, and she would be safely on her way.

He tipped her head back and kissed her right on the mouth. Right in front of everybody.

She shrank from the curious stares.

"Until we meet again," he said softly.

She fled into the car. An eternity passed; the figures of people began to flit by. She waved to Charles and then collapsed with relief. She need never see him again. She had escaped.

For the most part, Francie enjoyed the two summer months on the farm. She was eighteen and girls of marriageable age were scarce in the community. Her brothers took her to dances every weekend and sometimes in-between. What dismayed her was the obvious pairing of couples who openly displayed the most serious of intentions.

Although it was fun to be grown-up, she found that her parents thought of her as a child still. She milked cows, scrubbed floors, made beds, weeded the garden, yet felt a growing estrangement from her family, especially from her parents.

They knew nothing of the hard year she had come through. More and more Francie felt that she was among strangers, not in the way she had been with the French people, because even though they had shut her out with their language, they had treated her with respect: she was a teacher. Here at home she was no one to respect, no matter how hard she worked; she would always be just Francie, who couldn't amount to much on the farm.

She applied early for a second posting. In a few days she received an acceptance. Then she began to yearn to be respected again, to hold a job and do it well, to be held worthy of some admiration.

She began scrubbing the kitchen floor one afternoon. It was a standing joke in the family that the minute someone began to scrub the floor, any floor, Dad would find some reason to walk across the floor while it was still wet. At the right moment he would feel thirsty, and he would stride into the kitchen, muddy boots and all, and drink heartily. Perhaps he would be out of tobacco. At such times he walked through both the kitchen and the Other Room to get his tobacco can. Sometimes he walked through for no reason at all; his coming was as inevitable as the rising of the sun.

Francie's plan was to begin at the far end of the kitchen and work slowly toward the door, drying the floor well in the process. She had a feeling that she would never make it. Just as she finished soaking the floor in front of the doorway, sure enough, his boots sounded on the step.

She ducked back in time to avoid having her jaw broken. Her father stood in the doorway, his eyes fierce in a sooty face, holding up one arm where the blood ran thickly into his shirt sleeve.

"Qveek, bring de bazeen."

Francie cast about in her mind, searching for the thing he wanted. Bandages? Old rags? Ointment? The blood began to drip onto the dirty water on the floor.

"A bazeen! A bazeen!" he shouted. "Whatsa matter you?"

Her mind a blank, Francie scuttled toward the cupboard, where her mother was greasing the bread pans.

"He mean da basin." Mrs. Polanski's irritation showed itself. "Don't you know anything?"

Francie poured a dipperful of water into the basin and hurried to her father. He glared at her from under his shaggy brows, the pain in his voice accusing her.

"How come you so educated an' you don't even know what a bazeen is? What's de use of sending you to da school?" He placed his hand in the water. Immediately, the water turned a dark red.

"What you do?" Francie's mother bustled up.

"I cut de finger on de saw," he growled. "Bring me de rag to tie it up."

Francie did not dare begin to wipe up the crazy pattern of footprints on what had been a clean floor. And she knew better than to offer help to her father.

She stepped outside and pulled in a deep, satisfying draft of air. The

200

scent of wheat-musk drifted through the yard; the powerful fragrance of sweet clover hung in the air. It was late August, and she wanted to be gone.

After the bandaging and a cup of tea, her father returned to the shop. Francie finished the floor.

"Don' you know that Daddy calls a cabin a cabeen? A bazeen is a basin. You could think that."

Francie said nothing. She thought of all the accidents she had handled at school. She had looked after all the splinters, the cuts, the bruises, and no one had caught an infection.

Here, I am as nothing, she thought. If I could drive a tractor or fix machinery or make summerfallow, they would tell all the neighbors about it.

Next summer I'll not come home. There is really nothing for me here.

Before Francie left for her second school, Rosy came home for a day and came to see Francie.

"Oh, Rosy." The tears were close. "I am just so glad to see someone."

Rosy bubbled over. "Guess what, old pal?" She stuck her left hand into Francie's face.

"Rosy!! Not that old . . . old . . . ."

Rosy shrieked with laughter. "No, no." Then in an undertone she added, "But the old coot had lots of money. I'da married him if he woulda asked me. He ain't gonna be around too long. No. My guy's name is Walter Zonkiewitz."

Francie burst into laughter. Zonkiewitz? Of course. Rosy would never marry a Jones or a White or a McLeod.

"You really like him?" Francie looked closely at the speck of a diamond.

"He's it, Francie." Rosy was serious. "He ain't rich, but he has a little farm out West. I wish you could meet him and see what a swell guy he is."

"When will you be getting married?"

"Sometime next spring." Rosy dropped her voice. "Mother is too mad for me to bring him home yet."

"Why mad? I thought she'd be happy if you got married."

"It ain't that. Mother thinks that the only boys in the world are the Green Valley boys, because she knew their parents when she was young. Well, I told her the Green Valley boys stink! It made her screech!" Rosy grinned, remembering.

"Well, if you wait awhile and then bring him home, she'll get used to it."

"Maybe. But you know Mother: 'I'm not putting on any wedding for you. You ran away from home, and you expect me to give you a wedding yet?' " Rosy's face had lost its radiance.

"Me, I'm working until I have enough to buy a wedding dress and some clothes. And we'll put on the wedding ourselves. Francie, Francie . . . ." She looked into her best friend's eyes. "Promise me that you'll be my first bridesmaid."

"Of course!" Francie became excited. Then in a more serious tone she added, "I'll be teaching farther away from home this year. Just be sure you write me in plenty of time so that I can get someone else to teach for me."

Rosy's green eyes grew pensive.

"S'funny, you know, but I always thought that you'd be the first one to get married. You're too smart, Francie."

Something tugged at Francie's heart. "I like teaching. But this year my school is so much farther from home. So unless you pick Christmas or Easter to get married, I may not make it for your wedding. Or next July."

"July sounds pretty good. You wear any color you want as bridesmaid. Jackie's gonna be best man. Oh, Francie. I'm so happy. I only wish that you meet up with someone sweet."

"I'll write often," Francie promised.

There goes a little bit of me, mourned Francie as she waved good-by. She is just Rosy, but I've had more fun with her than everybody else. Without that crooked part in her hair and those clear eyes, she just wouldn't be Rosy.

CHAPTER THIRTY-FIVE

The school stood beside the highway. It had been renovated with grey and red siding. The tiny teacherage beside it consisted of a doll-sized bedroom and a kitchen-living-dining room.

"You'll just have eight kids." Mr. Wilson, the farmer who had brought her from the station, crinkled the corners of his eyes. "Three of ours, two from the district north of here and three young ones. Not a bad school at all."

The land lay heavy and flat all around the schoolyard. Well-tended farmhouses hid behind thick, green shelterbelts. Every field looked well-cared for.

"The board will throw a card party for you later on so's you get to feel at home," smiled Mr. Wilson. "Right now everybody's up to his neck in getting ready for the harvestin'. Been a bumper crop this year."

He helped to unload Francie's few possessions.

"Don't carry much for a woman."

His kind eyes crinkled again as he looked at her. "Jump in the truck and come and have some supper with us. We're a big family, so one more don't make no difference. You can save your cookin' for tomorrow."

Francie welcomed the invitation. The little teacherage held dark shadows in its corners, and it was getting late in the day to inspect it. She was dying to see the school. The outside looked so nice.

"Board put a lot of money into the school," Mr. Wilson boasted. "Figured we'd get a teacher sooner if we fixed her up a bit; didn't think we'd get one as good-lookin' as you."

He was being nice. Francie smiled.

"Course, with all them young bucks around here ready to settle down, you won't last too long. Lots of married schoolteachers in the district. About half the farmers' wives must be teachers."

The truck came to a stop before a neat, tall white house.

Mrs. Wilson, a slim, dark-eyed woman with a sweet smile, introduced the family. Francie was amazed to see so many seated around the table. The Wilsons did not look old enough to have eight girls.

Francie looked at the second oldest girl with care. Her thick dark bangs hung to her eyebrows. Her eyes were huge and brown. For the first time in years, Francie remembered the doll she had lost.

After the dishes were done, Francie asked to be excused. She was anxious to look over her new quarters, even though she might have to use a flashlight to do it.

Mr. Wilson packed the two oldest girls into the cab with himself and Francie. A full moon washed the schoolyard with silver. Crickets sang unceasingly in the ripening fields around them.

I wonder what it will be like here, Francie thought, getting out of the beat-up truck. I wonder whether I'll like it better living alone instead of boarding. I wonder how I'll feel about teaching at this time next year.

Mr. Wilson had brought along a gas lantern. He lit it with the help of his flashlight. The school room burst upon them.

The desks waited, varnished and gleaming. A long row of windows faced the north. And the floor! It was like new. The walls were smooth and unmarked.

Mr. Wilson noted her reaction.

"The board fixed it all up this summer. Put new siding on the outside too. We wanted to make sure that we got a teacher, because if we didn't, our kids would have to go all the way to town, twelve miles away."

"It really looks nice." Francie could hardly wait to get started.

"If you need any help, holler." Mr. Wilson carried the lamp toward the teacherage, the girls skipping alongside. "There's spoons and dishes in the chimney," he commented, rummaging through material stacked on a shelf.

"You'll be able to find everything in the daytime. I'll bring your stuff in now so that you can make your bed. Tomorrow I'll haul you a can of drinking water."

Francie lifted a stove lid and looked in. It was for coal and wood. A battered kettle sat to one side. She sighed with happiness at the thought of sitting in the kitchen of an evening, listening to the kettle singing and the clock ticking.

After Mr. Wilson drove away, leaving the lamp for the night, she pulled the dark green blinds to the sills, locked the door and sat in the old rocking chair beside the stove. She looked at the worn linoleum floor, the narrow kitchen cupboard that rose to the ceiling, the washstand with its pail and basin. It wasn't going to be that different from home.

Mr. Wilson appeared in the morning with a can of water and fuel for the kerosene lamp. He dumped a pile of split wood alongside the teacherage.

"Dad brought you a broom too," the oldest girl said.

"Think you'll be all right now?" Mr. Wilson's eyes crinkled. "Think you can manage this stove and the furnace at school too?"

"This is how I was raised," Francie answered. "All I need now is groceries."

"Okay. Get in with us and we'll take you to the small town south of here. It's only seven miles."

On the way back Mr. Wilson pointed out the different farms. Most of them looked impressive. The buildings were nothing like the ones around Green Valley or Field. The farmers here were better off than those in the southern part of Saskatchewan.

"The Greyhound bus goes right by the school every day," he said. "On Saturdays you can hook a ride into Meadowbrook and come back on the bus with your groceries. It'll be handy for you."

He puffed at his pipe and said, "I'd keep my door locked at night if I was you. This close to the highway you can't tell who might come along. Once the word gets around that there's a good-lookin' teacher living alone out here, you don't know what will happen."

Francie smiled at him.

"I mean it. There's a teacherage down the highway about forty miles. Last winter three fellows broke into it and raped the teacher. I don't want to scare you, but you can't be too careful."

Francie scrubbed the teacherage the next day. With her first check she would get herself a radio. She wound the clock and let it cluck away on the windowsill. She shook out the grates and built a fire in the old stove, then drank her tea sitting in the rocking chair.

It was one of those peaceful August days when the sun shone mightily in clear air over fields and prairie. A patch of sunlight fell on the floor through the open door. She rocked and drank her tea and felt at home. Outside the crickets sang.

The days slid by pleasantly. The children were so eager to learn that teaching them was a pleasure. Francie spent long hours preparing her work. She wanted the children to like school.

On Saturdays she caught rides into Meadowbrook. People who did not know her phoned to offer her rides. It was as if the community were in some kind of conspiracy to keep her happy.

Most of the parents were of Scottish, Irish or English descent. Mrs. Wilson was French. There were several grandparents living with the young marrieds. They did not leave the community but built small homes beside the larger ones.

"We're gonna put on a box social," Mr. Wilson told her one morning. "Harvest's done and it's time you met more of the people. Once winter sets in you won't get out much."

Francie had never been to a box social. With Mrs. Wilson's help she prepared a lunch and packed it in a shoe box.

The school filled with people. Some of the farm women, big and heavy, brought enormous boxes. Many of them no longer had children going to school, but they looked forward to socializing.

The boxes were piled at the front of the room on the teacher's desk. Children ran about everywhere. The men sat on the benches lining the walls, comparing bushels per acre. The women sat in groups away from the men, discussing canning and chicken killing. Francie sat quietly and watched and listened. She was quite comfortable.

The young bucks stood around the door, disdaining the wooden benches. They kept their hands in their pockets, laughing uproariously over jokes, pretending that they were not looking at the few girls present who, in turn, pretended that the young men were not there.

A cheer followed a short man carrying a fiddle toward the piano. With him was his wife, a sturdy, good-humored woman.

She plunked a key, and her husband began to tune up the fiddle. In a few minutes they were ready.

The strains of an old-time waltz were carried sweetly by the fiddle, while the piano served as a drum as well as a tune-carrier. The couple played only a short while. The crowd applauded.

"Everybody dance!" shouted Mr. Wilson, pulling Francie up. He was going to introduce her by having the first dance with her.

They swung lightly, easily to the music. It was a Highland waltz. For some minutes no one else got on the floor. Francie felt all eyes upon them.

Then they began to dance. Husbands partnered with wives, the young men with the remaining girls. The children ran back and forth along the benches.

The evening went quickly. Francie danced with every one of the young men and with several of the older men. Girls were at a premium; they never sat out a dance.

One tall young man who looked to be older than the rest of the young males kept wiping tears off his left cheek. Francie noticed that his eye seemed fixed and glassy.

"Are you coming down with a cold?" she asked, for want of something to say.

"No, I've got a glass eye."

Francie gawked. "How did that happen?"

"Oh, I was chopping wood, and a sliver flew up and went through my cheek sort of and damaged the eye."

"How do — did they put the glass eye in?"

"Easy." They both laughed. "I can pop it in and out like an egg. Want to see me do it?"

The liquor on his breath was making him bold. "No thanks," Francie said hastily.

One of the trustees began to auction off the boxes. The first one he held up was decorated as a little red schoolhouse.

"Who'll give me three dollars for this beauty?" he called.

There was a commotion at the door. Several voices called out.

The crowd laughed. Competition was going to be keen.

"Three-fifty."

Another chorus of calls.

Francie looked at the pile of boxes. They were so beautiful, some of them. She felt ashamed of her plain brown shoe box.

"Five dollars! Gone to Rick Jenson."

A slight, good-looking young man hurried from the doorway. He paid for the box, and as he turned to rejoin his friends, he looked at Francie.

She sat aghast. The little red schoolhouse! He had thought it was hers. The other young men around the doorway thumped him on the back and congratulated him.

Francie felt sorry for him. Anyway, anyone who had gone to so much trouble in making the box presentable surely had a good lunch in it.

She tried to look unconcerned when her box was held up. The man with the glass eye bought it for three dollars.

Then there was a bustling and much excitement. Francie's partner tore the paper off his box and looked inside. An incredulous look spread over his face as he read her name.

Rick Jenson had opened his box. All the young men around him craned their necks to see who his partner would be.

Francie heard exclamations. Then a tremendous roar of laughter.

And there went red-faced Rick Jenson carrying the box toward a thick-legged, heavy girl with coarse dark hair. The girl who was always last on the floor.

The young bucks in the doorway began opening their boxes. Francie knew the big question was "Who got her?" But by that time the man with the glass eye was making his way toward her.

"Looks like you're my partner for tonight," he smiled. She made room for him.

"It's not much," she apologized. "I didn't know that you put in other things besides sandwiches." Around them they could smell fried chicken, pumpkin pie, wonderful food.

But if Edward, her partner, was disappointed, he did not show it. He ate eagerly and talked about the farm. She guessed him to be about twenty-nine. She felt comfortable with him.

207

After lunch Francie sat out a few dances and watched the older couples do dances that she had never heard of. There was the Seven-Step, the Highland Fling and others. The dancing was graceful and dignified.

The winter came on strong. Wild winds whipped through the schoolyard, piling the snow high in blue, sweeping curves. It was Francie's job to light the furnace at the school in the mornings and to kindle a fire in her own stove as well. Throughout the school day she made regular trips to the basement to replenish the furnace.

After one such trip she stood with her back to the radiator in the wall. Through the windows she could see the sculptured snow-waves, running in a petrified sea of frozen snow. The children played happily, humming like contented bees.

I'm happy here, Francie thought. I like these children; I like this community. It's good to teach here.

That evening Mr. Wilson brought her mail when he came for his children. There was a letter from Rochester, and the handwriting was her dad's.

She could hardly open it. Going to Rochester meant cancer. Or something just as bad.

The letters were shaped carefully, well-spaced. Like her father, careful and deliberate.

Frynca,

The Mother is very sick. I take her to all the doctors in Regina but they cannot help her. I take her to Rochester by the train. She get more sick on the train. They have to use the stretcher to carry her off. The doctors operate on her gall bladder. She have only one stone but it is a big one. For three days now she is kritikal. I write you because I going crazy waiting. She not talk or move she don't know me. Oh Frynca I pray all the time that God will make her get better.

Dad

Going to Rochester took a lot of money; Mum had to be very sick if they took her that far. She thought about the young ones at home. How were they managing the cooking and the washing? Winter was a dangerous time too, because of the fires that had to be kept going.

A small envelope lay waiting to be opened. Claudette was to be married after Easter. Francie did not recognize the name of the bridegroom.

Her father had sent no forwarding address, so she could not write back for more information. She could only wait and wonder.

She reread her father's letter. It was the first time he had ever written her, and it contained so much anguish that she could not help but see her father in a new light. She wondered what had made him write to her. Just in case something happened, maybe, so that she would be half-ready.

The following week she received a letter from Nick. He wrote that their mother was improving, but slowly.

One blustery day the superintendent came to call for the first time, a tall man, balding a little and pleasant. He was much younger than any other superintendents Francie had seen. He wrote an impressive report. Francie read it with tears. The price, the price was high.

Several of the young men in the district asked her to go out. She went once or twice. When Francie told them that she would not get serious, they did not return. She knew what her mother would think of her if she continued to date without a sense of responsibility. She would say, "He spend money on her and take her every place, and then she too good to marry him. Poor boy. She take him for a sucker."

The family spent a quiet Christmas at home that year. Their mother was not ready to be discharged; Francie would not see her until Easter. There was no cooked wheat or passing of the Holy Bread, but Francie bought two blue candles for Christmas Eve. For her mother she spent almost all she had for a little gold watch; her mother had never owned one.

One blustery night Francie awoke from the dream drenched with perspiration. It was the old dream about Eddie. A rubber band came flying out of the dark and slapped Eddie across the mouth. The red blood spattered, and Eddie doubled over, crying. They all ran to him and tried to comfort him. Francie could not reach him. She struggled with all of her might, but her feet wouldn't lift off the ground. She fell forward and tried to crawl to him. She awoke to find herself tangled in the bedclothes and sweating.

With shaking fingers she lit the lamp. She did not want to go back to sleep too soon. She was afraid that she would dream the same thing over again.

The dream came whenever she was very tired. And it would bother her off and on all the next day. She would think that if someone could have been with Eddie, he would never have done it.

Advent was the long stretch of six weeks before Easter. As a Catholic she gave up dancing during that time as well as the weekly movie. The people in her community respected her faith. They left her alone. The dreary winter dragged on; night after night the wind howled around the corners of the teacherage. It was a time of spiritual desolation in man and nature. There came a time when Francie could not bear to think of the spring; it was too far away.

She knew that she was homesick. She picked at her meals and often did not eat at all. She would send an order for groceries into town, and the neighbors delivered it.

The nights were so long. A twilight hung over the prairie all day, and darkness came in swiftly and clamped down. It seemed to Francie that she lived from twilight to twilight. After the children were gone, she sat moodily at her desk or in her rocking chair, unable to pull herself together or summon the energy to make supper.

Francie visited a doctor and received a sound talking-to concerning her diet. She was put on a tonic and bought her first radio.

Her mother was home for Easter.

"Whatsa matter you!" she cried to Francie. "You so skinny!"

Francie blinked hard.

"You're not so fat either," she replied.

"Don' you like it dere, where you teaching?"

"I like it. But it's not the same as living in a boarding place and always having people around."

If they only knew, Francie thought, of the terrible loneliness in living alone, day after day, with only another day ahead.

"If you don' like it dere, you can find a school closer to home," said her father.

Closer to home. Francie looked at the old painted walls, the small crooked windows, the worn floor. Closer to home, but not too close.

CHAPTER THIRTY-SIX

Toward spring, she tried her hand at oil painting, then lost interest and let the brushes lie. She read until she could not sit any longer. She listened a good deal to the radio and embroidered tea towels for her hope chest. And then the letter from Rosy came.

Dear Pal,

I am working now as a waitress in a little café. I get real good tips. And I've saved enough to buy myself a wedding dress. Mother said she's not going to put on any wedding for me so we'll do it ourselves. I still want you to be my first bridesmaid. You can wear any color you like.

The day is July 2.

Gee, pal, I sure hope that you will find yourself a cute guy too. Am I happy!

Your friend,
Rosy

The superintendent came in May, stayed all one morning and at noon came to the teacherage to eat his lunch and to talk.

"What are your plans for next year?"

Francie buttered her sandwich slowly. "I don't know. I think I'll just stay at home."

He regarded her closely. It was clear to him that something was troubling her.

"You mean you don't wish to stay on here."

She shook her head. She wanted to get away. As far as she could. She didn't know why. But staying alone in the teacherage for the long winter had done it.

He chewed on his sandwich. "It will be hard to find a replacement. There are teachers, but then there are *teachers*. You've done a wonderful job with these kids. And you know that the parents think highly of you."

A lump filled Francie's throat.

"I know. But I just have to get away from here."

He leaned forward in his rocking chair. "I have a proposition to make. You want, and need, a change. I have a school about twenty miles south of here. A consolidated school. Two teachers. One handles grades one to four. The other grades five to eight."

Francie knew about that school. It was held in high regard.

"The principal is retiring," the tall man went on. "I would like to offer you his position."

She found it hard to swallow her food. Did he really mean what he was saying? The principal would teach grades five to eight and run the school as well.

He met her eyes with a level look. "You can do it. I've seen your work here. It would be more of a challenge, and you would not be as isolated as this."

The misery in her eyes touched him.

"Thank you very much," she said shakily. "But I don't know. I think I'll just quit teaching for a while."

He rocked in the chair and thought. Outdoors the children yelped like puppies.

Finally he rose. "Give me a ring if you change your mind. Immediately. I'll keep that position open until the last possible moment. I do hope you will accept it. The school needs you."

He smiled. "*I* need you." Then he held out his hand. "It has been a privilege to have known you, Miss Polanski. If we don't see each other again, I want you to know that I think you are a very fine teacher."

After the door closed behind him, she put her head on the table and cried until she began to wonder if she could ever stop.

When she received the superintendent's report, Francie sent it home for her parents to read. For the second time in her life, she received a letter from her father.

"Frynca . . . in all my twenty years as a secretary-treasurer of a school board I never seen such a good letter. You sure must be doing a good job there."

She would treasure the letter for the rest of her life. The worry that she had felt lifted a little. Spring had come, and she could not help but feel better.

At night the refreshing sound of running water came through the open window. The frog songs began. Wild game birds cronked their way overhead, and jackets replaced parkas.

A letter came one day with Mr. Wilson.

"Maybe your boy friend wants you to help him put in the crop," he teased. Then he changed the topic. "Are you getting enough to eat? You getting enough groceries?"

"Oh, yes," she said. "I'm never short. The trouble is that I'm never hungry."

The instant she said it she knew she shouldn't have. He looked at her intently, then let his eyes wander around the small kitchen.

"Mebbe it's not good for a young girl to live alone. Especially when the winters are like the ones we had these past two years."

The letter was from Jackie Prosvig.

Rosy was very ill. The doctor said that it was polio. She was in the hospital in Saskatoon, in an iron lung. It was very bad.

"Write to her, Francie. She needs to be cheered up. You were always her best friend."

Francie felt her way through the days that followed. Light-hearted Rosy, as irrepressible as a butterfly, trapped in an iron lung, very ill? Francie had seen a girl in an iron lung at an exhibition once. She could still hear the breathing of the machinery as it pumped life into the girl.

Until the exams were over, she could not go to see Rosy. In the meantime she would write a letter. A letter of hope, of cheer, the best thing she had ever written. She knew what kinds of things interested Rosy.

The letter wasn't easy to write. She kept putting it off because she felt so bad. Finally she wrote on the last day of school, a letter so fat that she could scarcely stuff it into the envelope.

She wrote about their school days, and did Rosy remember the vow they had made when they were thirteen? Her eyes misted over. The years had slipped by so quickly. She would go to see Rosy as soon as she got home.

The June sun greened the young wheat fields as Francie looked out at the passing prairie landscape. She lay back in the seat and tried to forget. Free. Free. A community picnic had been held on the last day of school, and they had presented her with a gift, and everybody sang "For She's A Jolly Good Fellow".

Those last few days the marking and the paperwork were still too near the surface. What now? She could go wherever she wanted. What did she want? Rosy to get well.

Nick drove her home from Field. She was almost afraid to ask.

"How is Rosy?"

"She was pretty bad. They say she woke up one night screaming that her legs were paralyzed. She got worse in the hospital."

"And now?"

"They're taking her out of the iron lung for a little longer every day."

It was good to see the shelterbelt once more, the trees tall and dignified, swaying in the west wind and wrapping the yard in a silken green circle.

The house seemed to be smaller than ever. All arms and legs, the younger boys looked at her critically.

"You got skinny this time," Danny commented. "Last time you got fatter."

"It was a long winter."

"She will get fat again when she milks da cows and picks da eggs," Mrs. Polanski said, plopping the boiled potatoes into a large white bowl. "Da farm is still da best place for da peoples."

I won't say anything, Francie thought, as she began to pick at her food. She would stay around, stay maybe for a week. Or two. But after that, she would have to go again, start again, she did not know where or why. If only Rosy would get better.

They heard the horse galloping from the south while they were eating. Someone was riding hard, and it was unusual because men did not ride horses hard by night.

Jackie Prosvig stood in the doorway, twisting his cap in his hands.

Francie's heart stopped.

"Rosy died this morning. Nick, we need you at ten o'clock in the morning to dig her grave. Mother wants her buried at Green Valley. Bring a spade."

They gathered beside the railway station at Green Valley to meet the train bearing Rosy home. A bitterness inside of Francie reminded her of how Rosy had hated Green Valley all of her life. Now they were bringing her back, back to stay forever in the place that she had despised.

They waited, not meeting each other's eyes. A rangy dog came around the corner of the platform and looked at them. He shook himself and his ears flapped. Far away a crow cawed and was still.

Hardly anyone in Green Valley was astir. There would not be many at this funeral.

The Polanskis were there, with the Chorneys, the Wilks and the Szodas.

They watched the train approach, then slow down. The faces of the trainmen were grave. One big car stopped at the loading platform. The big doors slid back slowly; the men carried the coffin out into the full sunshine.

Low moans of grief arose as the coffin was placed in a hearse. As the train mourned its way southward, they fell into step behind the hearse driving slowly up the rutted street to the church.

A barefooted child ran alongside the group, curiously watching the parade. Along the boardwalk an old man tapped with his cane.

The coffin was carried into the vestibule. Then the doors closed on the Prosvig family. The others waited outside in the brilliant sunshine on the day that should have been a wedding day for Rosy.

Then the doors were opened, and they filed by the casket. She lay in a sealed coffin, the top half of the lid made of glass, under which a bright red sign forbade the unsealing of the casket.

Because of her mother's request, Rosy had been dressed in her bridal finery. Her skin looked fair and white, her breasts flattened under the frills of her wedding gown. Her lids had lifted a little, and Francie could see the icy eyes underneath. Only the hands were Rosy's: short-fingered, chubby.

. . . Rosy was running toward her, her fine straight hair lifting off her high forehead, running through the tall grass of the schoolyard. To Francie, crouching behind the ragged caraganas, while Johnny Szoda counted to fifty behind the school.

. . . I hit Rosy, all for a silly game.

. . . There was never a time, Rosy, to explain.

And she said to herself as she looked for the last time at the face of her dearest friend: You meant so much to me, Rosy. And I never really told you.

She wept and could not stop weeping; she wept because her childhood had gone forever into the past and the last link had been broken with a wrench.

"Don't take it so hard." Mrs. Topchuk laid a warm arm on Francie's shoulders. "God wanted Rosy. She is at rest."

"She only twenty," sobbed Mrs. Prosvig. "God gives me a heavy cross."

The Prosvig boys stood awkwardly around the grave, their hands looking too large at the ends of their coat sleeves.

With a soft creaking the coffin descended. A fine stream of dirt rained in at the side.

"Throw a handful of dirt on her coffin," Mrs. Topchuk whispered. "It's the last thing that you can do for her. It means that she has gone home."

"Don't take it so hard, Francie," Nick comforted her. "Come on back to the car."

An uncontrollable fit of shaking overcame her as she stumbled over the dried prairie grass. They were burying Rosy right on the edge of the cemetery. She had been on the edge all of her life.

Without Rosy it would all be plain work and no more good times. Never a laugh when things got too much. It would just be work all her life and no bird singing.

Mrs. Prosvig and the boys came over that evening. They sat around the kitchen table and talked.

"It was her heart," the bereaved mother wept. "It was her heart, and the doctor say she lucky to die in hospital like dat." She turned to Francie. "She just got your letter."

Francie started. "My letter? Oh, I'm glad," she said.

"She just get your letter, the nurse tell me, and she laughed because it was such a fat one. She get the nurse to take her out of the lung and on the chair. Then she tell the nurse to go and get her some writing paper. Rosy say that this letter from her good friend and she want to answer right away."

Mrs. Prosvig wept.

"The nurse she going out of the room. She hear Rosy call out something, and she turn around and run back in. And Rosy she dead in her chair, your letter in her hand."

Mr. Polanski poured a glass of brandy for her.

"She never get the time to read it." She turned in anguish to Mrs. Polanski. "*Oi yoi*," she mourned. "She hardly home. Just go to school, den go away an' die. *Boza, Boza*."

Francie slipped outside. The night was full of the sound of insects. She struck her ankle hard against something that leaned against the house. It was the spade.

She walked down the road. Miles to the east, lights of farm homes twinkled. Families were sitting around tables, talking over the day, the times, the family things that were not spoken of during the busy day.

On three sides the thick dark arms of the shelterbelt embraced the wide yard and all that it contained. Francie passed through the trees and looked back.

Here she had grown up just enough so that she could go a little further by herself. Here she had returned after that first difficult year and then left again for her second posting. Then she had learned loneliness in living alone.

And the trees had grown. Little by little they had massed from scraggly little seedlings into strong, mature trees that bent with the winds and bowed with the snow, growing despite the cycle of death and resurrection.

She too had grown. Maybe even slower than the trees. She too could survive the wind and the snow. But she would no longer be afraid: there was always spring.

The moon passed behind a cloud, then came into view again. The prairie lay lovely in the moonlight.

Oh, Rosy, Rosy, she thought. I will mourn you all the days of my life.

"Nick, will you take me to Field?" Francie asked after the morning chores were done.

"Sure. Might as well take the cream in while we're at it."

Francie looked at the school as they jolted past. The white paint was peeling; the flag pole saluted the wide blue sky. Caraganas tossed in the wind beside the fence.

At Field she went into the telephone office. She gave the operator the number and sat down in the small booth.

From a great distance came a voice. "Hello. This is Superintendent Anderson's office."

"Mr. Anderson, please."

"Hello." The voice came on warm, strong.

"Mr. Anderson, this is Frances Polanski. Do you still have that position open?"

"Yes, we do. I hoped you would change your mind before the end of July."

"I have. I will accept it."

His laugh rang warm across the miles. "Good girl! We'll send you the application papers in the mail immediately."

On the way home they stopped at Joe's to deliver his mail. He asked them in for coffee.

"Well, Francie, time you got married. You're losing your looks. Gonna be an old maid."

He looked with pride at the two little ones lying on the floor playing with a kitten.

Joe had always been insistent.

"Look at all those nice Prosvig boys. Boys of your own kind. And that Wilk boy. Nothing wrong with him. You're not so young, you know."

The smell of wet diapers lingered in the air.

"You gonna stay home now for a while, long enough for the boys to catch you?" he grinned. Francie stopped smiling.

I once had a dear little doll, dears,
The prettiest doll in the world . . . .

"Joe." The need was urgent. "Whatever did you do to my doll — that one that Rosy gave me one time. You did something to it. What?"

He grinned over his coffee. "What difference does it make?"

"I just want to know. I went over that yard like a police dog. Did you burn it?"

"You really want to know?"

"I really, really do."

"Okay, then." The grin again. "I smashed its head against a tree, then buried it. In the manure pile."

"But why, Joe, why? Were you mad at me for something?"

Joe looked down into his cup.

"No, it wasn't that. We knew that you wanted a doll bad. But there was just no money. Then Rosy gave you hers. And then you played and played with that damned doll. You ate with it on your lap, slept with it, talked to it all day. And here we were, wanting you to play with us boys. But you

217

wouldn't leave that doll alone. So we had to do something so that you would come back and play with us again."

Tears sparkled in her eyes. "Thanks, Joe."

"Well, now you know," Joe grinned. "It took a while, but you started playing with us again."

They were silent on the way home. Nick whistled through his teeth, and a small song sang in Francie's heart. He had done it out of love. And all these years she had thought that he was mean.

"Well, sis, whatcha goin' to do next year?"

"Go back teaching. For another term anyway. I'll make up my mind each year as I go along."

The truck rolled to a halt in front of the house. A butterfly — gorgeous, silken — touched on the hood, opening and closing its wings in the sun. They watched it through the windshield.

"Guess you'll be like that butterfly," Nick said. "Here today, gone tomorrow." The butterfly swung into the breeze.

"Maybe that way is the best." She climbed down from the truck.